Coffin on Murder Street

by the same author

Coffin and the Paper Man
Coffin in the Black Museum
Coffin Underground
Coffin in Fashion
Coffin on the Water
A Coffin for the Canary
A Coffin for Pandora
A Coffin from the Past
Coffin's Dark Number
Coffin Following
Coffin in Malta
A Nameless Coffin
Coffin Waiting
A Coffin for Baby
Death Lives Next Door
The Interloper
The Murdering Kind
The Dull Dead
Coffin in Oxford
Receipt for Murder

GWENDOLINE BUTLER

Coffin on Murder Street

St. Martin's Press
New York

For information, address St. Martin's Press, 175 Fifth Avenue, New York, N.Y. 10010.

Library of Congress Cataloging-in-Publication Data

Butler, Gwendoline.
Coffin on Murder street / Gwendoline Butler.
p. cm.
"A Thomas Dunne book."
ISBN 0-312-07673-8
I. Title.
PR6052.U813C596 1992
823'.914—dc20 92-1074
CIP

First published in Great Britain by HarperCollins Publishers.

10 9 8 7 6 5 4 3 2

'In the real world, Proust would have killed Albertine.'

Gus Hamilton, speaking of the new play
written about Marcel Proust.

Coffin on Murder Street

CHAPTER 1

March 5

John Coffin, Chief Commander of the Police Force in the newly created Second City of London, made up of the old boroughs of Spinnergate, Leathergate, Swinehouse and East Hythe, sat in the window-seat of his living-room in St Luke's Mansions; he was preparing the text of his mad mother's diary for publication. The arrival of this diary had been one of the greatest shocks of his adult life. He had been brought up, fatherless and motherless, by an aunt and a grandmother who had fostered the notion that his parents were dead. It was later in his life that he discovered that his mother had not died when he was a child but had gone on to have numerous other relationships and at least one other marriage. Other discoveries had followed. Mother had been quite a character.

He was a tall man, going grey neatly at the temples with sharp clear blue eyes from which the innocent confidence he had had as a young man had long since faded. They were still kind eyes, yet wary. It was a good face, but held no promise of being easy. Life had toughened him. Presently he stood up, stretched himself and looked down upon the territory where he was responsible for maintaining the Queen's Peace as Chief Commander of the New City Force.

There was a killing taking place down there in Murder Street at that very time, but he did not know that yet. No one did, except the victim and the killer.

Coffin could look down on this world because he lived in the tower of a converted church. The tower of St Luke's and part of the church had been converted into three separate dwelling places, of which his apartment in the tower was the biggest and the most romantic. He could see the River Thames, he could get a glimpse of Tower Bridge and, if he was lucky and the weather was right, the top of St Paul's Cathedral. His authority stretched eastward and southward down the river towards Rotherhithe or Greenwich south of the river, but not including them.

He loved looking down on this London, his London, the new Second City of London, even though he knew better than most that the streets housed a great variety of thieves, housebreakers, pickpockets, sneak thieves, prostitutes, rapists and murderers.

But this was the new Docklands where many of the old warehouses and dock buildings, firmly built by their Victorian creators, had been turned into desirable and expensive places to live in. So the new rich had poured in, provoking some hostility from the old natives. A halt in prosperity had slowed the process down, and, while not making the poor richer, had made some of the rich much poorer. Not such a bad thing, he thought. All in all, the two communities were shaking down nicely together.

A bit of violence now and again, he would be the first to admit it, an occasional flash of social tension. But the murder statistics in his area were no worse than in the rest of the metropolis, which, considering, it housed one ancient thieves kitchen, still surviving in the original network of streets, was not bad.

His mother's diary made an interesting study, especially to the family circle which had been its first readers. Mrs Coffin had not been a woman of much education, but she had an easy, racy style of writing which led you on. Her life had lived up to her style, being also easy and racy, and leading you on. She had left three children by different fathers, dumped around the globe. One in London, John Coffin, the eldest by far; another in Scotland; and a third, the only daughter, in New York. It was possible there were others, but the trio who had discovered one another's existence by degrees, lived in some apprehension of more siblings. An extended family was one thing, but far-flung was ridiculous.

Laetitia Bingham, his half-sister, was the owner of the St Luke's Mansions complex where she had bought this old

Victorian church and developed the three apartments, of which she had sold one to John Coffin. She was turning the main church into an in-the-round theatre, and had established a Theatre Workshop on the rest of the land she owned. The Workshop was up and running, under the vigorous management of the actress, Stella Pinero.

Letty Bingham had just jettisoned her second husband (although her half-brother did not yet know this), and was planning to establish herself and her daughter in London. Letty was a successful international lawyer but her passion was the theatre. She pretended she was doing it all for her daughter who had just started drama school, but it was really for herself.

William was the third sibling, who had taken to law; he was a Writer to the Signet in Edinburgh. One way and another the law was in the blood.

The law, and a bit of drama, because you had to account for mother somehow. Perhaps her mother had been a Gaiety girl? And her father? Well, at one point in her diaries, she claimed he was King Edward VII.

Surprising this pull of the law, John Coffin thought, pouring himself a drink and taking a rest from his mother's diary, because that lady herself had shown no respect for any law judging from the way she had gone on. He did wonder how much of her diary was fiction. That episode in the Hamburg hotel, for instance, with the man who had claimed to be a member of the Romanov family and who had given her a diamond tiara. Where was that tiara, he asked himself; had Mother pawned it?

And what about that story of travelling by car from Glasgow to Edinburgh with a man who told her when they arrived in Morningside that he had his dead wife in the boot, and had left her mother in the cellar back home. He could believe that one, reflected Coffin. People could behave that way.

Drama, fantasy, and lies, mixed with a modicum of truth, that was the cocktail his mother had mixed.

Publication of Ma's memoirs was a joke, of course. Letty's idea: she had arranged the typing of the diaries.

Private publication, she said, and then we will try for TV and film rights. Make a mini-series, the material is there, but we must first establish our copyright. Surely Letty could not be serious? What did her husband think of the idea? Did she still have a husband? Coffin had his doubts, Letty had not said anything, but he could read her lovely face.

He put aside the typescript, removed his spectacles (a recent and regretted addition to his life), and went on to his next task. Stella Pinero had persuaded him to a little amateur acting.

The Friends of the Theatre Workshop, an association of energetic local ladies, had started a playreading group. Once a year a public performance was put on. As always, they were short of men. Coffin had no illusions about why Stella had enlisted him. He had been drafted, he was a conscript. Lately another man had joined, a quiet character who seemed willing to stay in the background and indeed had not attended the group lately, but Coffin was hopeful that the shortage of men was on the way out, although perhaps not with that one.

To his chagrin, he discovered in himself a faint sense of rivalry. He should be ashamed of himself. 'I don't care for the fellow, that's what it is, not jealousy as such.'

With surprise, he had discovered he was enjoying the acting experience. Drama obviously was in the blood. Ran in the family.

No great part had been allotted to him, Stella was not going to push him too hard.

They were doing *The Circle*. Somerset Maugham was having a comeback. He was the butler.

'Luncheon is served, sir,' he said. He tried it another way. 'Luncheon—' deep breath—'is served, sir.'

That was his best line. He had another: 'Lady Catherine Champion-Cheney—Lord Porteous.'

You couldn't do much with that, the important thing was not to get tied up in the names and fall over your feet. But he had a bit of business with a tea-tray later on that he thought he could work up nicely.

It could have been worse, he could have been the footman. All the footman said was, 'Yes, sir.'

They had eliminated the footman. It didn't seem to matter to the plot, speeded it up a bit. Coffin reflected that only in the low wage, pre-Equity days of the 1920s when *The Circle* had first been produced could a writer have allowed himself both a butler and a footman on stage.

He went to the door of his sitting-room, opened it, and gave a bow: Luncheon is served, sir.

Letty Bingham and Stella Pinero, the famous actress, now installed as Director Elect of the new theatre (as yet only half built) and Acting Director of the Theatre Workshop were running a Festival Month. It would raise money; money was always tight. It would bring publicity; publicity was always valuable. Things were rolling forward, with four plays now in preparation, the casts engaged. Life was hotting up.

The four plays were *The Cherry Orchard.* The early Rattigan: *French Without Tears.* Arthur Miller would be represented by *Death of a Salesman*, because Miller, like Maugham, was having a renaissance, and Ben Travers came forward with *Rookery Nook.* She was also doing short runs of plays with small casts. Stella had cast the plays with cunning and some shrewdness, hoping to cater for all tastes and entrap the favour of the critics. The favour of critics was like a wary beast that you had to lure to you and then entice to your bosom.

If only half the famous names signed up by Stella arrived in due course to play their parts, and attracted all the tourists that were hoped for, then all the sneak thieves, dips, confidence men and petty criminals from outside the Second City and as far as Hong Kong and Australia would swarm in to join the native criminal population.

A few miles up river, over Waterloo Bridge, up the Strand and turn left, you were into Virginia Square. This square of tall dusty houses now converted into offices was small, blocked off at one end by the back of a large chain store, and lined on one side with coaches setting off on various tours round London. Tickets could be bought from itinerant sellers carrying small boards which displayed the names and prices of the various tours, and covered with advertisements themselves on caps, shirts and jackets. One or two of them had been mugged for the money they carried, it was a job not without hazard.

A Tour of Westminster Abbey and the City Churches; See Harrods and Visit The Tower; A Mystery Ride round London; A Total Terror Tour. See the Most Evil Places in London. Guaranteed Trembles. The Ultimate in Fear.

The coach firm which ran the Terror Tour was called Trembles Ltd, and you might joke that the coaches were owner-occupied because the two brothers Tremble who owned the firm were also the drivers. One brother did the Mystery Tour and the other the Horror. The classy tour of Westminster and Harrods was advertised but did not actually exist. Anyone who asked for it was persuaded to take one of the others. Horror or Mystery, it didn't matter which, the itinerary was more or less the same, the Horror being the more popular.

The Trembles had thought of this particular tour because of their name being what it was. Before this they had run tours to Spain, but you could have enough of Spain and sun and they had, and also of passengers who got drunk and run in by the local police and they were fed up with this too. A change was as good as a rest. The Horror Tour was never likely, they thought, to bring in the police. Also, the coaches were getting old and no longer up to the long runs. It was a modest business, always teetering between profit and disaster.

In fact, this tour was very popular with foreign visitors. It did most business in the evenings when customers were young, noisy and happy. Sometimes a little drunk and amorous, but always very willing to be frightened. But not too disappointed, in fact, if they were not, and the tour was, to tell the truth, not very terrifying. There was a coffee-bar at the back of the bus with a big Thermos and people helped themselves, but the tour usually ended up at a pub renamed not long before as the Ripper and Victim, known locally as the Rip and Vic, before a swift ride back.

The Terror Tour bus was small, because it is easier to arouse terror in a small group than in a large one. It was painted a sombre dull black and the windows were shaded green. So were the lights inside.

Not crowded tonight, thought the driver as he collected the tickets, and rather an elderly group. So much the better, he might get home early. On the other hand, more bodies, more money, and he was hard up. He sighed. The horses had not been running well lately. Those that could fall down had fallen down, those that should have finished first had finished last. It was Friday, a spring evening in early March.

He had much on his mind. He was, he felt bound to admit, a man who liked to oblige his pals. Perhaps it was a weakness, but there you were. He had an old friend, known to him all his life, they had been at school together and their fathers had worked side by side in the Docks. He liked him, but what a talker!

Tremble thought back to the young Tremble who had been led into all sorts of trouble by this same persuasive friend. Like the time they'd caught a Russian spy. Except he hadn't been. Poor chap, a survivor of Hitler's camps and then caught by two kids and locked up in a broom cupboard. Dad had tanned his backside for that exploit.

People didn't change. Russian spies, Libyan terrorists, IRA bombers, and a murderer, a great circus of them, all walking out of his pal's mind down Regina Street. Murder Street. And what were you to believe?

He mused: after all, it would only be an extra bit on his trip. Might amuse the punters.

Still, even among friends, nothing was for nothing, and cash was always useful.

The ghost of the young Tremble stirred inside him, issuing a warning. What was he getting into? As always with his friend, he had the uneasy feeling that he was taking part in a play, the plot of which had not been fully revealed to him.

He closed the door of the coach, and at the appointed hour set forth.

At 9.20 p.m., he was over the water in Coffin's territory, had passed St Luke's Mansions (where Coffin was learning his part) and the Theatre Workshop without comment, although both were brightly lit. But they were not in pursuit of brightness, but of darkness. The coach turned down a narrow road, badly lit.

'Here we are in Murder Street,' he announced. The coach passed slowly down the road.

Here on the left, at No. 6, the murderer Dr Brittany did away with his wife, his mother-in-law, and the cook, with arsenic. That was in 1914, just before war broke out; he escaped but he was caught in the end and hanged on Armistice Day. Three doors down, and again on the even side of the road at No. 12, the axe murderer, Joseph Cadrin, did in his victims and buried them in the garden.

'How many, sir? It was never rightly established, the bodies being cut up so. Nineteen twenty-seven, that was. A lot of the victims would have been tramps and dossers.'

He slowed the coach to a crawl so that they could all get a good look and flash away with their cameras, taking photographs if they wanted. Sometimes he stopped and let them out, but not tonight. He didn't think they felt like it somehow. He didn't himself.

'That's all on this side, except just towards the end there was a young woman found dead in the basement, though that could have been suicide.' He sounded regretful. 'But on the other side of the road, odd numbers, four people and a dog died in a fire in No. 7, arson, that was. Yes, they have rebuilt that house, sir, but you can see which house it was, looks newer. And here and here . . .' He went through the catalogue: at No. 15 (no, there was no No. 13 but 15 would have been it if there had been) rape and suicide; at 23 a double murder; and at 29 a single death by stabbing. Yes, it was a longer road on that side, the old match factory cut into the other side.

He changed gears and put on some speed. Time to get on. He felt quite tired himself. Goodness knows, they'd all swigged enough coffee en route, ought to be as bright as crickets. But no, sodden was the feeling.

9.30 and they drove off into the darkness. There are some darknesses which seem to swallow people up. This one did.

The bar of the Theatre Workshop was a great meeting-place. That evening a small but animated group had gathered after the curtain had gone down. It was the custom for the cast of the play then in repertory to appear in the bar for a drink after they had taken off their make-up, where they could meet and talk to some of their faithful audience.

Most of the audience and almost all the cast of the current play had melted away home, but a small hard core of Friends of the Theatre Workshop remained talking to Stella Pinero who was sitting in one corner. A few people were hanging on because they had heard that Nell Casey, star of a transatlantic famous soap, and booked to play in the Festival, might appear.

Here too was Gus Hamilton, current star at the Old Vic, who would be joining the Festival in *French Without Tears* and *The Cherry Orchard*. He was also teaching a group of local students in a Drama Workshop. Getting to Know the Bard, he called it. He was doing it for peanuts, just one peanut, as he said himself. Gus was never greedy about money but he was shrewd about how to advance his career. He was standing on his own, drinking a glass of white wine, a posse of his admirers having just left.

There's something I ought to tell him, thought Stella. Then it happened before she had a chance. Oh dear, she thought, Gus is going to be furious.

Casey came in through the swing door and met his gaze across the room. She stood still. 'My heart stopped,' she told herself afterwards. 'Just for one second, I stopped breathing.'

They moved towards each other, reluctantly, but irresistibly impelled.

Casey began to breathe again, but her breath was hard inside her like a knife.

'I thought you were dead.'

'Not funny. You knew I wasn't dead. I'm still on the Equity list. You could have looked.'

'I've been in the States.'

'I was on Broadway.' Off Broadway, but that was smarter.

'Not that kind of dead,' she said. 'Not dead dead.'

'Is there another kind?'

'Dead to me.' Her voice dropped.

'You always had a duff hand with dialogue, Casey. I've told you that before. It's why you haven't been more successful. You can't give a line the right weight.'

'I am successful. And you played off Broadway.'

'Aha,' he said triumphantly. 'So I've come back to life, have I? Not dead at all.'

'And you got lousy reviews.'

'Better than you did, dear, for your extremely lousy Amanda.'

'Dead spiritually and emotionally,' said Casey.

It looked as though they were about to embark on one of the stand-up fights that had broken their relationship in the first place. They had a fascinated audience all round them, drinking it in. Casey and Gus at it again.

Then Gus held out a hand. 'Come on, Nelly. Kiss and make up.'

Casey swung on her heel. 'You ought to have stayed dead.'

John Coffin, walking into the room, thought: Who are these people who are behaving badly? Years and years of knowing Stella Pinero and having a stage-struck sister had not accustomed him to the idea that a scene was words but not deeds and a quarrel was not for ever. Probably not even for the next ten minutes.

Still, this one had looked real.

The girl, tall, beautiful, reddish hair (he liked red hair on a woman but not on a man), a thin and delicately boned face—did he know her face?—was talking to a group of three, then moving on, being hailed, kissed and exclaimed at. Someone asked her if she had 'brought it with her'. He made his way across to where Stella sat. 'What was all that about?'

'Oh, you've turned up?'

'I said I'd be late. So what was it?'

'They knew each other well once, and were going to be married. May still be,' she added thoughtfully. Only indefinitely postponed. Owing to injury.

'What got in the way?' From the manner in which they assaulted each other he would have said they were a perfect match.

'Something rather nasty. A death.'

'Oh?'

'Don't prick up your detectival ears.'

'Bad word.'

Nell Casey finished her tour of the room and ended up by Stella. 'That was painful.'

'I should have warned you he was here.'

'Are we both going to be working in the Festival?'

Stella prudently held back the information that they were cast in the same play, the Rattigan. Wonderful publicity to be got from their pairing, she had to put the show first. 'Apart from work, you need never meet.'

'We have met,' said Casey.

'Isn't it about time to call it a draw?'

'No,' said Nell. '*Niet, non, nein.* Is that clear? No, no, no. I'll never forgive that shit. And you heard him just now.'

To Stella's relief, she turned to John Coffin, and held out her hand. 'I'm Nell Casey. I know who you are, I've seen your photograph in the papers.'

'Surely not.'

'Yes, and I saw you on TV. You were over in Los Angeles on some policemen's conference. You said . . .' She stopped there, perhaps she couldn't remember what he had said. 'Well, it was about women as victims.'

'I ought to have had my mouth shot off.'

A tall figure, bespectacled, with greying hair and a small white beard, who had just come into the room, tapped Casey on the shoulder. 'So you got here.'

She spun round. 'Ellice! I didn't expect you.'

Neither did I, thought Stella, a little disconcerted. Ellice Eden was a famous and caustic theatre critic, who had not so far been too kind to her productions although professing undying admiration for Stella herself. 'Lovely actress,' he always said. 'Lovely.' Unmarried himself, he was famous for a special sensitivity towards actresses, while asking the question if women could ever reach the height of the greatest of men. Garrick, Kean, Olivier, did they stand on their own?

Duse, Bernhardt, goddesses, he said. Among moderns he praised Ashcroft, Redgrave, and Bloom. Nor did he despise the screen. Hepburn, marvellous. Monroe, now there was a talent of a very special kind. Streep? He was still watching and assessing. But the reservation about the supreme greatness of women remained, so actresses were careful with him.

He had shown a special liking for Nell Casey, and true admiration for her professional skills. She was so young, she had a long way to go.

'Came to see you. It's been quite a gap.' He held her at arm's length. 'You look more Pre-Raphaelite than ever.'

'"By the margins willow-veiled, slide the heavy barges trailed." You always did like the river,' she laughed.

He pulled her towards the bar. 'Come and have a drink.'

Stella and Coffin were left alone.

'What's the story about the death?'

'Surprised you don't know. Casey and Gus were part of a company, avant garde little group called Boxers, they were touring Australia. They were in Sydney for a month. Gus ran a little class within the company, he likes teaching. One of the kids fell for him. A lad, of course, they were pretty bisexual, that company, some tours are. I've looked round on occasion and thought: Not a proper man here. Anyway, this lad hung around Gus, that sort of thing.'

'So?'

'Gus said he didn't encourage him. Well, perhaps he didn't. Two schools of thought about that. And then Nell moved in and kind of mopped him up. So they say. Anyway, it got pretty messy,' Stella said. 'He was found dead.'

'Where?'
'Does it matter?'
'It might.'
'In a car park adjoining the theatre. In a car, from the exhaust. It could have been suicide. But there were bruises, enough for doubts. Was he attacked, or was he not? Brilliant chap. Got all the medals and loads of praise. Gus came in for a lot of criticism, and some suspicion. Was he jealous, people asked, and if so, what sort of jealousy: sexual or professional or both?' Stella thought a bit more. 'He and Nell broke up amid tears and blows.'
'When was this?'
Stella made a guess. 'Not so long ago, but before Casey went out to Los Angeles and the part in the soap we all know about, and Gus struck it big in Shakespeare. Say a couple of years.' She shrugged. 'So one's sort of forgotten about it, and thinks those two ought to have done. That long.' She looked across the room to where Gus was ordering himself a drink. She frowned. Back on that again? She would have to keep an eye on Gus.
'Was the truth about the death ever established?'
'I don't think so, I don't really know.' Stella sounded faintly surprised she should be expected to know. 'It was in Australia.'
Far away and long ago.
'Nothing to do with you.'
'No, of course not.'
Across the room, John Coffin could see Gus inserting himself into what he clearly hoped was a neutral group, neither on his side nor Casey's, or who perhaps had never heard the gossip, anyway. Coffin felt sorry for the man. He knew what it was to feel a pariah: all policemen did. Sometimes you felt an alien in a hostile world.
'I believe you set this up on purpose. Arranged the whole thing,' he accused Stella.
Stella pursed her lips together. 'It's time they made it up. But I wanted Gus. I tried to get him to do a new play about Proust and then *Othello*. It was going to be a double on jealousy, but he said no.'

'You're a dangerous woman, Stella, and you could have created more of a situation than you realize,' he said, observing Nell Casey's rigid stance.

The party in the bar was increasing in size rather than diminishing as word got round that not only Nell Casey was there but Ellice Eden also. Max from the Deli round the corner, who ran the bar as a private venture, never minded staying on late. He was a man of business who nursed his profits carefully.

Nell and Gus stood at different ends of the room but were without doubt the two most courted members of the party, twin suns with their own powers of attraction. People drifted back and forth between them. Ellice Eden sat by Stella and held his own court.

In Murder Street, the real name of which was Regina Street, the small body of this particular victim had already been neatly packaged and any mess tidied away, ready for burial. It had been efficiently done. The murderer was a tidy, efficient person.

Regina Street, which knew its name but did not rejoice in it, harboured a floating population in its crowded houses, most of which had been subdivided into what the landlords called 'studio flats'. This meant one room with a midget kitchen and a shower room tucked into a cupboard. Most of them were let furnished, this bringing in the most profit for the smallest outlay. Very few people stayed long, especially when they got to know the local name for the street, and observed the tourist coaches studying them. There were one or two old inhabitants.

One was called Jim Lollard and as he was an old dockworker who had lived there since before the war, he was generally regarded by those of the inhabitants who noticed him at all as having been unloaded from the Ark. He was the only one who had a whole house to himself, and the interest to devote to it. His house was the one freshly painted and with a single bell with but his name underneath it. Since he had retired with a nice lump sum and a steady pension from the Dock Labour Board, he had spent most of his time decorating his house, inside and out, and tending his garden. He took evening classes in carpentry and upholstery and was willing to do odd jobs for anyone. At a price.

'His house is his hobby,' said Mimsie Marker tolerantly. Mimsie sold newspapers outside the Tube station at Spinnergate and knew all the old inhabitants of the district, being one herself.

But she was wrong. His house was not his hobby but his life's work. His hobby was murder.

He was well known to the police. As a murder addict, he frequently reported crimes that had happened, or were about to happen, as well as some that had never happened and were never going to happen.

He never bothered with a substation, but always directed his attention to the headquarters of the new Force in the big building a stone's throw from Spinnergate Tube station. Thus his name and his face were known even to John Coffin, from whom, because of his rank, all but the most august criminals were sheltered.

'You'll cry wolf once too often, said the sergeant on the desk one day, leaning across to Jim Lollard.

'What do you mean?' Defensively.

'You'll call murder and we won't believe you and it'll be you. You'll be the victim.'

Lollard drew back. Aggrieved. 'I'm doing a citizen's duty. I could report you for saying that.'

'You do,' said the sergeant. 'Now hop it.'

Lollard was stung into further speech. Truth to say, he had had it prepared and meant to get it out. 'You don't take account of what you've got in this district. Polyglot, that's what it is. Muslims, Hindus, the Irish. You want to watch them. I do.'

'We've got special units dealing with that,' said the sergeant.

Lollard was not to be stopped. 'I've got it all on paper, don't you worry. I keep a record. And I'll see it gets noticed.'

'Oh, pop off, dad.'

'You lot wouldn't know a crime coming if it got up and waved its hand at you,' Lollard flung angrily over his shoulder as he departed, nearly knocking over in his anger the only other regular caller at the station, a young freelance journalist always hopeful of a story. So to make up to the young man, Jim Lollard took him for a drink at the Rip and Vic, which although expensive had good beer and an atmosphere that jelled with his own.

That had been some months ago, but the comment from the sergeant had rankled. He had seen several suspicious circumstances since then and was convinced that he had his eye on at least one killer and that a mass murder was on the cards. But he had plans. Ideas catapulted out of his mind, one after the other. Get attention, he told himself, publicity is what you want. Set up a scene they can't ignore. His imagination accelerated.

He saw the newspaper interviews. He would produce his records, show his diary of events. Let them see the kind of scoreboard he kept on the kitchen wall. Sell it, there would be money in it. He'd get on the Wogan Show. He saw himself sitting there, telling the tale.

Two of the items on his scoreboard related to the last two weeks. He always dated them, sometimes putting what the tide was on the river. In his old days as a waterman this had been important to him.

Mr Lilly, what does he do with his cats? Eat them?

And then: *A strange fellow in No. 16. Will bear watching*, ran one scrawl. *What's he doing here, not our sort, and what has happened to him?* He had the darkest suspicions and had told a neighbour who let rooms what he thought. She laughed, but he'd show her. Show her something, anyway, to surprise her; he had his plans made.

Later that night a tentative telephone call came through to the Thameswater headquarters asking if they had any information about a tourist coach that had entered their area earlier that evening but had failed to return to base. Had there been a road accident? Had the coach broken down anywhere?

Sergeant Bond phoned around, but had to return the answer that nothing was known. He had zero to report.

When was the bus last seen? That was not clear, no one seemed to know. They had been sighted in Murder Street.

'Regina Street,' corrected the sergeant who lived not far away and did not like the nickname.

And the coach had not called in at the Ripper and Victim pub. But then I wouldn't myself, reflected the Sergeant. Tourist trap, the landlord overcharges you.

The party in the bar of the Theatre Workshop was showing signs of breaking up at last.

Stella Pinero was speeding it on its way. 'Come on now, you lot. I shall want you all in for a workout tomorrow early, then rehearsal—' for she was producing the next play in repertory herself—'and then there will be a meeting of all of you to hear details of the Festival productions. I will be handing out castings and you will be meeting Stan Odway and Jean Allen who are co-producing.'

The names struck awe in some of those present who started to melt away. Odway and Allen were hot stuff, names to conjure with, and Stella had been lucky to get them, all present acknowledged that, but they were tartars and you needed all your strength to cope.

Coffin, who was tired but had been hoping for a quiet half-hour with Stella, decided to depart himself.

The door opened and a dark-haired girl came into the room. She was carrying a bright-eyed little boy.

'I'm sorry, Miss Casey, but I couldn't get him to settle without saying good night to you.'

The child held out his arms and Casey gathered him up.

'You should be tougher with him, Sylvie.'

Sylvie, who had a charming French accent, started a confused explanation, muttering about something or someone being missing. A favourite toy, perhaps? Coffin raised an eyebrow at Stella.

Nell had rented a flat in The Albion, which was hard by St Luke's Mansions. The Albion had once been a public house, exceedingly seedy in appearance and not at all respectable, but it was of great antiquity, with cellars that looked as though they could have been there since the Domesday Book was compiled. Geoffrey Chaucer was said to have stayed there and Charles Dickens to have taken his friend Trollope for a drinking session there. Since then it had fallen on hard times, until converted recently into costly new apartments. Owing to the recent drop in property values most of them were as yet unsold, and the owner was turning them into furnished rented properties on short lets. Stella was suggesting them as homes for a number of her visiting stars in the approaching Festival. All expenses tax deductible, as she was pointing out.

'Her child?'

'Of course.'

Across the room, Coffin saw Gus staring hard at Casey and the boy. Casey was picking up her coat and hustling Sylvie out of the room. Stella followed. He moved forward and got the door open for them. The child gave him a smile as he passed in his mother's arms.

Nice kid, he thought.

And then: So that's what she brought with her.

And that wasn't all she'd brought. Long years of experience had made his nose sensitive.

He could smell it, it was all around her: Trouble.

CHAPTER 2

March 5

Late that evening, March 5, Ellice Eden was reading the newspapers as he took his nightcap. He had been too busy that day to get at them before. He had all the dailies delivered as a matter of business, plucking out of them all the reviews of his fellow critics. He cut out those he did not like and stuck them on a board with a sharp and vicious pin. Those he approved of he put in a drawer and asked the writers for a drink at the Groucho after the next show. He liked some of his rivals, he had a kindly streak inside him, although not all performers would have agreed with this judgement if they had suffered from his acid pen. But it was universally acknowledged that he was more often right than wrong. Which was, as one unhappy victim had pointed out, no comfort at all.

There was an auction at Sotheby's of the theatre objects he collected, such as costume, bits of jewellery, even the odd wig and piece of furniture or china connected with famous players or plays. He had a notable collection. He also had a modest collection of Victoriana, pictures mostly. He ticked what he might bid for.

He poured himself a cup of chocolate, which he drank with cream and very hot. Since the days of efficient servants (Oh Bunter, oh Jeeves, where are you now?) had long since passed, he had made it himself.

Today, however, he had finished with the critics (two to fix with a pin), and was reading the news. Something there troubled him.

He poured out another cup of chocolate and, after a moment's thought, padded across his golden Afghan carpet to fetch a bottle. He had recently acquired a taste for malt whisky and was presently experimenting with Glen Fiddich.

It was a strong measure but was allowable tonight. Morning almost. This morning. He drank it, then went back to his chocolate.

Presently he reached out for the telephone. It was late, but theatricals never sleep early and he knew this one did not. His toes did a sort of dance inside the blue and white slippers which matched the blue and white silk dressing-gown from Turnbull and Assher. In his youth he had breakfasted once with Noël Coward in the house in Gerald Road and had decided that he too would look like that one day if he could afford it. (Although not so red of face.) Now he could afford spotted silk dressing-gowns, and he even had a maisonette in Gerald Road to go with it, and very convenient it was.

He was a man who liked to dress with style and present a well-manicured appearance to the world. Hair, face and hands all received daily attention with lotions and creams.

From his window as he stood sipping his chocolate, hand on the telephone, he could see the police station. He knew some of the faces over there and a very decent set they were.

'Gus dear, there you are. Did I wake you up?' He didn't name himself. If Gus Hamilton did not recognize his voice, so much the worse for him. 'How are you? What about lunch one day? We haven't talked for a long while. Admired your work.' Not perhaps you yourself, my dear boy, not your character and your ways, but you are a peerless actor. In the making, anyway, not perhaps Olivier yet. 'But it's about Nell. Yes, our Nell. Your Nell, my Nell.'

Gus could be heard muttering something.

'All right, as you wish, not your Nell. But the child? The picture I have just seen in the paper of Nell, clutching a largish infant. How did that come about?'

Gus muttered that it was nothing to do with him. Very likely not, thought Ellice, won't disagree with you on that, but babies are not produced by a kind of spontaneous conception whatever your views on virgin birth. Two parties are required, even if one is represented in a test tube. Not that he thought that was how it had been with Nell Casey. No, indeed.

'She has said nothing about it. Kept very quiet. A mistake.' Every woman was entitled to one mistake, but Nell had made more than her share in his opinion.

The explosion of anger that Gus delivered over the telephone surprised him.

He had meant to get some information from Gus, not to call up a storm.

Ellice began to put the telephone down, not having, as he had intended, asked Gus to lunch. He would invent some other treat for that young man.

He had not, of course, been quite truthful in what he said to Gus. With his excellent intelligence system he had picked up news about the child. She had not exactly kept quiet about it, but not spread the word either. Her own business, she had implied.

But what he had not expected was to see such a large, handsome and healthy child. Somehow a frail, delicate little creature would have been more suitable for Nell.

Nor had he expected to see Nell looking down at the boy with such evident love.

Sad, he thought. Very sad. Oh Gus, oh Nell, what a pair of star-crossed lovers you have been. It's a tragedy. Shakespeare, Euripides, Racine. On that scale.

A new voice took over on the telephone. 'What have you done to Gus? He's in a terrible state.' The girl Gus currently shared his flat with, a singer. Ellice knew all the gossip.

'You ought to watch over that young man,' he said seriously. 'He's dangerous.'

The voice went on at him again.

'I know, dear,' said Ellice, 'I know you say Gus is a very private person.' Whatever that meant, not a bright girl, this one, just lovely long legs and a way of picking up clichés. 'But we don't want any of this Here we go and Vengeance is mine says the Lord and I am his instrument, do we?'

Like John Coffin, he too smelt trouble. He was tired now, but he was glad he had looked in at Stella Pinero's outfit that night, always nice to see Stella. Not a great talent but a real pro.

CHAPTER 3

Still on March 5

There was a special scent for trouble, Coffin thought. Somewhere between sour smoke and vinegar. The exact smell varied according to the quality of the trouble. The very worst of trouble took your breath away, it was so sharp, so acrid. He had smelt it once or twice in his life and hoped never to smell it again.

It wasn't the sort of thing you mentioned, especially if you were a senior police officer, because other people might not smell it. Possibly did not. But everyone had something, he guessed, some little forerunner of trouble about. To some it might be a pain in their big toe. Or indigestion. Or even just a strong desire to quarrel with their wife. He had no wife himself. He had one once, but that was long since, and she lived now in another country and he bore her no grudge. Hell it had been at the time.

He walked home to his flat, Stella having eluded him, and considered what trouble Nell Casey could be bringing with her. Gus, certainly, was high on the list. In fact, he might be the trouble.

Certainly connected with it, he thought, as he put his key in the lock.

He did this with a certain pleasure. He liked his handsome oak front door, old as the church itself, with a great lock whose brass key weighed down his pocket. He liked his home, of which he was quietly proud, and of himself for owning it. He had paid his sister, who had converted the church, a pretty price for the place, but it was worth it. Up in his tower he felt at peace, and peace was not a thing that came easily in his life. In the course of his career, he had had many homes in different places, some decidedly scruffy. Now he lived in his church tower with a sweeping view of his bit of London.

He walked up the winding inner staircase, past his kitchen up to his sitting-room on the top. Above him he had the turret and a tiny roof garden where his cat sunned himself among the geraniums and daisies which were all the flowers that Coffin managed to grow. They were, he found, indestructible plants, which even he and the London climate could not destroy.

Tiddles, the cat who had chosen to live with him and who answered to no name or any according to mood, sidled up to him, suggesting a little snack would be acceptable.

Coffin liked to say he lived alone, but while he had Tiddles he was never alone. Tiddles, although a quiet animal, had a strong presence. He was not to be ignored, as witness the feeding bowl in the kitchen, the sleeping basket complete with plaid blanket by the window (he rarely inhabited this but a cat liked to have a bit of property), and the supply of his favourite food, minced beef, in the refrigerator.

'Later, boy,' Coffin said to Tiddles, throwing his coat on a chair. He had decorated this room with his few good bits of furniture, several large bookcases, and his treasured large oriental rug. Letty had ordered him to buy a Chinese rug because she said it matched the ceiling, but he had resisted her advice and bought a Bokhara. On the walls he had three biggish oil paintings which he had bought himself, backing his own taste. You had to be strong with his sister Letty or she bullied you. He loved her, though, and was delighted to have her in his life.

For so long, he had not known he had a sister, although he had suspected he had a sibling. Then this beautiful, clever, enigmatic sister, Laetitia Bingham, had identified herself. Life had then delivered a bonus in the form of brother William. He did not love William, but he was prepared to like him and he certainly respected him. He suspected that his half-brother was, as they say in Edinburgh, a 'warm man', and Coffin who had never made more than his salary had to respect a man who could make money. Willy might be warm but his money was never burnt. William was both canny and cautious and that inheritance must have come from his father's side of the family, from his mother's it was impossible. Only in his marriage did William show a streak of that lady, for his wife was flaxen, buxom and extravagant. It was William who had come across his mother's diary in some old property left for safe keeping with the family that had brought him up, read what she had written with a mixture of shock and amazement at her racy ease, and Letty who had suggested the diary should be published. 'Not exactly the memoirs of an Edwardian lady but the frank, honest account of a real woman's life before, during and after the war. That is how we must sell it,' she had said.

Frank, Coffin admitted; honest, he doubted. He thought Ma might be a bit of an old liar. It almost seemed as if she had written for publication. A mystery there. He would probe it, and one day might get to the bottom of it. Meanwhile, it gave him something to exercise his mind on in the wakeful stretches of the night. A recent recruit to the ranks of insomniacs, he had plenty of those.

He checked his answering machine: no messages. His telephone remained quiet. Such inactivity was unusual, since he had instituted the rule that he received notice, even if briefly, of all important activities involving his force, whatever the time of day or night. He never wanted to be caught off guard. He was well aware that the social tensions in his area between those who had and those who had not, between the new inhabitants who had paid a lot for their property and did not want it sullied by the proximity of the old inhabitants who had ways of their own, not to mention various racial undercurrents, made for an inflammable mixture. If there was going to be a riot, he wanted to be the first to know.

As he handed out some food for the cat and then prepared for bed, he found he was more worried by the quietness than by a stream of messages. He checked again all the machines that ought to have been speaking to him, but found nothing wrong with them. Just a very quiet night.

Tiddles, fed and let out through the window which gave on to a roof so that he could descend, tail waving, upon the town like a Restoration gallant, had gone about his business, and Coffin poured himself a drink.

He would have to come to some resolution of his relationship with Stella Pinero. That was why he wasn't sleeping. He loved Stella, had loved her for years, but Stella engaged in her own career and living elsewhere was one thing, Stella always on the premises was quite another. They had tried it once, in the distant past when they were both a good deal younger, and it hadn't worked.

I jolly nearly did her in, he reflected, that night she threw the saucepan at me and I threw it back. Stella had missed; he hadn't. It had been the instinctive action of a good games player, but it had brought him up short. Violence towards Stella was not something he wanted to exhibit. He had helped her up, asked her to forgive him and moved out. Shortly after Stella had gone on a long tour of a Rattigan play with the first company, and he had gone on a course in Cambridge. They had not met for years.

Over, he had thought, all over. But it was never over between him and Stella, it was like a disease they had both caught, in which there were many remissions (in one of which he had married, and in another, Stella had done so) but no real cure.

She was part of his life forever, and living, moreover, only a stone's throw away. Those facts had to be faced and dealt with.

I'll do that tomorrow, he thought.

Tiddles leapt back in through the window, his fur smelling of the fresh air.

Coffin turned his mind to other things. Odd about the child. No, not odd at all. Everyone, all young achievers, had one these days, in or out of wedlock, they were fashionable. Even if you didn't fancy one for its own sake, then it was the smart thing to do. But this kid was loved, you could see that.

Was it Gus's? The age was about right, according to the chronology of the story as transmitted by Stella, who was actually accurate about things of this sort. She could be madly wrong and ill-informed about matters of national importance but about personal details she could be relied upon.

A night without a single crime, he thought, a peerless, uncorrupted night. What a treat. Nothing to think about.

He and Tiddles were just about to go to bed, they shared one, not from Coffin's choice but because Tiddles offered none, he was always there, soundly asleep with his head on the pillow. The utmost freedom allowed to Coffin was to take the other pillow. He had Tiddles and Tiddles had him.

He was just choosing which book to read in bed when the telephone rang.

'Sir?' It was the duty officer at his headquarters. 'Just to inform you that a coachload of tourists on a trip through the City has disappeared.'

'How many?'

'Twelve plus the driver.'

Thirteen people missing, then. A bumper crop, the peerless evening effortlessly racing ahead of itself and creating a record.

Still, no reason to believe they were dead or otherwise harmed. Just missing.

'No accident reported?'

'No, sir, not in our districts or outside.'

Of course not, that would have been the easy answer and he would not have been bothered in the small hours. It was now nearly one o'clock in the morning.

'Any messages, demands for ransom, anything of that sort?'

'No, sir. Silence.'

'There may be something later.'

'Not a very rich firm that runs the tours, sir. And the people they get on the tours aren't in the millionaire class.'

'They'll turn up,' Coffin said confidently. They'd have to, dead or alive, you couldn't easily dispose of that many bodies.

'Of course, sir.'

'Let me have the details,'

'Just faxing them, sir.'

The sight of Tiddles's well-licked food bowl made Coffin feel hungry himself, so he put together some coffee and a sandwich, not a neat one, which began to fall apart. He stopped in the window of his sitting-room to take a hasty bite.

By this time, the faxed pages were arriving, slipping out of the machine and neatly disposing of themselves. Along with them came information about several committee meetings tomorrow, a multiple accident on the motorway (not in his area, but a number of people had been killed and that was bad), and a survey, with graphs, of the fire risks in all the police stations in Thameswater. None of which statistics he wanted at this moment. A fax about a suspected child murderer who was believed to have moved into the district was different. He paused to read:

William Arthur Duerden, believed moved into this area. Suspected of several child murders (details attached) but no proof. He goes under several aliase. (names attached). Born 1945. Five feet four, brown hair, blue eyes, no distinguishing marks. May alter appearance with wig and contact lenses.

All this paper just waiting there to spring out at him.

He picked out what he needed to read. That was the trouble with machines, the desire to take over was built into them. They always wanted to do too much. Otherwise they broke down and were called failures, and scrapped. Naturally no machine wanted that to happen, it was better to overdo it.

Whoever had kidnapped, murdered or mislaid thirteen people had overdone it. Thirteen was too many.

The missing coach belonged to Trembles Tours Ltd, a licensed operator having two coaches. The drivers were the twin brothers, John and Alfred Tremble, who owned the firm. The brothers always set out their route and approximate timetable and informed the traffic police. They had never been in any trouble and had no record.

Now one of the brothers, together with his coach and all his passengers, had disappeared.

'Damn.' His quiet night had gone. Crime in his bailiwick was like the rain over England: if there was one dry day, then it levelled up the next day with a steady downpour. The average was always the same in both cases: high.

He drank his coffee and went back to studying his lines. No doubt Maugham would send him to sleep. There was a kind of deadness behind its smart dialogue and dated good sense. He wondered if Stella and the ladies of the Reading Club had been wise to choose it? But they were supposed to know their audience and tickets were selling. He had a suspicion it had been chosen because a prominent member of the group had red hair . . . like Lady Kitty.

Over one of Lady Kitty's speeches, he nodded off to sleep, but one last thought rolled across his mind.

So I was right, there is trouble, trouble in triplicate, but not Nell Casey's trouble, not the trouble I smelt, that's still on the way. This is extra trouble.

But trouble was what he lived by and it paid his wages.

Nell Casey had taken her son home, first borrowing a pint of milk from Stella Pinero.

'I'd forgotten what London was like for shopping,' she apologized. 'Shops all closing at six o'clock sharp.'

'Not quite that bad any longer, not round here, anyway. Mr Khan down the road by the Spinnergate Tube stays open till midnight, and Max's Deli about the same.'

'Not all night, though.'

'Not all night.' Stella handed over the pint of milk. She hardly drank milk herself, but the dog loved it and in spite of what her neighbour John Coffin believed, the cat Tiddles spent a lot of time eating and drinking in Stella's establishment. The dog, of course, was a privileged animal, having once saved Stella's life. Or from a fate worse than death. The story as Stella recounted it never lost drama in the telling. Still, it had been a bad enough episode in truth.

'I'll pay you . . .'

'Don't bother, love.' Stella repressed a yawn, and pressed Nell's hand gently. 'Off you go, I'm dropping where I stand, even if that kid's wide awake.'

A pair of bright bird-sharp eyes met hers as he leaned over his mother's shoulder.

'What was the matter with him, by the way?'

'His dog. Seems to have got lost.'

'Bonzo,' said the child lovingly.

'You brought a dog from the States? Did you smuggle it in?'

'It's not a real dog, a toy dog, stuffed.'

'Bonzo, Bonzo.' Now it was beginning to be a shout. Very soon there would be tears.

'He doesn't look tired at all,' said Stella. 'I admire

stamina in a man. You'll have to put him on the stage, Nell.'

'Heaven forbid, I'm going to make him a stockbroker who'll earn lots of money.'

'Isn't he a bit heavy for you to carry?' If he is Gus's son, Stella speculated, then he would be. That man has heavy bones. Any one who had been on a stage with him knows that. It shakes.

'Yes,' said Nell shortly. 'Come on, Tommy, shut up and find your feet. You can walk.' She stood him on the ground. 'We're still on New York time, you see,' she said turning back to Stella. 'That five hours doesn't seem so late to us.'

'You wait till morning.'

Nell and Tom walked slowly, hand in hand, round the corner to The Albion. It was March but not cold and there was a moon. If they made a strange couple, mother and small son walking through the empty streets, Nell was not aware of it.

Presently she looked up at the church tower where, high up, a light still shone. A figure could be seen in profile.

'Look, a man eating,' said Tom.

'Yes, a man, still up. Just like us. I don't suppose he's eating.'

'Eating,' said Tom firmly. He was a child of one idea at a time.

In the flat, Nell said to her French au pair: 'I think he's hungry. Give him something to eat.' She handed over the milk. 'How did he manage to lose the dog?' Considering that Bonzo had come with them on all her tours, surviving overnight stays in motels, plane trips across the American continent as well as two flights across the Atlantic, it was strange he should go missing now.

'Tom says that after the journey Bonzo needs to go into the garden,' said Sylvie simply. 'So I put him in the garden.'

One of the things that Nell Casey liked about the girl was that she took Tom seriously. She took the boy seriously herself, but she could see that a slavish adherence to Tom's dictates could have its drawbacks. She sighed. 'You've looked all over the garden?'

There was a communal garden for The Albion, nicely laid out but not large.

'Everywhere in the garden,' said Sylvie firmly. 'And Tom helped. Bonzo is not there.'

Tom, busy drinking a mug of milk, a feat which demanded all his attention, did not set up a wail for Bonzo, but his eyes staring at them over the mug were unrelenting. Bonzo or else, they said.

Nell knew what that meant: a child who would stay awake, who would not cry but would keep up a constant low keening sound, more painful to listen to than deep sobs.

It's all an act, she said to herself. He's a performer, can't blame him for that, but I don't feel strong enough for one of his performances tonight. Seeing Gus again had shaken her more than she wanted to admit. She didn't want to give Tom a smart slap, not what a good mother did, but it had worked on occasion.

She struck a bargain. 'Let Sylvie put you to bed and I will go down and look in the garden myself.'

Sylvie protested that it was too late, too wet, too cold, but a judicial nod from Tom let her know she could go ahead.

'Oh, Miss Casey, someone tried to call while you were out earlier this evening, but by the time I got to the door, whoever it was had gone.'

'Oh? Well, they might have waited.'

'I was slow,' apologized Sylvie, 'I am afraid I was. I called out Please wait. But Tom was on his pot and I must stay with him.'

Nell nodded. She knew the importance of Tom and his pot and the rituals that went with it. Heaven forbid you should omit them or tamper with them in any way, or the worst happened.

'Not important,' she said.

Who knew she was here? A small card stuck by the bell said CASEY. In Los Angeles and even more in New York, people had seemed happier to call her Casey. She liked it. Casey felt free and vibrant and, although very female and attractive, sexless in an interesting kind of way. Not one to be put down. An achiever, that was Casey, and Tom was a bit of her equipment like a Gucci handbag or a bottle of Giorgio. But now she was in London, she couldn't help noticing that the English air was converting her back to Nell. Nell would lower her voice a decibel or two, would probably drop that scent and wear another (the new Guerlain, say?) and admit freely that Tom was the person she adored.

'I didn't expect anyone,' she said.

'It was a man, I think.' Sylvie picked up Tom and stood there with him straddled on her hip.

'Oh, why?'

'Heavy feet,' said Sylvie thoughtfully. 'On the stairs. I opened the door and heard the feet. Then the front door shut. That was heavy too.'

As the two disappeared towards bed, Nell went to get a raincoat. The flat was small but conveniently arranged, she had a bed with what amounted to a bathroom and dressing-room attached. They had been here over twenty-four hours but not all her clothes were unpacked yet; however, she knew where to find her raincoat.

She took a quick look round the room before she left it. A wide bed, pale wood for the dressing-table . . . Not bad for a furnished place, she had known worse. Many worse in her upward career. It was nice to have a bit of money to burn, the TV series had done that for her. But now she was back, to do some serious theatre work, starting with the play for the Festival. Her agent had already sent some scripts for her to read. It was a beginning. This flat would make a very good base from which to operate.

Stella Pinero had been so encouraging and helpful, she really liked Stella, admired her as a performer, respected her as a person. Stella had been through the mill and knew what it was like.

She felt optimistic and happy, lovely to have things to look forward to, lovely to be back in London.

If only Gus wouldn't mess things up. There was no love left between them, surely there wasn't, but Gus was a powerful and disturbing force in her life. She had great regard for his talent, which was huge and still growing, but as a man he could be frightening. The guy that had died in Sydney had been torn in two by Gus, destroyed as a person and as an artist by Gus's criticisms in class, never mind any sexual element that might have come in, through her or Gus. And she didn't think Gus knew what he had done. The memory troubled her. Almost everything about Gus troubled her.

I didn't like the way he looked at Tom. She went down the stairs, unlocked the heavy front door to let herself out into the garden. *I ought to have brought a torch.* But there was light coming from a street lamp.

She could see the garden walls where a strong cotoneaster grew, and the edging of flowerbeds of daffodils and tiny irises. A conifer stood up in the middle of a patch of lawn. The garden ran round the corner of the house before terminating in a high brick wall. This corner garden was nothing but a strip of grass. The street light barely reached it but light came down from lighted windows in the flats above. They were the windows in her own dwelling.

A bit too eager, she said to herself. *Gus definitely looked a bit too eager. I hate that look on his face.* She wished he hadn't seen Tom. Why was she frightened of Gus? He couldn't hurt her, couldn't hurt Tom. *I can look after Tom and myself.* She had been independent and self-supporting for a long while now. It had been a hard slog but she had done it. The two of them could afford a reasonable way of life now. Which included Sylvie, who was responsible for the loss of the valued Bonzo.

He wasn't in the garden. She had searched and the Bonz was not there. Since he could not walk, someone or something had taken him. An urban fox or a rat? But would any creature of right mind want an aged stuffed dog?

If it was hungry enough, perhaps.

The thought of there being animals around here hungry enough to eat Bonzo made her shiver. She hadn't cared for Bonzo, he had been too much trouble to her, the constant focus of alarm and crisis, nor did she care for his black and white spotted coat and his bold and leering eyes. Eye, one lost. Still he had deserved better than being a London meal. But if so, wouldn't there be a bit of Bonzo left around? A calico ear and bit of tail, a scrap of stuffing?

She looked around again. Nothing.

But under the oak tree was a small mound with a piece of wood stuck into it.

If I didn't know that it couldn't be, she told herself, I would say that was a grave.

A small grave with a tiny inscribed wooden stake.

She knelt down on the damp earth and in the light from the street lamp tried to read what was written. On one side was the faded name: *Rosa alba*. Just plucked from the garden here, she thought, but this is no rose and she was not reassured.

On the other side was one word, fresher, and unfaded, it appeared to have been written in black pencil and it said:

TOM.

CHAPTER 4

March 5 to March 6

Nell drew out the little wooden slip, she couldn't bear to leave it there in the mud with Tom's name on it, and crept up the stairs. The flat was quiet. Tom's room was dark but with the door left open, as he liked. Sylvie was locked behind her own door, she was playing a pop record but very, very faintly.

Must get her a Walkman, thought Nell as she moved past, keep her happy. If you have a Tom in your life, then you also need someone like Sylvie, that is, if you are a working mother. There had been a period when Nell had been a solo parent and it had been tough. Either way it was tough: if you were working, then you paid someone an arm and a leg to look after the beloved offspring, which left you penniless, and if you were unemployed (and that happened frequently in the theatre world) then you did it yourself and were still broke. But to have a child, that counted.

Nell stood by the child's bed. He was deep in sleep already, on his back, arms flung wide, his face flushed with the comfort of his slumber.

'You all right?' she whispered, touching his warm cheek gently. Yes, he was well and happy. He had been abused by the misuse of his name, but he personally was not touched.

But Nell felt the threat. Inside that tomb was Bonzo, but it could have been Tom.

She went back to the sitting-room where she dialled Stella Pinero's number. For a time there was no answer, still she hung on, praying that Stella was home, alone and not entertaining anyone. The chances were good. Stella hadn't looked in that sort of mood.

'Hello?' Stella's sleepy voice.

'It's Casey. Nell Casey.'

'You still on New York time?' said an aggrieved Stella. 'I was asleep. What is it?' She was awake now and beginning to be alarmed. 'What's wrong?'

'I've found Bonzo.' Stumbling in her speech, Nell told her. 'In a grave.'

'Oh, come on now, Nell.' Stella fumbled on the bedtable for her spectacles and put them on. She thought she could feel more awake and sensible if she had them on. She listened while Nell described what she had found. 'You don't know that the dog is in there.'

'No, all I could think about was getting back to Tom.'

'He's safe?'

'Oh yes, asleep.' In a desolate, small voice, Nell said: 'I don't know what to do.'

'You stay with him. I'll come round.'

Stella dressed herself, considered waking the sleeping mongrel Bob to come with her as protection, then dismissed the idea. He was apt to be too enthusiastic and thorough as a guardian.

But she took a torch and the trowel she used for her window-boxes. Bonzo was unlikely to be buried too deep.

As she walked round the corner to The Albion, she glanced up at the tower where John Coffin lived. A yellow light shone.

'Oh good, he's still up.' It was reassuring. The two had many brisk disagreements, even quarrels, usually but not always her fault, but he was a strong, comfortable presence in her life. A good deal more than that, indeed, but she wouldn't dwell on that now.

Strengthened by this thought, Stella went into the garden. The moon was up now and she could see about her without difficulty, although the moon lengthened and darkened shadows.

No one seemed about, which was just as well since she desired no audience for what she was going to do. There was the oak tree, and yes, there underneath was a small mound of newly turned earth.

So Nell had not been imagining things. *Never thought she was for a minute,* Stella assured herself stoutly. *Not a scrap of imagination in Nell Casey, one of her drawbacks as an actress, feet too firmly planted on the ground.* Big feet, of course, it was one of the things you noticed about Nell, her hands and feet were on the large side.

Her own feet in their light slippers felt damp and cold on the grass. She was muttering under her breath to keep her courage up. 'Wish I'd brought some gloves, I'm getting earth all over my hands.'

A worm moved sluggishly away from the trowel, a brown and pink creature not wanting to be disturbed.

Stella took scoops out of the earth, it was soft, and easy to move. The trowel struck something, not hard like wood or stone, but softer. She stopped digging for a moment and sat back on her heels. 'Oh dear, I don't believe I'm going to like this.'

Dropping the trowel, she brushed the earth aside with her hands. There was a cardboard box about twelve inches long and six wide; the sort of box shoes come packed in. In fact she could see the lid said *Armstrong Shoes.*

She lifted the box out of the earth, laid it on the grass beside her and lifted the lid.

Bonzo was there but he had been strangled. His head had been twisted round so it rested on his back. Something odd had happened to his feet, they had been extended and twisted too.

As far as you could murder a stuffed dog, Bonzo had been murdered.

Stella stood up. *Only lightly buried*, she thought. *Buried but meant to be found.*

How on earth could she show this to Nell Casey? On the other hand, Nell was up there waiting for her, she would expect to hear what Stella had found. How could she not tell her?

After some thought, Stella knelt down on the grass again, put Bonzo back in his box, and reburied him. She pressed the earth down with a firm hand, making all as tidy as she could. If you looked hard, you could see signs of disturbance, but probably no one would look.

Then she rang the bell for Flat No. 3 and when the answerphone spoke, announced herself.

'It's Stella.'

'Come on up.' The door opened for her and she made her way up to Nell Casey's temporary abode. Nell had the door open and was waiting for her.

She drew Stella in. 'So? What did you find?'

'It's Bonzo, all right. He's in a box and just under the soil. Not deep.' She had left the trowel behind. Damn, must remember to collect it on the way home. 'Before you ask: I left him there. He didn't look too good, poor Bonzo. I don't think you'd like him.'

'No.' Nell put her hand to her head. 'What am I going to say to Tom? I promised him I'd find Bonzo.'

'Well, you have done. But you can't give him that particular Bonzo. Can't you get another one?'

'Tom wouldn't stand for it,' said Nell, all mother figure. 'He'd know. Probably throw it at me.'

'You'll have to tough it out, Nell.' No child would want to play with the Bonzo down below.

'Couldn't we tidy him up?'

'You can make up your own mind in the morning when

you've had a look. But there's something else. Think about it, Nell. It's not good what's happened. It looks like a threat to me, one directed at Tom.'

'I know,' said Nell unhappily. 'Not Tom now, Tom next time. So what do I do?'

'You know that or you wouldn't ask. You tell the police, see what they can do.'

'Yes.' Nell accepted it. 'Tomorrow. But Tom? What about Tom? Shall I send him away? Hide him? And Bonzo, how on earth will I handle that?' Nell Casey sounded distracted.

'Hell, I don't know what you're going to do about that. But my advice on the dog is a straight cash offer.' She had formed her own opinion of Tom, and she thought money would speak.

'Yes,' said Nell thoughtfully. 'I believe that would work with Tom.'

'Never known it fail,' said Stella briskly. Her own daughter always took a rake-off in either disaster money or triumph money, it sweetened the world remarkably. It was known either as incentive or bribery, according to how you looked at the world. She called it comfort money, herself.

She kissed Nell and gave her a consoling hug. 'Go to bed, get some sleep. I won't say it'll seem better in the morning but at least you will have the strength to face it. I'm off.' Must pick up the trowel, she told herself.

As she held the door open for her, Nell said: 'Do you think the police will take it seriously.'

'I know one who will,' Stella promised. Or she would know the reason why, she told herself.

Cars were parked at intervals along the quiet street, but she had no sense of being watched or followed as she turned in to St Luke's Mansions. She looked up at the window in the tower. Still alight.

Should she call now? But even as she looked the light went out.

Before she drifted off to sleep, one question worried her. How had the person or persons who grabbed Bonzo known he belonged to Tom? For that matter, who had known about Tom, his name and who he was? Nell Casey and her son had only been in the country for a few days.

The same question was worrying Nell herself, as she lay in bed. It must be someone who knows us, she thought.

Some person, somewhere, in this country she had come back to, hated her and Tom enough to torment them. She had an enemy, but who was it?

A secret enemy was a frightening thought, but an enemy who moved in one's own world, whom you know, perhaps had liked and trusted, that was even more frightening.

'But there's another way of looking at it,' Nell said to the silent interlocutor who was conducting the inquiry inside her, 'someone whom you know to have a grievance.'

Someone like Gus.

Sleep was not going to come easily tonight. It was haunted by thoughts of Gus, whom she had once loved, and still admired, and whose character she knew to be striped about equally with generosity and anger. He was capable of anything, probably.

John Coffin slept soundly, his dreams not disturbed by fantasies of the missing coach with its pilgrims to horror, nor even by the child murderer who might now be one of his own flock. He had learnt long since to dismiss the worries of the day as far as his work was concerned. He had built up an efficient CID force, ably backed by the uniformed men. Let them get on with it. They had radio telephones, fax machines, and a computer network to help them. He could let them get on with it.

That said, he had enjoyed being a detective, puzzling out the truth of a crime, looking for the evidence and then putting one patient piece after another into the jigsaw until he had the truth. After that came the job of getting a case together and conviction in the courts, and there, he had to admit, he had not always been successful. There were one or two men and several women walking around who had escaped the law. They probably hated him just as much as if they had gone down. He got several hate letters a week.

More sometimes. This too did not disturb his sleep.

Stella Pinero, however, could always disturb him, and she did so now. The telephone rang by his bed, waking him up.

'Stella?'

'Yes, of course, it's me.'

'What is it?'

'Come down and have breakfast with me and I'll tell you.'

'I don't eat breakfast.'

'Not true. I've seen you having a croissant and coffee at Max's.'

'Well, I wasn't going to do that today. I'm in a hurry.' Not quite true, but if Stella detained him too long, then he would be. Holding the phone away from his ear while he removed the cat from his chest where Tiddles seemed to have spent the night, he could hear her voice still talking. 'Peace, Stella, I will come down. Put the coffee on.'

When he rang her bell, she opened the door at once, looking businesslike in spectacles with her long hair tied back.

'I like you looking like that.' He kissed her lightly on the cheek.

'Like what? Come into the kitchen.' The smell of coffee was floating towards them. Other people's coffee always smelt better than your own and Stella's could be relied upon. She had learnt how to make a good rich brew in her first job as ASM to Douggie Fraser, who liked his food, and had kept up the standard.

'Like a power lady. You are a power lady.'

'Have to be.'

Stella had not slept well but she had turned her wakefulness to good use. She had risen, showered and dressed in her white linen track suit, and then settled down with her notebooks. There was always plenty of work to do, it seemed to get more not less as her ambitions and those of Letty Bingham flowered. Also, Letty was always mean about money and kept the theatre on a rolling budget which demanded Stella's constant vigilance to avoid going cap in hand to Letty.

Cash was always one of her preoccupations. Hence the

Festival, the Charity Night which the Friends of the Theatre were organizing (up to them in theory, but in practice Stella liked to keep a sharp eye on what was going on . . . there was trouble about tickets, they would keep allocating the best seats to their own friends), and the Workshop for Students which Gus was about to conduct, and she'd kill him if he misbehaved. A good grant from Thameswater Educational Authority was involved here, they mustn't lose it.

'Come on then, tell me what's worrying you.' He had finished his first cup of coffee and was holding his cup out for another. He had his own worries. Before coming over to her, he had taken a quick look at his fax sheets. There was a fire in the tunnel near the Spinnergate Tube station and a train, complete with several hundred early commuters, was held up there. A man had just reported that he had blown his wife's head off with a shotgun in his house in Poland Street, Swinehythe, and the coachload of tourists was still missing. Two potentially major incidents boiling up, with the only good bit of news being a late fax suggesting that the man in Poland Street was a fantasist who had no wife and no gun.

Briefly, Stella told him. He heard her out, then put his coffee-cup down smartly. Suddenly the coffee sat sourly on his palate.

'Damn, oh damn.'

She was surprised at the force of his reaction, but not alarmed. 'You take it seriously, then?'

Oh yes, he did. But this did not seem the moment to tell Stella about the arrival of a suspected child murderer in Spinnergate.

'Come on, let's go and look at this dog.'

For a moment, he considered bringing in the whole CID apparatus. Scene of Crime officer and all. But what crime? None had as yet been committed. Assault on a stuffed dog hardly seemed to be enough.

'Bring the trowel you used before and a pair of gloves.' He wouldn't handle anything himself, and traces of Stella must be all over everything already.

It was a perfect spring morning with a pale blue sky and a soft breeze. Just the morning for a little digging.

Stella led him round to The Albion, and pointed out the site of the burial. 'There, under the tree. You can see the earth is heaped up.'

'Yes.' Earth was sprinkled over the grass. 'Anyone could see.'

'I thought I left it tidier than that. It was darkish, though.' And she had been upset.

There was movement behind them, and there was Nell Casey, holding her son's hand. He was wearing an immaculate pair of jeans and a shirt with TOM embroidered on it. No trouble in identifying who he was, thought Coffin.

'Good morning. Saw you from the window. So we've come to look.

'Should the boy be here?' asked Coffin bluntly.

'Can't leave him, Sylvie's just popped round to the deli to get some milk and croissants.'

'Well, take him for a walk while I do some excavating.'

But Tom had spotted something. Wrenching his hand away from his mother's, he ran over to the bushes.

'Bonzo, Bonzo,' he cried in triumph, pointing to a low branch on the cotoneaster. 'Bonzo in the bushes.'

There, suspended by his neck, looking a wreck, yet somehow quite relaxed and comfortable, was dear stuffed Bonzo.

Tom seemed unmoved and unalarmed by the damage done to Bonzo; perhaps with a child's selective vision he did not even notice. He reached up and plucked Bonzo down, holding him firmly to his bosom. Nell made a noise of protest but her son ignored her.

Coffin looked from him to the little tumulus, then turned to Stella. 'Open it up. Let's see what we've got here.'

'Well, nothing, I suppose.'

'I'm not so sure.'

Stella knelt down and got to work. She regretted the green stains on her white trousers but this was no time to be selfish.

'With gloves,' commented Coffin. He ought to have been feeling better about things, just a joke of a dubious nature here after all, but he had that nasty feeling at the pit of his stomach that suggested otherwise.

Slowly, with nervous hands, Stella moved the earth away until the cardboard box was uncovered. 'Still there,' she said.

'I see that.' Coffin knelt down beside her. 'Give the gloves to me.' Without disturbing the box *in situ* he lifted the lid which was lined with plastic film. It came away with a little sucking noise as if it had got stuck.

Inside was one small, perfectly formed child's hand. Severed at the wrist.

And streaked with blood. A bloody hand.

CHAPTER 5

March 6 contd

'Stella, take Nell and the child upstairs.' Coffin's voice was rough with tension, 'take her up there and keep her up there. I don't want her to come down again.'

'Right, come on, Nelly.'

'I heard what you said, but I don't think I want to go up and be hidden. I want to see. There's been a child murdered.' Her voice was rising.

'We don't know that,' said Coffin absently. 'Take them up, Stella. I'm going to do some telephoning.'

There was a call-box on the corner of the road outside The Albion, he shut himself in, ignoring the interested gaze of a lad who ought to have been delivering the newspapers.

He gave his instructions briskly. 'Get plastic sheeting over the whole area. Keep an eye on it. No, nothing else. I don't know yet if any crime has been committed. Oh yes, send a policewoman over. NOT uniform.' He could give the orders, cut corners, arrange things as he wanted them, and he did. Not always, but when it suited him. 'To Miss Casey, Flat Three, The Albion.'

'Classy joint,' said the CID sergeant who was taking the call. 'And the Old Man is there himself.' John Coffin's code name was WALKER, but you only used that in certain circumstances. 'A WDC, he says. Would you like to go, Mary Anne?'

Mary Barclay, the Anne was extra, a joke which she privately resented, was keen to go.

'What is it, though?' She was a girl who always liked to get things established and as clear as possible. Anything to do with the missing coachload of tourists? Still unaccounted for as far as she knew, and that really was weird.

'Don't know, might be a nasty, might not, but if the Boss calls we answer.'

Mary Barclay prepared to depart. 'There's a bit more than that, though, isn't there?' she said, knowing him.

'A child is involved,' said the sergeant towards her back without looking at her. 'He said that much. He's waiting for you there, he'll tell you the details.'

'Ah.' Reluctantly he met her eyes. Brown, sympathetic eyes. Both of them had read the item about the suspected child murderer thought to have moved into the area. And the Sergeant had lost a child last year. His son had gone out to play and never come back. He had been found afterwards, in the canal. Drowned. Not foul play, exactly, they said. Murder by his peers. Three six-year-olds, having a game.

Mary Barclay drove off, glad to get away from Sergeant Jeremy Kay, she was so sorry for him that it felt painful.

On the other hand, she thought, if I've got to face an anxious mother that's not so good, either. But it's the job. She had only been a CID officer for six months after a tough apprenticeship in the uniformed branch. But she liked her work and liked the district where she had grown up. To know so many people and have them know you was both a help and a hindrance; it made them tell you some things and hold back on others.

Nell Casey? She knew that name, she had seen one or two of the episodes in the soap *Destiny* in which Nell had appeared, although it was tripe. Ripe tripe. But the clothes had been lovely; she had read that Nell was out of it now, and had come back to England to be made legitimate on the stage.

A uniformed constable was already covering an area of earth and grass under a big tree when she got to The Albion.

Coffin met her in the hall.

'We'll talk here.'

Upstairs, Nell Casey and Stella were looking out of the window, down to the garden.

'What's happening?'

'A policeman in uniform is pegging down a sheet of plastic.'

Nell shivered; she still looked white. 'It was horrible.'

'Are you feeling better now?'

'Oh yes.' She looked across the room to where Tom was playing with a train, but he had Bonzo by him and was keeping a protective eye on the animal. An attempt to remove Bonzo from his custody was likely to produce a storm. 'As long as he is.'

'No one touched him. You nearly fainted down there, you know.'

'You knew it wasn't a real hand, didn't you?'

'Not straight away. But at a second look.'

'I didn't take a second look,' said Nell with a shudder. 'It looked like real blood, though.'

'I think that was real,' said Stella thoughtfully.

But the hand was of plaster, the very perfect model of a child's hand. Not exactly a museum piece, but a good piece of work. The Victorians had liked that sort of thing. Some loving mother had had that piece made. Perhaps of a dead child.

Better not think on those lines.

'Queen Victoria had models of all her children's hands. Of their feet too, for all I know.' Not much of a joke, but it might lighten Nell's mood of doom. Not unjustified, she must admit. And a small smile did touch Nell's lips. 'We had one as a prop when we did Housman's *Victoria Regina*.'

'Is that where it came from, do you think?'

'We borrowed ours from a local antique shop, as I remember. He got a credit in the programme and a couple of free seats.' A wide boy name Les Llywellyn who knew as much about antiques as you could read on the back of a postcard but knew how to make money. 'I suppose it went back.'

The young policewoman detective, who said her name was Mary Barclay, came up into the apartment and asked gentle questions, taking statements from both women, Nell Casey first because she was the mother of Tom, and then Stella, making notes as unobtrusively as possible. Downstairs, John Coffin had told her to handle the whole thing with tact. She had meant to do that in any case, but she was also observing Nell Casey and Stella Pinero with passionate interest. They both looked a bit pale and beaten up, not that you could blame them, and smart clothes were not in evidence, but, yes, a definite glamour hung around them.

Sylvie, who was in charge of Tom, had also been spoken to but seemed to know nothing. But you couldn't be quite sure of that, thought Mary, who was better able to judge a girl so near her own age. Sylvie might know something. She saved that thought up for future use.

Stella Pinero took herself off to her own apartment, protesting she wouldn't go if she didn't have a meeting.

WDC Mary Barclay saw her to the door.

Time for Tom also had to have his minute with her, sitting on his mother's knee, clutching Bonzo.

'I think he'll have to give Bonzo up for a while,' Mary whispered to Nell Casey. 'Tests, you know.' Coffin had instructed her to get possession of the stuffed animal. Peaceably if you can, he had said, but by brute force if you have to. Not the easiest of her jobs.

Nell shook her head. 'Not a chance.'

'He'll have to, Miss Casey.' Was she Ms, Miss or Mrs? Mary Barclay did not know but took the safest route, actresses were always Miss, the days of Mrs Siddons were long over. 'Either I shall have to take it off him or you will. Better you, really.'

But getting the dog away from the boy went better than Mary expected, surprisingly easy, in fact. The boy didn't have much of a vocabulary but what he had he was efficient with.

His mother had sat down on the floor and asked straight out for the dog. And straight out, she had set a price.

'A pound if you let me have him.'

No response.

'All right, two pounds. And you'll get him back. He will, won't he, Mary?'

'You will get him back,' Mary had promised, not knowing if he would or not.

'More,' Tom had said with a winning smile. 'More dollars.'

'The deal is in pounds,' his mother reminded him.

'Is that more?'

'It is.'

'Yes, Tom will.' But he still held on to the animal. 'Each day.'

'What, each day Bonzo is away? Come on, Tom.'

'He won't be away long,' said Mary hastily. He might never come back, who could tell what Forensics would get up to, but it was a lie in a good cause.

'All right,' said Nell, 'you've got me over a barrel.'

As she took the toy away from the boy and put it in a plastic bag, Mary thought: Wonder if he could have done it himself?

But no, that was a wicked thought, although in her experience kids could be wicked. But still, he certainly couldn't have buried the plaster hand and he didn't look old enough to have written his name.

'Can you write your name, Tom?' she asked.

His mother answered for him. 'He can't,' she said coldly. 'No more of that, please.'

'I had to ask.'

She put a few questions about the plaster hand, but Nell Casey knew nothing more.

Mary Barclay did not pass on the information about the arrival in the district of the child murderer.

'Keep a watch on him, Miss Casey. Probably nothing to worry about. But if anything does alarm you, you can always call me.'

Why did she have the distressing notion that she and Nell Casey would be seeing a lot of each other?

As well as the alleged child murderer who had just moved in, they had their own authenticated, fully certificated bunch of child molesters all on the register.

They had names, addresses and records. These were the lads who had been caught, sentenced and served their term.

In addition, there were all those undesirables they did not know about, who still moved murkily about the undergrowth. Life was full of joy, Coffin thought.

What the local mob were calling The Missing Bandwagon had still not turned up. By now the Press had heard about it and were besieging the Headquarters by Spinnergate with requests for information. There were two good pubs there, one a free house and the other with an excellent cuisine (best bangers and mash in London), so it was not a hard beat to walk.

The coach had been missing for almost twenty-four hours, and the coach-driver's wife, normally the most permissive and relaxed of women, was anxious. She was used to her husband being away a great deal, it was the job, but he was good about telephoning if he was going to be delayed. This time nothing. Silence.

She had spoken twice on the telephone herself to her brother-in-law, the other partner in the firm.

'Gert, I know no more than you do: nothing. At first, I didn't think much of it, I've had tours go missing before, temporarily. But never in London, and never for so long. I'm real worried about the coach.'

'I'm worried about my husband.'

'Of course you are, Gert, of course you are,' he said hastily. 'So am I.'

Somehow, he felt this was not quite enough, and the silence at the other end of the telephone reinforced this impression.

So he added, by way of explanation: 'But it's the insurance, you see, if anything's gone, well—' he sought for a word—'what you might call wrong, I have to put in a claim within twenty-four hours. The policy says so . . . Is Alf insured? Personally, I mean.'

'My God, what a terrible thing to say to me just now. And no, he isn't. You know him better than that.'

Unfortunately they both did.

'The police are out looking.'

'He won't like that, you know he won't,' said his wife with conviction.

They both did.

All over London, police units were keeping an eye out for any sign of the missing group. Naturally, the search was sharpest in the Second City of London where the tour had last been sighted. The Force commanded by John Coffin had the keenest responsibility.

Comments among the police ranged from the bawdy, making frank suggestions about where the coachload had gone and with what activity in mind, to the idea that a spaceship had come for them and they had gone off in it, a bunch of elderly ETs.

But underneath there was worry: it was beginning to look less good with every hour that went by with no sighting. The Force was stretched because of the fire in the Tube, but the blaze was out and so that particular crisis was now over, but it'd taken a lot of men off other duties. But they had the usual patrol cars out.

One patrol car had paid particular attention to a group of deserted Dockyard buildings, an empty office block and an old warehouse down by the Bingley canal. The canal itself was due to be turned into a marina with a hotel complex beside it, but planning permission was being disputed so that no work had been done.

The offices were empty and derelict and the rats had moved in. The young uniformed constable swore, kicked a ratling away, and left.

He returned to his car where his driver, a young WPC, looked at him in surprise.

'You weren't long. And look at you! Are you all right?'
'I don't like rats. Swarming with them in there.'
'Ah, I've heard there was a plague of them. It's the warm weather and all the rubbish. It suits them.'
'I'm not going back in there.' Not without a rat-catcher. Did the Force have one? If not, it should have.
Wordlessly she drove on a few yards. 'What about the warehouse?' She nodded to the gaunt building ahead of them. 'Want me to go? I don't mind rats. Used to keep white ones when I was a kid.
'These were not white,' he said with a shudder. 'Not white and nice at all, believe me.' He was getting out of the car. 'No, I'll go.'
'If you scream, I'll come across and help,' she said, settling back into her seat. She thought of having a smoke, but her colleague didn't smoke and was against breathing in someone else's fumes. Enclosed in the car she could hear nothing, but she could see him.
Suddenly he started to run. Someone was banging on the great double doors leading into the old warehouse. He could hear a voice, a woman's voice. 'Let me out, let us out.' The voice was hoarse, as if she had been shouting and shouting. 'Open the doors, damn you.' There was hysteria in the voice.
He waved towards his colleague in the car. 'Come and help me open these bloody doors.' But she was already out and running towards him. The voice on the other side of the door had gone quiet. 'I'm coming,' he shouted. 'Hang on.'
He was a strong young man, but the doors were heavy and old and stuck. He got them open a crack and peered through. 'Oh the Lord Harry! . . . Jess,' he called back. 'Get on the radio. We need help here.' And plenty of it, he thought.
He got the doors far enough apart to force himself through. It was dark inside but a strong streak of light came through the aperture so that he could see the coach parked in the middle of the warehouse.
The woman who had been banging and shouting was

slumped on the floor. He attended to her first. She was alive but looked poorly. He propped her up against the wall. 'Help's on the way. Hang on.'

Then he went over to the coach and stepped inside. He saw the driver slumped across his wheel, but on investigation he was found to be breathing, heavily but strongly. From the driver's seat the constable shone his torch along the rows of seats.

Passengers seemed to have collapsed into them. Slowly he went down the centre aisle, stopping at each seat to examine each person. Breathing, alive, but out cold. But one or two were stirring. One or two had vomited. Eyes opened.

He came to one seat and touched a chilling hand. He shone his torch in the face.

'This one's dead,' he said.

Because it was a major incident, John Coffin came down to the warehouse himself as soon as the word came through to him.

Ambulances were lined up on the forecourt where lorries had once been loaded with tea. The police surgeon was on hand, as required, but the ambulance men were good judges of an unconscious person.

'Dosed with some sedative,' the first arrival had summed up, 'hopped up with alcohol in some cases.'

The driver smelt faintly of whisky and was a bad case, still breathing stertorously, while others were already coming round, but looking rough.

'Drugged,' said the police surgeon briskly to John Coffin. 'Not lethal doses, though.

'And the dead man?'

The police surgeon shrugged. 'People react differently. Or he may have got more. Of whatever it was.'

Coffin walked down the coach to where the dead man lay across the back seat. Inspector Archie Young showed him the way. Lights had been rigged up so that he could see well.

'I know that face,' Coffin said.

'Yes,' said DI Young. 'What was he doing on the tour? It's Jim Lollard. We all got to know him, you as well, sir. He saw to that. He's cried wolf often enough and now someone's got him.'

Stella and Nell Casey were lunching in the bar of the Theatre Workshop. Trays of lunch were sent across from Max's Deli. He liked to do this trade, it paid, and kept his name active in theatre circles. His daughter, the Beauty one, had brought the trays across. She was anxious to inspect Nell Casey, although slightly disappointed to see that Nell was smaller and less made-up than in the soap, and wearing jeans, which anyone could wear (she was herself) and not the designer originals she had hoped for. The voice was the same, though, very lovely, although back to being more English.

Nell was in *French Without Tears*, playing the *femme fatale*, Kay, who tries to seduce the whole male cast, but gets her comeuppance in the last scene.

Gus, inevitably, was the wary sophisticate, originally played by Rex Harrison, who does not get seduced.

Nell said to Stella that she would not have minded playing that part either, but sex discrimination was still too strong to let a woman play a man, so she would grit her teeth and let Gus have the last word.

Tom and Sylvie were out to spend the first instalment of Tom's Danegeld, with Sylvie under strict instruction not to let him out of her sight.

'You ought to have some protection yourself, Nell,' said Stella, biting into a chicken sandwich. How many calories she wondered; still, the job she did demanded as much energy as a lorry-driver so that her weight was stable. Give or take a pound or two.

'I can look after myself. I'm strong. I took self-protection classes in New York. I didn't live in a very upmarket district, didn't have the money, so it seemed a good idea. A lot of women do it, it's so easy there.'

'Catching on here.'

'Just walk in and join a class, as easy as having your face

lifted. You can just walk in off the street and get your jaw-line tidied up. Over here you practically have to have a signed certificate that you are in your right mind.'

'Not if you're an actress,' said Stella.

'Now let's talk work.' For the next half-hour Stella filled in more detail about the work plan ahead. Bits of theatre gossip passed between them.

Nell began to look more relaxed and Stella congratulated herself. They walked across to the theatre so that Nell could familiarize herself with her working conditions.

'Dressing-rooms are adequate but not luxurious,' Stella warned her. 'Money being tight, I concentrated on good rehearsal and workout rooms.'

'Can I have a look?'

'Mm, sure. This way.' Stella went through a fire door (Letty Bingham had been very firm about these and they were always kept closed), and turned into a large, well-lit room. If it looked like a shed, that didn't matter; it was good, usable, adaptable space, exactly what rehearsals needed. 'Lovely to have this to use so that we don't have to go out to rooms at the back of pubs or old social halls. And I usually manage a good timetable so that even if, as happens, we have a couple of plays in rehearsal, each has its place on the rota.' She looked at her watch. 'Empty now.' . . . Oh damn, but this was to herself.

The room was not empty for there was Gus, walking round shouting as he busily conducted his teenagers in a workshop session on *Hamlet*, and *Rosencrantz and Guildenstern are Dead*. Several of the group were in the centre acting according to his instructions. Two of them looked baffled, one was crying and the third, a girl, had mysteriously picked up a black eye.

'I said be physical, not brutal,' Gus was saying. 'You silly sods.' His audience gave a joyous whoop, this was the sort of talk they liked. Beat politeness any day. Gus swung round as the two women came in.

'Oh, sorry, Gus, didn't expect you to be here.' Stella put a protective arm round Nell and began to draw her away. 'We'll leave you to it.'

'Saw the place was empty, just moved in.' Gus all over, he was a great mover-in to unoccupied places, not exactly part of his charm, but certainly part of his power. 'Oh, Nell, wanted to see you.' He was standing on the balls of his feet, rocking slightly. There was a threat there. 'I want to talk.'

'Some other time,' said Nell turning towards the door. 'Later.'

He caught up with her. Stella stood aside quickly. 'No, now. Question and answer time, love.'

'Not in front of all these people.'

'They can't hear.' This was true. Left to themselves, his class was raising its own din, as several of them moved into the acting arena and others disputed the interference. Stella could hear at least three Hamlets on the go and a couple of Ophelias, precipitating themselves noisily, but differently, mad. 'And I don't bloody care.'

'I don't want an audience.'

'Not like you, dear.'

Stella said hastily: 'There's my office just down the corridor.'

'This place will do.' Gus had a grip on Nell Casey's arm. 'The child, he's mine, isn't he?'

Nell did not answer.

'Yes or no.'

She shook her head.

'How old is he? When was he born? I have a right to know.'

Nell pulled at her arm and Gus pulled back. Her foot slipped on the matting and she slid backwards to the floor. 'Damn you, Gus.' She got up, white and shaking.

'I'm sorry,' he began.

'No, you're not, you enjoy it.'

Stella got herself between Nell and Gus. 'That's enough, you two. Come with me, Nell. Gus, I think your class needs you.' When Stella liked, she could pull rank and she did so now. Gus nodded, made a muttered apology and turned back to the small near-riot behind him.

Stella took Nell to her office, sat her down and gave her a drink. 'No questions asked, but clear things up with Gus before work starts in earnest. I won't stand for any nonsense in working time. You can do what you like outside it.'

Nell decided that she needed something to restore her morale and some new clothes might be the thing. After all, London fashion was subtly different from New York, clothes were not quite transferable and she might as well patronize the home team. She thought of names like Muir and Hamnet and Conran and Charles. John Boyd, but no, she wouldn't buy a hat. You needed to be in really good face for that and she was still suffering jet-lag skin. Besides, hats of all things were tricky, highlighting differences of skin, bone and sex, in a way you wouldn't expect. Her hair had suffered from the travel too, but she could deal with that herself. Nell had long ago learnt to do for herself what was needed. Money had been too short most of the time.

Tom and Sylvie had returned in triumph from their shopping expedition, having located and purchased another Bonzo. He was not, after all, unique. Hamley's had plenty of him. Bonzo Two he was now called.

They had been too excited to eat, so Nell took them to Max's Deli. She put on her dark spectacles but there was no one from St Luke's Theatre present. Mostly it was a pleasure to have fans and admirers come up and greet her, but sometimes she wanted to be anonymous. That was how she felt today.

She placed her handbag on the table beside her, an elegant soft leather pouch from Chanel. She checked her money and credit cards. All there. Next to them, tucked into a side pocket were three letters. Yes, they were there, as they should be. She valued those letters.

She gave Tom a long and loving look. What hostage to fortune a child was.

'Ice-cream?' she said. 'But have a club sandwich first.' She looked around. No, Max did not do club sandwiches, too American, but she could smell a buttery, oniony and peppery smell, and there was a big bowl of Parmesan. No, they would not starve. She picked up a packet on the table.

'Have a grissini,' she said, 'while I order.' After lunch, she set off shopping, taking the Tube from Spinnergate and changing at Piccadilly Circus for the line to Knightsbridge. She went in and out of shops, picking up this and that, little items, small but eyecatching. It was calming, like a drug, and what her spirit seemed to need. A compulsion not to be resisted. Tom and Sylvie had sought and been given permission to go to the park across the way.

'After your rest,' she had said.

'With Bonzo Two,' announced Tom.

'I should leave him at home.'

Tom shook his head.

'Up to you. But there won't be Bonzo Three if he goes missing.'

So Nell had put on what she called her 'Casey' face, and enjoyed her shopping. She returned, carrying several boxes and carrier-bags bearing illustrious names. At least one of the plastic bags was loaded with small choice objects that had taken her eye. She had been in a compulsive mood. One way and another she had had quite a haul.

She got out of the taxi (you really couldn't carry a dress from Yves St Laurent on the Tube) and met Sylvie and Tom just returning home.

Tom seemed as gay as a grig but there was a sort of look on Sylvie's face. She thought perhaps Sylvie was not too pleased to meet her just then. Tom had Sylvie's jacket draped over his shoulders.

'Why is Tom wearing your coat?'

Sylvie thought about it. 'He was cold,' she produced.

'But it's quite warm.' Actually, the boy looked overheated. 'Do take it off him.' And when Sylvie hesitated, she whipped it away herself.

His shirt was grubby but not too dirty, and he waved his arms about, certainly not complaining of being cold.

As he danced ahead into The Albion, she saw the back of his shirt.

Across it was a great handprint in red. It looked like blood.

'How did that get there?' she asked sharply. 'Is he hurt?'

Sylvie shook her head.

Nell grabbed the child and took a closer look. 'How did that get there, Tom?'

'Man,' he said happily. 'Man.'

'What man?'

'Man,' he repeated.

Nell put her hands to her head. 'Who is tormenting me?'

CHAPTER 6

Still March 6, then through March 7 to March 8

Although you couldn't leave it there, and Nell Casey said so at feverish intervals to Sylvie, it was hard to know how to advance. She couldn't get any more out of Tom, who varied Man with Person, a new word in his life and one that pleased him, thus confusing them completely.

Was the Person a man? Or did sex not matter to Tom and Man not mean man but a person who might be a woman? It was even possible to believe that Tom knew what he was doing and was confusing them for the hell of it.

It looked like a man's hand, though. The size. A right hand.

They had gone straight upstairs to the flat, Sylvie carrying Tom and Nell following behind in a protective way. There ought to be a lift, she grumbled to herself.

Under questioning, Sylvie produced nothing that was helpful. She admitted that they had been playing hide and seek with another small child who was out with her mother and that there had been a brief space of time when Tom was out of sight.

'But we were in a pretty part of the park,' she said tearfully, as if that in itself had constituted a protection, 'by the duck pond with flowerbeds all around us.'

'Were there other people near you?'

'Many, many,' said Sylvie, with tears running down her face. 'People walking, ladies with dogs, other children.'

'When did you notice about Tom's shirt? When did you see the blood?'

'When he came back from hiding.'

'You found him?'

'No, he just came back. And I say: What is the matter, Tom, why do you come back? He had that look, you know how Tom can look when he has done something he knows is naughty but he has enjoyed it.' Still the tears fell.

Nell knew the look exactly. 'And he showed you his shirt.' Nell was getting impatient, she was chiselling the facts out of Sylvie. Dry up, girl, she wanted to say, and get on with what happened.

'No, he just laughed. But I thought he was not happy, that something might have happened. Then I see the shirt, so we come straight home.'

'And did you see who could have done it?'

Sylvie shook her head.

Nell turned her son round. 'I suppose it is blood? Yes, it looks like it. Could have been an accident. Did anyone have an accident in the park? No, don't answer,' she said. 'You didn't see and you don't know.'

She sat back on her heels in the middle of the room with her packages, those lovely garments she had bought with such joy, distributed all around her.

'Get that shirt off, Tom.'

He held his arms up and let her pull it off. She stared at it for a moment. The blood was dry now, turning brown as the oxygen in the air got to it.

'Wonder if it's human blood?'

'What will you do?' asked Sylvie; she looked white.

'You frightened of blood, Sylvie?'

She nodded. 'Makes me sick.'

'Well, I'll tell you what I'm going to do. I'm going to put it in a plastic bag and take it round to the police . . . You and Tom have some tea and spend a bit of time watching television . . . There's a chocolate cake in that box.' She smiled and patted the girl on the shoulder. Sylvie flinched away from her: Nell didn't like that. What the hell's up with you, she thought, but she kept calm. 'It's all right, I'm not angry now, although I was at first. But just keep an eye on him in future, right?'

'Right,' said Sylvie, allowing herself a small tentative smile.

That girl's a fool, Nell said to herself as she gathered up her boxes and bags and went to her bedroom, but I think she's a kind fool and that's something.

Sylvie was already stagestruck, loved working for an actress, and had barely hidden ambitions to be an actress herself. This was one of her reasons for working with Nell Casey. Her father was a famous and successful film producer, which was Nell's reason for employing her. They both had their motives.

Nell rang the local taxi service, and walked down the staircase, the plastic bag containing the stained shirt under her arm, to wait for the cab.

'Take me to the main police station,' she said to the taxi-driver. 'I suppose you know where it is?'

He was one of the silent sort, which suited Nell, and he nodded without a word. It was a short drive, past St Luke's Mansions, down the busy main road towards the Spinnergate Tube station and then a sharp right turn. The new police station was a large, blunt-faced building that had not tried for elegance and had barely made functionalism. When you looked at it you had a shrewd idea that the roof leaked somewhere and would always leak, and that the people who worked in it were not so happy in it as they had hoped to be.

The taxi-driver leaned out of his cab: 'Want me to wait, miss?'

'No, I can walk back.' She had memorized the route like a cat, she had not got used to spending money freely and, as a matter of fact, had not got that much to spend. Her little circus took a lot to carry round with her and then to house in the comfort they expected. Nor would she be earning much with Stella Pinero, but there was something good coming up which her agent was negotiating for at this very time. The new Ayckbourn was casting and she was being asked for. A lead part too, and he always wrote marvellous parts for women.

She was surprised at the smart reception area, not like *Hill Street Blues* or Cagney and Lacey at all. Surely British police stations could not be newer and more comfortable than those across the Atlantic? Not beautiful, though. Commonplace was how she would have described it, as if the architect had not really thought too highly of the people who would use it. Or even much about them at all, and much more of the records, papers, books and computers they would need.

She asked the uniformed man at the desk for WDC Mary Barclay. The name rose to her lips unprompted.

She got a look of surprise, but a telephone call was put through and Mary Barclay presently appeared through the swing doors at the end of the corridor.

'Hello, Miss Casey. Anything I can do?'

'Talk, please,' said Nell, through dry lips. There was a clean, clear look in Mary Barclay's eyes as if she could see right through to the essential you. That's the professional look, Nell thought, flinching away from it nervously.

'Right. Follow me.'

Mary Barclay took Nell through to an interview room. Still clean, still reasonably comfortable. A faint, just a very faint institutional smell on the air.

'Let's have it.'

She listened quietly to Nell's story. Then she said: 'Have to ask this. Sorry, but I must. Is there any chance the girl, Sylvie Meruit, could be doing these things?'

'Don't think I haven't thought of that,' said Nell. 'I mean, of course I did. But I can't believe it.'

'What do you know about her? References and all that?'

'Her father is a very well-known film producer,' said Nell slowly. 'I didn't think she needed references. I've worked with him.'

She had done more than that, together they had had a very pleasant, little fling. Or call it what you will. It had been both pleasant and intense. More on his side than hers, oddly enough, because it was usually Nell who went overboard. Physically it hadn't worked too well, she had been unlucky there. These things took time. Then his family, including Sylvie, had come over and the affair had ended. Just as it should do, because neither of them wanted his wife upset. She was in fragile health.

In fact, she had died rather suddenly. It was one of the reasons for bringing Sylvie away with her: to give her a lift, help her get over it.

Get over what? asked a hard little voice inside Nell Casey's head. Her mother's death or her father's affair?

But Sylvie can't know about that, Nell answered herself. It had not been an utter secret, things like that were never an utter secret in the world she moved in, but the relationship had been declared past history as soon as Sylvie came over from Paris.

Past history for Nell was easy. She could put things behind her fast.

All except that one thing connected with Gus, which still rankled. She had liked that kid in Australia, really liked, and he had really liked her.

'Can't believe it of Sylvie,' she said aloud to Mary Barclay, putting aside all her reservations about the girl. 'Not Sylvie, she's such a nice child.'

But WDC Barclay registered the slight delay in answering and drew her own conclusions. Something there, she thought.

'Besides, Tom likes her. He'd pick up any bad vibes, I know he would. And he wouldn't fail to say, either.'

'He's very young.'

'But no fool,' said Nell stoutly.

But children can be deceived, thought the policewoman from the depths of her troubled experiences, children can be so easily deceived, led and misled by those they love.

'Fond of the girl, is he?' she asked.

'Very.'

'It was sensible of you to bring the shirt.' She took up the plastic bag with the soiled shirt in it. 'It does look like blood. I'll get it looked at.'

She was reassuring to Nell, said she would come round and see the boy, have a word with him, see what he had to say, then talk to Sylvie herself.

'He won't say anything more to you, and I don't suppose Sylvie will.'

'Worth a try,' said Mary Barclay easily. 'I have to give it a try. Couldn't face the Sarge without.' She made it light, not serious at all, as if no terrors could ever break in.

She did not say that the police everywhere were on the alert for William Duerden, looking for him all over the district, and that this was her real worry, not any suspicions of Sylvie.

Get Duerden, the Boss had said. If he's in my bailiwick I want him. Unexpressed by John Coffin was his feeling that Duerden was already operating.

Nell walked home, grateful to have the air on her face. She felt sick inside: she had set the machine in motion, but she could not leave it there. Tom was her responsibility. Somehow, she would have to protect him, while getting on with her own life. She couldn't afford to stop work.

If it was Gus doing this, perhaps that was what he had in mind: to drive her out of the theatre. He had always hated her work, pretended he hadn't, but she knew better. He thought she was too light, too detached, not involved. Not female enough. Not true. She worked in a different style but her work was just as true and valid as his. That was one of their troubles, the clash of two different visions.

He wouldn't hurt a child, though, she thought. But it might be some devious scheme to get his hands on Tom, to claim him as his own.

Over my dead body, she told herself.

She called to Sylvie as she let herself in to the flat in The Albion. 'I'm back. That policewoman will be round soon. So don't go out.' Sylvie had the evenings free if Nell was home.

Nell gathered up the script with the notes that Stella had given her and sat by the window, working. She had a beautiful voice but she was finding it hard to get into the speech patterns of Rattigan, the 'thirties way of speech was subtly different, but it was important to get it right. Speech patterns influenced body posture, she believed.

She looked out of the window. No one there.

A dead body lay under the harsh lights in the police mortuary. The only victim of the missing coach was being investigated. The other passengers were quietly passing the time in their various homes and hotels while awaiting visits from the police. They had been told not to talk to the journalists clustering around like flies over a succulent piece of decay.

To the police all the passengers had told the same story: they had felt sleepy, gone to sleep and woken up to find themselves locked in the old warehouse. The heavy doors were stuck and impossible to open.

They had a memory of being driven in and told by the driver it was going to be a true horror and something they would never forget. It had been, only not in the way they had expected.

Some passengers were angry at what had happened to them, others just miserable, and all were puzzled. At least two were in hospital and one was dead.

The driver was questioned at more length and was still detained in hospital. The police had quietly suggested he would be better there for the present and the doctors had agreed. He was segregated from his passengers, all of whom had been medically examined before leaving. The majority of them had been passed as fit by the doctors, and allowed to depart.

Doped, but coming out of it now. The drug had not yet been identified positively, but the informed guess was that it was a common sedative easily bought over the counter which could be used as a sleeping tablet. Dormex was the brand name. It was allied to one of the anti-allergens. As a drug it came out of the same family.

The driver had been sicker than most, or perhaps more tired to begin with. He still seemed dazed, as if he couldn't believe what had happened to him. Or was he just acting that way? DI Young had his suspicions.

Tremble was genuinely bemused and his head ached

worse than any hangover he had ever had; it was a relief to keep his head on the pillow and see no one. He did not want to see his wife or his brother, nor the policemen who kept popping in and out with questions. He felt confused, with his head full of thick lead, but alert enough to pick up that he was under suspicion. Of exactly what he was not sure, but of something. He was questioned at first by a young plain clothes sergeant, only he didn't quite catch his name. Second time round he was questioned by a full inspector and this time he took pains to listen to the name. Or perhaps he was just more awake by that time.

DI Young. Not a friend, he thought.

In the room, sitting in a corner, but not saying anything, was a tall older man, with bright blue eyes.

This man he did not introduce himself, nor did Tremble know him, but he had the feeling he ought to have done. Might even like to, he looked a decent chap. Only, with policemen, as Tremble well knew, you could never tell. Looks could deceive. Might be a real swine underneath that calm look.

He wished he could remember exactly what lies he had told.

John Coffin was sitting in on the interview, to the embarrassment of DI Young, who had had no choice in the matter, had to say yes, of course, sir, as politely as if he was pleased. The word had already gone in that the Boss would be dropping in on them all without warning. It was just his turn. The Boss was doing it to them all.

Coffin had good reason for this.

One of the local MPs interviewed on the radio had said that he was not happy with the policing in this area. Was it racialist? Too casual, too laissez-faire? Was the Chief Commander up to the job? He might be asking a question in the House.

The attack was probably political, an election was coming up in what was a marginal seat, but you had to play politics. You had to protect yourself. Coffin knew this and had learnt to play the game.

He had let it be known that he would be dropping in on all units, unannounced, to take a look around.

This apart, these two cases worried him.

A dead man, Jim Lollard, dead in strange circumstances, and a child murderer on the loose. A man gearing himself up for action, by all the signs. Coffin had read the report of Mary Barclay and he didn't like it. Yes, he was worried and taking a very personal interest.

Now he took in the scene in front of him. Driver Alfred Tremble was sitting in a chair dressed in hospital pyjamas and gown, looking sorry for himself. He was a small man with a long nose and greying hair, it was easy for him to look depressed. The good cheer that coach tour drivers were supposed to radiate towards their customers had not existed with him. He was a natural for terror tours.

Yes, he said, he had driven to the warehouse. No, he'd never been there before and hoped never to go again. But he'd been told it was the scene of a horrific mass murder and hadn't been touched for years. Genuine unspoilt scene of the crime and well worth a look.

And was it? DI Young said, keeping his voice neutral, masking his scepticism.

No, not really, swept and garnished except for the odd mouse dropping, it had looked in the coach headlights. But honestly, Guv, he'd been half asleep already, sagging at the wheel. He'd known something was wrong.

You drove in? DI Young had asked. What then? Who shut the doors?

Tremble said he thought it was one of the passengers.

Wasn't that odd?

Not really, Tremble had tried to say. He'd expected it, part of the show. Drive in, doors close, lights off, then floodlights would come and there would be the spectacle.

Who shut the door? DI Young had persisted.

Tremble had licked his lips, taken a drink and managed to answer that one with a loss of memory statement. Couldn't say.

But the question was put once more. Even he could see it was a crucial question: Who shut the door?

Tremble said again that he couldn't remember. He was aware of not being believed.

There was silence in the room, then DI Young asked: 'And who told you this tale, which you say you believed, about the mass murder?'

The silence went on and on. Tremble thought they would sit there for ever until he answered.

'Jim Lollard,' he said at last.

Jim Lollard, late of Regina Street, otherwise known, and principally by Lollard's own efforts, as Murder Street.

Lollard couldn't confirm or deny this, he was dead.

Tremble pressed his hands to his eyes. 'I've got a terrible headache. Can I have a drink?'

'Shifty chap,' said DI Young as they were talking it over afterwards. The scene had moved to the Incident Room set up in the old church hall next to the Rip and Vic. Handy spot, he thought, feeling thirsty. 'Always has been.'

'You know him?' asked Coffin.

'Of old.'

'Keep at him. He's lying, I think. Keeping something back.'

'We won't leave him alone.' It was a promise, and one which Tremble had felt hanging over him. More was to come, and no one knew it more than Alfred Tremble.

Coffin and Archie Young discussed the case, Coffin sitting there with the various reports and statements laid out in front of him. 'I'll have to be off soon,' he said, aware of the next engagement, the next committee, this time one in Central London. There was never enough space for everything.

In the room with them was Superintendent Paul Lane and Sergeant Alison Jenkins. These two had arrived to discuss the elusive child murderer. They were aware of the importance of grabbing the Chief when you knew where he was.

Jenkins had had experience in looking for people like William Duerden. She knew what to look for, the signs of their presence in a community, but this time she was having no success.

He seemed to have vanished off the face of the earth. But he had done that before in his career. It was one of his tricks.

All local known perverts being rounded up and interviewed. Just in case they had contact with Duerden.

'Not usually a coven,' said Lane.

'No rules,' said Coffin.

'Agreed. But they tend to be loners.'

Alison Jenkins said nothing. Not for her to interrupt the top brass. But she had her own thoughts.

DI Young said: 'I've heard a rumour that a paedophile group is in the district. Haven't been able to get anything positive.'

'May only be a letter-drop. Postal address but no actual meetings,' said Jenkins.

'Yes, I wondered about that. But my informant thought it was for real. Actual bodies meeting.'

'Is he reliable?'

'It's a she. And yes, I think so.'

'Work on it,' said Coffin.

The meeting ended on this note, and Coffin took himself off. The others went off to the Ripper and Victim for a drink. He would have gone himself, but there were certain things protocol demanded.

He returned to his office, dictated some letters, and in the car on the way to his meeting allowed himself to think about Nell Casey and Nell's child. There was something deeply disturbing in that set-up. What was going on was irrational and abnormal. A good thing Stella was there. Stella could be maddening, but she was a very sane lady.

Also drinking in the Ripping Vic (his own special nickname for the Ripper and Victim) was a young journalist. He sat in the bar and sipped his lager, making it last, while he thought out what to do.

Jim Lollard was dead.

He knew something about Lollard.

Should he tell the police? Or write it up first? A scoop, as they used to say, and in his private mythology still did.

It was only wise to keep in with the police. It was also wise to keep in with his editor.

He went back over his talk with old Lollard. He remembered the words and could recall the angry voice. 'There's going to be a multiple crime, I see the signs. I tried to tell the police but they wouldn't listen. Cocky chap, that sergeant. Well, he'll find out I was right. I can see a roomful of people. All with their eyes closed. Flopped about anyhow.'

The young man sipped his lager. 'You got second sight?' he had asked.

Lollard hadn't answered directly. 'Oh yes, death there all right,' he'd said with some satisfaction.

So there had been, admitted the young man. Lollard's own death, as it turned out.

Lollard had probably been mad, living there on Murder Street. There, where so many people had met violent ends over the years . . . He'd lived there for so long, thought about it too much, let it get on his mind. Gone off his rocker.

Or had he known something?

He put down his lager to make a few notes. Across the room, he saw the police group come in. He recognized them, of course. He had attended enough Crown Courts, had hung around the police headquarters in Spinnergate often enough to know their faces and put a name to them. It was his job.

He watched them talking and laughing. He knew already that Young was working on the coach hi-jacking. (That was the headline in his own paper although he knew and the chief news editor knew that hi-jacking it was not. Or not precisely. Something both more and less.)

He drank slowly, considering the little nugget of information he had inside him. Lollard had probably told him the tale so it would be in his newspaper. So in a way he was letting him down by not rushing it in. Get his byline on it. Our reporter writes . . . A special insight from our reporter. Sounded good. He was tempted.

But a certain wise caution held him back.

In the first place, his news editor played golf with DI Young and was said to belong to the same Masonic Lodge as Superintendent Lane. There was a channel of communication between all three and you could never tell what messages about him might pass down it.

That was one thing. Secondly, like a stray dog left outside in the street, he felt a strong, elemental desire to insert himself into that cosy group.

He stood up, unwinding his thin length, took his drink with him and went over.

'I know something,' he announced. 'Old Lollard knew there was going to be a scene of mass murder.' It hadn't quite worked out like that, but Lollard had talked about death. He thought there might be more than one. As it happened there hadn't been, only his own, but it might not be for want of trying. 'Call it precognition if you like, but he knew.'

They looked at him as if he was mad, but they were certainly taking it in.

'Sit down, sonny,' said Lane, 'and tell us all.'

Pompous bastard, thought that young man. But he sat down. He was in. The stray dog was inside and wagging his tail.

The other straying dog, the first Bonzo, had yielded up a little information on the forensic laboratory bench.

Twenty-four hours after listening to the interview with driver Tremble, and having heard about the tale from the young journalist, having inspected several other departments and presided at several committees and tactfully refused to be interviewed on the lunch-time radio news programme about the criticisms from the MP, Coffin remembered about the dog and telephoned to ask for progress. He was working alone in his room, but every so often he thought about Tom and about Nell Casey. Stella had telephoned him about the episode of the bloody shirt, and he had read Mary Barclay's résumé of her interview with Sylvie and the boy. Which in turn had been sent to Superintendent Paul Lane and Alison Jenkins, both of whom were approaching the affair from another angle.

Nothing the boy or Sylvie had to say was either helpful or pointed positively to Duerden, but it all made Coffin's nerves twitch. Yes, he wanted to see that report.

The report was duly delivered to him on the evening of Thursday, March 8, rushed through at his urgent request, to the accompaniment of various jokes by the cynical and wary scientists who worked in the police laboratory. Still, it made a change from their usual investigations.

There were no fingerprints, the nature of the furry skin made this impossible.

Nevertheless, his attacker had not worn gloves, so there were traces of sweat on the fur. This would be helpful if they ever had a suspect under investigation when his or her DNA profile could be offered up for matching.

More helpful was the information that there were traces of make-up on the animal. On the inside of the skin, so these traces were unlikely to have been left there by anyone other than the hand with the knife.

A woman, then?

Or stage make-up?

Coffin raised his head from the report. But what about the plaster hand of a child, stained with blood? Anything in the report about that?

No, nothing. That was still pending.

Likewise the bloody shirt, which had come into the laboratory too recently to have been worked on yet. It was still sitting in its plastic bag, waiting.

A kindly hand had stitched up Bonzo so that he looked decent in case he was handed back to his owner, but he was still locked up in his sterile envelope, so he was not due to go home yet awhile. If ever.

Coffin went back home to prepare himself for a read through of *The Circle*, which was going to be held in the house of one of the Friends of St Luke's Theatre. She was Chairperson of the committee and also a power in the Dramatic Society. In addition, she was playing Lady Kitty. Melanie Milkington Strange was a powerful lady. She was known locally as Milly M.S. and was both feared and admired. Stella Pinero liked her very much, but then she and Stella fought at equal weights. They did fight, as Coffin well knew having observed one or two dust-ups, both ladies having clear strong views on matters such as the choice of the plays for the Theatre Festival season, the casting of such, and the erection of a marquee in the ground behind St Luke's for the serving of a buffet supper after the performance. Milly M.S. was also, *ex officio*, on the committee of the Festival. She had a hand in everything, and had contributed money generously to all funds. In short, she could not be ignored, although Stella would override her when she had to do so, shouting loudly that all policy decisions were hers and hers alone.

Milly gave good supper parties, but after an evening of being Lady Kitty Champion-Cheney was apt to put on a few airs and graces, as acting Lady Kitty went to her head. She was also inclined to forget that John Coffin was not a butler but only playing one. He had got bored last time, buttling for Milly and ministering to the miseries of Sybil Deansly, the pale blonde whose acting ability was severely taxed by the small amount of it she was required to display as the young wife, Elizabeth. There was a sense in which Elizabeth was the heroine of *The Circle*, but everyone knew that Lady Kitty was the best part. Milly knew this too.

So he thought he would give her party a miss and take Stella off for a light supper at Max's. Max's Delicatessen had recently equipped itself with a small supper parlour where you could eat after the theatre. Max never seemed to go to bed. He had put in his bid to supply the marquee food for the Festival and this was another bone of contention between Stella, who was on Max's side, and Milly who wanted the food to be provided by a new caterer from Covent Garden. Stella was sticking out for using the local firm.

She was on stage that night, as she liked to take an occasional small part, but he left a message on her answering machine, suggesting a meeting at Max's.

Then he went off to his own session. It was without the

book tonight. Well, no trouble to him. He had nothing much to say, but it might be tricky for poor Sybil. He smiled, feeling no mercy. He rather enjoyed watching Sybil act badly, she was so deliciously distracted, half miserable, half pleased with herself, that it offered a pleasure peculiarly its own.

The rehearsal was round the corner in the Scouts' Hut. He would mark out the stage himself, and set out such small props as they needed. It was his other world at the moment, far away from child murderers and dead men who could foretell the future. He stepped out cheerfully, hoping the hall was unlocked and that the caretaker had put the heating on.

He never got there. Before he was half way round the corner, he met Nell Casey herself.

She was in a hurry, almost running. She threw herself towards Coffin.

'Thank God I've found you. I was looking for you. Tom is missing.'

He took her arm. 'Steady on. How long has he been gone?'

'I don't know,' Nell cried. 'I was out. Working. Lunch.' The words came in small bursts. 'I had a meeting with my agent and then an audition. He was home with Sylvie as usual.' She took a deep gasping breath.

'And?'

'When I got back they weren't there. No sign of them. And they haven't reappeared. And it's long past Tom's bedtime.'

He steadied her. 'There's no reason as yet to believe he's come to harm. Calm down.'

She turned her face towards him, there were tears on it.

But how extraordinary, he thought, one eye has tears in it and the other is quite dry.

She's an actress, he told himself, she can achieve effects. Even force tears if she wants.

Something strange about this girl, he thought as they hurried towards The Albion.

All right, she loves the boy . . . I think she loves the boy. She's the mother. If he is her child, and not a prop she has arranged for the occasion. But there's something extremely odd going on.

The root of the mystery is in this woman. It all stems from her.

CHAPTER 7

Still March 8

The little apartment was empty but showed signs of Nell Casey's anxieties. Her coat, with an umbrella and small handbag, were thrown on the floor in the hall. A pile of letters and a newspaper were scattered near them, as if she had picked them up and dropped them when she realized the place was empty.

'I stood at the door and called,' she said. 'But there was no one here. I rang the theatre, but Stella was not around. The matinée had ended late and she had gone off for a discussion with the director. I spoke to the stage manager but he hadn't seen them. Sylvia and Tom wouldn't go there, anyway. Then I ran outside looking for them. I looked in the garden.'

'And there was no sign of them?'

She shook her head. 'No sign they had ever been there. I waited. You know how one does, hesitating, thinking what to do. I hung around, wondering, trying to damp down my fears. But then I started to panic. Where were they? What had happened. Then I came looking for you.'

It was amazing, he thought, how good she appeared, even in her distress. Her hair looked untidy, but it was fashionable to have wild dishevelled curls, she had bitten off her lipstick, but pale lips were in vogue. He saw her beautifully manicured hands, with the long strong fingers. Well cared for, he thought, slightly tanned (might be make-up?) but elegant. She had lost one earring, but anyone might do that. And it was even fashionable just to wear one solitary jewel (hers were of pearl, pink and gleaming), so she might have started out that way. She was beautifully dressed in a pale tweed suit. A tall girl, with a strong bone structure, she looked well in tailored clothes. She had had an audition, he recalled and a meeting with her agent. Did you dress like that for an audition? Had she dressed herself with something else in mind?

He could smell her scent, strong and sweet and synthetic, and mixed with it the sweat of sudden emotion. She was wound up all right, but what was she really feeling?

He pushed her into a chair. 'Let's sit down and talk this over. Where does it start? Tell me about today.'

The day had started well.

Yes, she had gone for her audition, a reading, nothing much to it, difficult to read cold, Ayckbourne always was, she didn't know if she had got the part. She had dressed up for the part because she was nervous. Her fingers had flexed anxiously as she spoke of this. Yes, in an office off Bond Street. Then she had walked round the corner to see her agent, not stayed too long, and then walked to Piccadilly.

A message left at her agent's had invited her to lunch at the Ritz with Ellice Eden. Lunch with Ellice was both a ritual and a threat in the profession. No one refused, he was too powerful for that, but you went at your peril.

It was so easy to fall into trouble with him (and she had done, in the past), if he was in a rotten mood and then there would be bad notices for your next play and probably the one after that. So it was as well to read the signs, the significance of which was handed on by word of mouth from survivors of such lunches. If you were offered a champagne cocktail, accept, it was a good sign. You were in favour. If offered a second before lunch, refuse. At lunch, let Ellice choose the wine (if he went for mineral water only, forget it, you might as well get up and go home, things could only go from bad to worse) and do not eat red meat. Never ask for soup.

Nell had arrived, feeling nervous but hopeful, because she knew he liked her as far as he liked any woman, and been offered a champagne cocktail before she even sat down beneath a tree in a pot.

'I've been looking forward to you coming back to London.' Ellice Eden sat in a chair opposite, bright-eyed and alert. 'That stuff you were doing on TV over there was not worthy of you.'

'No?' Nell was cautious. 'Earned well, though. The money was good.' She had been grateful for the income.

'Money isn't everything, especially at your age. I know what I'm talking about, don't think I don't. I've been poor. But talent has to be served too. You have talent.' He leaned back in his chair. 'Another drink?'

'No, thank you.'

He rose. Let's eat then, shall we?'

The Ritz and lunch, Nell knew, was for those on the way up. When you had really arrived it was dinner at the Savoy.

Just as well it was lunch, she told herself as she sat down, and not dinner anywhere. She had clothes for a smart lunch but not for a dinner, except somewhere casual like Max's Deli.

'Soup? Or something else?' He put on gold-rimmed spectacles to read the menu. '*Oeuf en gêlée*, perhaps?' His eyes glittered behind the spectacles.

Nell took a risk. 'I think smoked salmon.'

She had chosen well. 'Splendid. Plain, straightforward, a wise choice. I'll join you. Then we'll both have venison.'

She hated venison, but venison it would be, and she would look happy with every substantial mouthful.

'They hang it very well here. Just the right length of time. Nice and high.'

Malevolent beast, she thought, he's doing it on purpose, he knows I hate meat.

'I expect you're wondering why I've asked you to lunch?'

'Oh well . . .' What a question. 'You do ask people to lunch.'

'I'm known for it.' He nodded to an acquaintance across the room. She longed to turn and look, it was bound to be someone celebrated, someone she wouldn't mind meeting. 'It's my way of working.'

So this is work. Nell silently absorbed the idea. I'm work. Lunch at the Ritz is work, dinner at the Savoy more work. Well, good for you, old boy.

He was independently wealthy, she knew that. Lavatory fittings from Grandpa, so she'd heard. The statement that he knew what it was to be poor was not true and never had been. Or not poor by most people's standards. A lot of his power lay in this financial independence. That, and an innate, instinctive, unlearnable taste: he knew what was good. He had a palate for the theatre as some have for wine. And he had a passion for it, which was perhaps what mattered most.

Here he and Nell met on common ground; she too had that passion.

'Talking of work,' he went on over the venison. 'I'm glad you're back this side of the Atlantic. How did today's audition go?'

'Oh, you know about it?' Nell was surprised.

He nodded. 'Of course. When Charles told me he was casting the new Ayckbourne, he thought of you at once.'

Nell doubted this. In her opinion there were several strong contenders for the role of the doughty, sharp-tongued heroine, from Maggie Smith downwards, but she was glad to be in the running.

'I'd like to get it,' she admitted. 'Marvellous play, marvellous part.'

'It would make you.'

Nell thought she had been made already, by her own exertions, but to star in the West End, and Her Majesty's Theatre had been hinted at, would be a big step up. No mention had been made of salary but she would take that up when the time came. If it came. She wanted to believe in all this but a sense of unreality pervaded her. She hadn't slept much lately, she had so much on her mind.

'How's the boy?' asked Ellice over coffee.

'Oh yes, did you meet him at St Luke's?' *Had he?*

'Saw his picture. Nice-looking lad.'

Nell smiled gratefully but said nothing. They might be on dangerous territory. Ellice Eden was not known as a child-lover. Rather the reverse, as several child performers had found to their cost.

'Don't let him go on the stage, dear.'

'He's a bit young to think about anything like that.'

'In the blood, though, I expect. Not that he looks like you.'

Nell was silent.

'Sons often look like their mothers, but not in your case.'

'I don't think there's any rule,' said Nell uneasily.

'I expect he's more like his father?'

'There's no accounting for genes,' responded Nell vaguely. She drank some coffee and pre-empted any speech from Ellice by asking for a second cup. In another minute he's going to ask who Tom's father is. Or was.

But the moment passed.

Ellice led the talk off to theatrical gossip.

'Marvellous woman, Stella Pinero. The theatre would be lost without her. She's really the guiding force behind St Luke's. She persuaded Laetitia Bingham into it, you know. I was there when they met at a dinner-party. Stella did it in about three minutes flat. A joy to watch. I think I introduced them. Penny Hayden was the hostess and of course she never knows who she's asked to dinner. If she knows the face she can't remember the name and if she knows the name she's forgotten the face.'

'I don't know Lady Hayden.'

'Keep away from her, dear. At least for the moment. When the right time comes, I will see you meet.'

'Oh, thanks.' A little tipsy with wine and excitement, Nell leaned back in her chair. She had kept her head and not let anything out that she didn't want let out. That in itself was a major achievement with Ellice, who was famous for being able to winkle out what he wanted. She could see what he was getting at: whose child was Tom? None of your business, she thought. Time to go, another glass of wine and she might say more than she should. She pushed her chair back. 'Been a lovely, lovely lunch, Ellice. Thank you.'

He reached out his hand and took hers. 'I want you to leave this lunch perfectly happy.' She was touched by the sincerity in his voice. He really minded.

'I am, I am.'

And so she was.

Nell had gone home, flying high, happy in the blissful expectation that her career was about to accelerate. She had been right to come home. London was home. It had been fun being Casey, she half regretted the dropping away of that bright, tough persona, but Nell, after all, was who she was. A person who had her pretences but less of them than Casey.

She had considered taking a taxi all the way back home to The Albion (Casey would have done so), but Nell frugally took over and chose the Underground from Green Park, changing at Piccadilly and then again at Charing Cross for Spinnergate.

At Spinnergate she emerged to have a brief conversation with the lady in the lavishly flowered hat who sold newspapers from a stall on the pavement.

She handed Nell the early edition of the evening paper. 'Got a paragraph about you in it, Miss Casey. And a lovely picture of you and the boy. In the "About London" column.'

'Oh good. Any publicity helps.'

'So Miss Pinero always says,' said Mimsie Marker. 'Sells papers, anyway. You'd be amazed how people buy them if they've got their face in it. Mind you, we're lucky round here. We have a lot of local murders and that's always good for trade.' She handed over Nell's change. 'The latest one in the old Hacker's warehouse is going nicely. It's the coach tour that's the selling point. Look at the driver, I say. He'll be in it somewhere.'

'Think so?' said Nell.

'Take my word . . . Saw your little lad going off for his drive. Good job he isn't twins, you've got a handful there.'

Nell walked on, looking at the newspaper, reading about 'the coach tour to Terror Land', as the newspaper headline called it, which had involved the death of Jim Lollard. Funny business, she thought.

There was nothing in the paper about the search for William Arthur Duerden, suspected child murderer, for this was a matter the police were keeping to themselves.

As Nell walked the few yards to The Albion, she remembered what Mimsie Marker had said about Tom going off for his drive. Not Tom, she thought, some other boy.

But she hurried her pace, the edge of her mood clouding somewhat. In at the front door of The Albion, up the stairs, never a soul to see, there never was, the other inhabitants seemed permanently immured behind their doors, with sounds of movement and smells of cooking but never a face to be seen, then unlocking her own door. She could hear her telephone while she fumbled with the key, but by the time she was inside it had ceased.

'Sylvie? Tom? I'm back.'

No answer. Nell went from room to room, looking for them. Oh well, Sylvie was allowed to take Tom for a walk. They weren't prisoners.

She changed her clothes, made some tea, and waited. And waited. The light began to fade from the spring sky.

Anxiety seized her. She telephoned Stella Pinero; not available. She spoke to the stage manager: no knowledge of Tom and Sylvie, they had not been seen.

It was at this point that she ran out to look for John Coffin.

'I'll take you back to The Albion,' Coffin said. 'And we'll start doing some more telephoning.'

Silently Nell let herself be led back. This time, a woman's face appeared at the door of the flat below.

'Are you all right, Miss Casey?'

'Yes,' said Nell mechanically.

'I heard your telephone ringing and ringing this afternoon and no answer. Then I heard you run down the stairs. And you left your front door open.'

'Did I?' Nell, followed by John Coffin, went upstairs, leaving the woman staring after her in concern. Yes, she had been rude, but she had no concern left to spare for good manners.

Inside, Coffin sat her down. 'Come on now, we're going into this. When did you last see the two of them?'

Nell stared out through the window. 'Before I left. They were in the kitchen . . . But I think they may have gone somewhere in a car. Someone took them.'

'You didn't tell me this.'

'No. I'm telling you now.' She hesitated. 'I heard about it. But I didn't believe it was them.'

'Who told you?'

'The woman who sells papers down by the Underground.'

'Mimsie Marker. She's a good witness.' The best. Hard to fault Mrs Marker's eyesight, powers of observation and memory. 'What did she say?'

'She said she hoped the boy enjoyed his ride.' Nell added: 'She meant me to know, I think.' As if she had spotted something wrong.

'We'll get hold of Mimsie.'

'She won't be there still.'

'I know where Mimsie lives.' He went to the telephone and dialled Mimsie's number, one of them, she was reputed to own a handsome villa elsewhere and also a house in the country, but he gambled she would be in the old family home.

'Hello? Mimsie, John Coffin here. Just a question about the Casey boy. You saw him in a car?' Nell, listening, heard the telephone crackle. 'Right. Sure it was him? All right, Mimsie, I believe you. You're sure? Who was with him? . . . Really? Thanks, Mimsie.'

He turned back to Nell. 'He was in a taxi and Sylvie was with him. No one else.'

'I don't understand. Why should they do that? It's not like Sylvie. Where would they be going? She hardly knows anywhere in London.'

'Hold steady. It's good news. If they were in a taxi, then we'll trace it. Someone ordered the cab and the driver knows where he took them.'

He picked up the telephone, ready to take action, but before he could do so they both heard the door to the flat open.

Sylvie and Tom bundled into the room. Tom looked cheerful if tired and dirty and Sylvie looked cross.

Nell sprang towards them. 'Where have you been? I've been so frightened. Why did you go off in a taxi? Who sent it?'

Sylvie pushed the hair from her forehead. 'You did.'

'Me?' Nell recoiled in surprise.

'Yes.' There was an edge of anger in Sylvie's voice. 'You sent the cab and a message to meet you at the Natural History Museum in Kensington. And then you didn't come.'

Her voice rose. 'We waited and waited. I took Tom for a look around at the fossil animals. Then we looked for you again. And I telephoned several times but you weren't here. So in the end, we came home on the Underground. But we got lost.'

'Hungry,' said Tom loudly.

The two women stared at each other in open hostility. Coffin looked from one to the other.

Now which, if either, is telling the truth, he asked himself.

CHAPTER 8

The late evening of March 8 on to 16

'It's hard to know which one was telling the truth,' said John Coffin, over his much delayed meal with Stella Pinero in the new supper room at Max's Delicatessen. It was possible Max had overreached himself in the decoration of this room, which he had based upon memories of a room in Vienna full of gilt and red plush, and he was nervous of its future, aware he served a fickle public, but meanwhile it was proving popular, always busy and crowded. Very crowded this night, but he always had room for Stella Pinero, and prudence itself dictated a welcome to the policeman. He liked the man, although sometimes Max said to himself that the crime had gone up round here, not down, since Coffin moved into the neighbourhood.

They were eating one of Max's special dishes, an omelette filled with seafood and served with a hot tarragon sauce. You had to eat it immediately it was cooked, and with flat bread. A green salad later, not with. Max's orders. Then a sorbet to refresh the palate.

Stella took a mouthful of her omelette and since Max was not looking, a bite of salad too. 'You'll get it out of them.'

'I shall see the taxi is traced. Mimsie says it was the local service, Dockside Cabs, that helps.' He knew the owner of the firm, a man with a record, but now allegedly going straight.

'I feel I've dragged you into this, that if you hadn't known me, Nell and her problems wouldn't have come your way.'

'I'd have heard of them,' he said, thinking about William Duerden.

'But not taken a personal interest.'

'I don't know about that. I might have done. It would have interested me.' Especially with a suspected child murderer loose in my district. I certainly take a personal interest in flushing him out.

There had been no news and no sightings of anyone like William Duerden; he seemed to have disappeared. They must have lost him somehow, and that rankled. Men like Duerden should not be mislaid, yet they had a marvellous facility for melting into the undergrowth, had such men.

'Still, you could have been writing all your memoranda and reports and sitting on all your committees . . . See, I know how you work, and you needn't have taken Nell so seriously.' Stella sipped her chilled wine and took a mouthful of lemon sorbet. She watched her weight keenly, but ate carefully, the sorbet and wine were her treat of the day.

Coffin smiled. Stella thought she knew about police work, but in fact she didn't at all. Not the reality of it. It was nastier, harder, and tougher than she knew. I've protected her from that knowledge, he thought. But he knew better than to say so to her except in anger (as he had done once), because the ardent feminist in Stella would have said: Bloody cheek.

She'd have meant it too, while paradoxically enjoying the protection.

But she was right, he certainly had other problems, other puzzles, such as the death of Jim Lollard. It was a real case for the record books, that one, with the coachload of drugged tourists. But he could trust the team headed by DI Young, because he knew his man. Archie Young would ferret away till he got at the truth. So leave that with him.

But this problem, Nell Casey and Tom, was for him.

'Some coffee?' Max had appeared with silver pot in one hand and a cream jug in the other. He prided himself on the strength and heat of his coffee.

'Shan't sleep if I do, but yes, Max, I will. No cream.' She let Max fill her cup and agreed, yes, brandy would be lovely. She was always a bit high after a performance, the adrenalin pumping around. But it was a good feeling and one she treasured as a perk of the job.

'What do you know about Nell Casey?'

'She's a damned good actress.'

'Apart from that.'

'I've played with her once or twice. She always behaved well, kept the rules, punctual, knew her lines, wore a wig if she had one as if she was born to it. I don't think I know more than that. Except the usual gossip, of course. I've known Gus longer.'

'What was the usual gossip?'

Stella shifted uneasily. 'Oh, you know, about Gus and their quarrel. But they always quarrelled. Something in their chemistry, I expect. And, of course, lately . . .' she hesitated.

'And?'

'Well, the boy. Whose child is he, that sort of thing.'

'And what do people think?'

'Gus thinks he is the father, of course. But I think the

question is open. Tom doesn't look like Gus. She had a bit of a fling with various characters while in the soap, so I hear, but no details. Sylvie's father was one of them.' Stella shrugged. 'She just appeared with the child ready for the next season's filming.'

'I suppose Tom is her child?'

Stella looked surprised. 'How would I know? Do you mean you doubt it?'

'I don't know what to think about that young woman.' From his own background, with a defaulting mother, he had strong feelings about the mother–child relationship. Things were not always what they seemed by a long way.

Over the coffee, he said: 'Let's make an hypothesis. Tom is not her child and Nell is lying all round. She is setting up all the incidents and Tom is in no danger. But why?'

'That would be the question,' said Stella sardonically.

'So let's try again. Nell is telling the truth and Sylvie is the one doing the lying, creating all these incidents because she hates Nell, hates the child whom she believes to be a product of a union between her father and Nell.'

'Is that how you arrive at the truth?'

'You have to form a picture in order to know where to look,' he said. 'All right, you form the wrong picture, but in disproving it, you move on to what might be right.'

'Looking for proof?'

'Of course.'

It was one way of working. The other way, the orthodox police way, from which he did not entirely divorce himself, was to collect a heap of facts.

'Why wouldn't Nell say about the boy?' he asked. 'Be open.'

'Because she's like that,' said Stella stoutly. 'It's her business, after all.'

They finished their meal and walked back to St Luke's Mansions in silence.

'How's *The Circle* going?' asked Stella.

'Fine, I think. I'm not very good,' he said with modesty, hoping to be contradicted.

But all she said was: 'All right for the butler?'

'Good enough for that,' he agreed, accepting Stella's verdict on his acting skills. 'We could do with some more men in that group.'

'It's always the same with these amateur outfits,' said Stella. 'Always more women than men.'

'We did have one recruit, small quiet chap, but he's disappeared.'

'Well, don't you do that. The more activities I've got clustering around the Theatre Workshop, the more help I get locally. Funds and so on. And your sister keeps us on a pretty tight budget. Not that I blame here. Where is she, by the way? I haven't seen her for some time.'

'I think she's having a little domestic difficulty.' And the name of the game, he suspected, was divorce.

'Ah,' said Stella knowledgeably. 'Thought it might be that. She'll come out on top, though.'

At her door Stella paused, she looked worried. She was nervous about going intc the dark alone.

'Want me to see you in?'

'No, that dear dog of mine makes me feel quite safe.' Already, behind the door they could hear the preliminary snuffings and sniffings of Bob, who, having satisfied himself that it was indeed Stella out there, would soon burst into excited yelps.

'You looked thoughtful.'

'Yes, there's going to be trouble when this new business about Tom gets out. And you know from whom.'

'Gus?'

'Gus. He's spoiling for a fight with Nell. Has been for days. He was foul to his class today. I stood in and watched. Fortunately they love him, enjoy being bullied, little masochists. The great man showing his mettle, they think.'

'He may not find out. I shan't say anything and neither will you.'

Stella said nothing. 'Good night. Here I come, Bob. Yes, it's me.' And to a crescendo of barks, she passed inside. He heard her voice. 'It's me, it's me. Good boy, down now, down. Oh, mind my tights, you beast.'

*

But of course Gus did learn of what had happened the day before. On the Friday morning, he went into Max's Deli to have some breakfast before taking his class in a development of *The Trojan Women* (he had decided to make a virtue of having more girls than men in his class), and Max's daughter, the Beauty one, told him as she served his coffee. As well as being a Beauty she was also a gossip.

Gus listened as he crumbled his brioche, and that famous dark look came over his face.

Beauty watched with interest; she thought he was madly attractive and she adored that glowering look. Not that she would want it directed at her, but turned towards Nell it was highly desirable.

'Yes, Sylvie told me when she came in for their morning croissants. But we all knew something was up when we saw Miss Casey running down the road.'

Gus got up, flung some money on the table and left without drinking the coffee. It was a highly dramatic moment and one of great joy to Beauty. She cleared away the coffee and crumbs and took herself off. This was not the sort of thing she told her father, a small secret pleasure of her own.

Gus met Nell in the courtyard of the Theatre Workshop. Behind them the builders were busily constructing what would be the main auditorium inside the old St Luke's Church itself. At the moment most of the workforce were sitting in the sun having their midmorning snack. His own class was assembling in cheerful groups, several ladies of the Friends of St Luke's Theatre were having a consultation about a flower display, and Stella was conducting a small row with the works foreman. Nell was just walking peacefully back from an exercise session designed to loosen up her throat and chest muscles to help her strengthen her voice. She was humming quietly to herself on one low note as instructed. A couple of others of the cast were with her, also humming.

An audience had thus assembled itself for the scene.

Nell saw Gus coming towards her and tried to disappear into the crowd of ladies doing the flowers, but he saw her. 'Nell, I want you.' He grabbed her arm.

'All right, all right. Don't shout.'

'I'm not shouting.' Nor was he, but a perfectly produced voice was audible all around the arena. Spectators afterwards said it felt like an arena.

'I've just heard what happened yesterday. On top of all the other things I've been hearing about.'

'Oh, you have, have you? Nothing to do with you, Gus, so clear off.'

'I think it is something to do with me.'

'Is it you doing it all, Gus? Is that what you're saying? Some obscene spite campaign? I have wondered about that.' She wrenched her arm away. 'Not a nice man, are you, Gus?'

He went quite white, a member of the audience reported later to husband and child in the safety of her own house, and his eyes went red. Yes, I swear it. Red with rage.

'You are a rotten mother and a bitch to boot. That child is not safe in your care.'

'He's not safe anywhere near you, you mean. Tom's been safe enough with me all this time. I brought him up, remember? It's only now you appear on the scene he starts to be in danger.'

Gus said through his teeth, but every word perfectly audible: 'I'll kill you, Casey.'

Nell recovered her poise: 'You want to watch that temper of yours, Gus,' she said coldly. 'It's got you in trouble before, remember?'

Then the pair of them moved out of earshot. Nell Casey stalking ahead with Gus running after her, they were still quarrelling when they moved out of view, but nothing could be heard.

Their audience returned quietly to their own lives, but every moment had been savoured.

'Bad scene,' said Stella soberly. She was beginning to wonder what she had done in bringing these two together in her Festival. She crossed her fingers. Theatre people are always superstitious, as behoves those in such a chancy craft, and she was no exception.

*

Several days passed in relative quiet. As quiet as anything ever was in John Coffin's life.

Driver Tremble was still in hospital. They had kept him in over the weekend, and on Monday and Tuesday (March 13, he registered the date with superstitious gloom) he had had two more short interviews conducted by DI Young, with each party getting more and more irritated with the other, as Tremble continued to look dazed and unable to remember exactly what had happened on that night, and Young to feel more and more doubting.

But Young knew he was getting closer, he could read Tremble's eyes and see the look behind them. Quite soon, Tremble would break and tell all.

Archie Young reported as much to Superintendent Lane, who in turn informed Coffin.

At the same time a check was going on of all known paedophiles in the district, of which there were more than Coffin cared for, both male and female.

Years in his job had informed him of the sexual aberrations of both sexes, he was too sophisticated to be surprised at anything, but the pursuit and abuse of children by women still saddened him.

'I would like to say I don't understand it,' he said to the woman detective as she came to him with the special report he had asked for. 'But I suppose I do. In a way.'

'For generations,' said Sergeant Alison Jenkins, who had done a special course at Cambridge for this work, 'women have known how to soothe babies by stroking or sucking their genitals. In some women it just develops from there.' She sounded more tolerant than she really was.

'But this woman—' he picked up a case history—'she beats all.'

'Well, she's one we don't have to worry about,' said Alison Jenkins. 'She's inside and will be for quite a bit.' She gathered up her papers. 'I think there is an active group of paedophiles operating from a papershop in Magdalen Road and I think our man Duerden may have been in touch. My contact there was distinctly shifty about him. Wouldn't say yes, but wouldn't say no.'

'But no leads as to where Duerden is now?'

'No. My contact implied that there were no addresses and no dates to be had. Duerden, if he was in touch, was handling himself cagily, I'd say. Keeping all information about his movements to himself.'

'Moved away? Out of the district?' said Coffin hopefully.

She shook her head. 'Can't say. But my contact is nervy.'

I'm nervy myself, thought Coffin morosely.

'Who is your contact?'

'I'd rather not say, sir.'

'Trustworthy?'

'As far as I know, sir,' she said cautiously.

'Would Duerden have been using one of his known aliases?'

She shrugged. 'My contact did admit to two new characters in touch with their group. He may have been one of those two. The names used were Deacon and York.'

'Mean anything to you?'

She shook her head. 'No. Not yet. But I'm working on it. Sometimes takes a bit of time to build up an identity profile.'

Coffin considered. 'Let me know when you get anything. Personally.'

'Will do, sir.'

'Any of them likely to have been playing games with the Casey child?'

'Not for their pleasure,' said Alison. 'Not their style. In their way they are straight.'

'Pleasure,' said Coffin angrily. 'Who said anything about pleasure?'

Somewhere in the jungle of his territory some creature, probably humanoid, abnormal and dangerous, was moving. He could sense it.

She had something else to add: 'Another activity started up that may or may not have something to do with the papershop group. A couple, man and woman, have been going into school playgrounds, talking to the children. They say they are searching for kids for a play they are putting on. In two instances they have taken photographs and got addresses before being chased off by the school staff.'

'Pity.'

She shrugged. 'Had a car handy. Just got in and sped off.'

'No one got the number?'

'No.'

'Have those children been accosted at home?'

'Not as yet, and the parents have been warned.'

'Good.'

But he didn't like the theatre motif appearing.

On the evening of the third day after this, it was a Friday afternoon, Tom and Sylvie were playing in the garden at The Albion.

Sylvie sat knitting in the sun, keeping a wary eye upon Tom. She had picked up the suspicion that hung over her, and didn't want to get into further trouble.

A car passed slowly in the road outside, drove on, then turned and came back.

Sylvie noticed the manoeuvre and turned to study the car. A dark maroon car, she did not recognize the make but they were all Japanese anyway. The car moved away.

The Albion stood at the apex of a triangle of land, its garden bounded on two sides by road. The maroon car drove slowly round the block and came up on the other side of the garden. The side where Tom was playing.

Sylvie sat down and resumed her knitting. It was a complicated pattern which occasionally demanded all her attention, but she could see Tom at play by the laurel bushes. There he was, that was his head.

When she looked up again, he was gone.

CHAPTER 9

March 16

In a case like this one, the last person to see the missing person inevitably comes in for some suspicion. Thus the weeping Sylvie was questioned and questioned again. She was interviewed first in the flat in The Albion, in the presence of Nell Casey, and then taken down to the police station and interviewed again. Nell did not go on this expedition but a policewoman stayed with her at home. Nell seemed stunned by what had happened. 'I can't tell you anything,' she kept saying. 'I can't understand it.'

Paul Lane, on the direct instruction of the Chief Commander, John Coffin, had taken charge at once himself, he had his sergeant with him and WPC Mary Barclay was present. The interview room in the new police centre hard by the Spinnergate Tube station had already achieved the slightly battered air which comes so easily to rooms through which any number of people pass. Archie Young was still engaged in the coach case and the death of Jim Lollard, but he knew that Tom was missing. The news had spread fast. There was something about the disappearance of a child missing that everyone found painful.

Sylvie had stopped crying by the time of the second interview, but she looked white and frightened.

'I was knitting. I had my head down only for a minute and then he was gone. It was the car. I know it was the car.'

'Describe the car again.'

'A dark car. Maroon or deep brown. Even black. No, it was dark red, I think it was dark red. It came round once and I was suspicious. Then it went away, so I thought I had been wrong. Imagining things . . .'

'But the car came back?'

'Yes, down the road on the other side of the garden . . . I didn't know it could circle round the back of The Albion.'

'You weren't looking when Tom went?'

'No. I was listening, but not looking. Not just at that very minute.'

'So you didn't see the actual abduction?'

'No, no,' she cried out. 'I saw nothing.'

'Did the boy call out?'

She hesitated. 'No, he didn't cry out . . . That's strange, isn't it? He must have known the person who took him.'

'That could be the case,' said Superintendent Paul Lane. 'What about the car? Did you see who was driving?'

'No. It was speeding down the road. Oh, so fast.'

'And you didn't get the number?'

She shook her head dumbly. The tears started to flow again. Sylvie was a pretty, slender girl, who was usually attractive and appealing, but now her eyes were swollen and her face was puffy. 'Poor Tom, poor Tom. He's a dear little boy.'

'You liked him?'

'Of course, very much, everyone does.'

'How do you get on with his mother?'

'Well, well,' said Sylvie. 'I like her too.'

'No quarrels?'

'Sometimes she has been cross with me,' said Sylvie with reluctance. 'But we have never quarrelled and she knows I am doing my best.'

They let her rest then.

'Strange how that girl's always the one around when things happen to the boy. The dog, the telephone summons supposedly from the mother. A lot of it we only have her word for.'

'Wonder if she's got a boyfriend?' said Mary Barclay.

'You think she's in it with an accomplice?'

'Could be.'

'And we forget about William Duerden?' asked the Sergeant.

'No, by God we don't,' said Paul Lane in a voice louder

than he knew. 'We keep on looking for him and we get the hooks into the papershop lot. Magdalen Road, isn't it? We've had trouble with the man who owns it before. And we try to pick up the couple who have been hanging around schools. They used a car, remember?'

'No, not forget.' Mary Barclay, put in her contribution. 'Just bear all possibilities in mind.'

'I go along with that,' said Paul Lane.

'And the motive for the girl?' pressed the Sergeant, who had liked the look of Sylvie.

'Money, a ransom,' suggested Mary Barclay.

'I don't believe Casey's got any money.' Lane looked sceptical.

'She could probably raise it.'

Actresses could do anything.

When they carried the report of the interview to John Coffin himself, he said: 'I wonder why the girl took the job as minder to the boy. Her father's a rich man, she's got a Baccalauréate, she could aim higher. I think we need to know more about that young woman and her motivation in life. She may love Tom, anyone would, he's a nice kid, but I wouldn't call her a natural child-carer.'

'But don't forget Duerden,' he ended. 'I still want him.'

Duerden was still there in the undergrowth, but in the case of the disappearance of a child, all things had to be considered. You had to suspect the family.

In a case like this one, the mother inevitably comes in for some suspicion. Thus Nell Casey was questioned at the same time as Sylvie without being allowed to speak to the girl.

Nell had been working, involved in a pre-rehearsal at a church hall the other side of Spinnergate which, in spite of Stella's best efforts to keep it all under one roof, had been dragged into use as rehearsal room; Nell had been in company with several others of the cast, all engaged in going over some moves with the producer of *French without Tears*. Then she had taken a taxi to St Martin's Lane to try on a wig.

'I didn't see anything, I was working. I thought Sylvie was in charge. I thought Tom was safe.'

She was angry. 'You knew Tom was under threat. You ought to have had a watch on him. What about the other things—the dog, the plaster hand, the blood on his shirt? What are you doing about them? They must tell you something.'

The answer was: Not very much. 'We're working on them,' said Mary Barclay. If they caught someone, then these articles might be valuable evidence in court, but until then they were just so many strands blowing in the wind.

And meant to be so, Mary Barclay thought, this plotter was clever and devious.

She had been under the eyes of her producer and three members of the cast of the play for the early part of the afternoon, and later, even in the taxi, she had had the designer of the set with her. The wig had to be just right, she explained tearfully.

This first questioning was done by Mary Barclay. The second was tougher.

'I want to go now,' Nell said. 'I want to go home. And I want to see Sylvie. Where is she?'

'Superintendent Lane wants to ask you a few questions first,' Mary Barclay said.

'You're asking me exactly the same things as she did,' said Nell angrily some time later. 'There isn't anything more I can say. Find the boy, find Tom.'

'We will do,' said Paul Lane. 'We'll find him for you.' He wished he believed it.

'I want to see Sylvie and I want to see John Coffin.'

'You can't go to him,' said the Superintendent shortly. 'I am in charge.'

'You suspect me, don't you? Somehow you blame me. I can see it in your face.'

'It's routine to question the family,' said Paul Lane.

John Coffin himself came into the room just as Nell was leaving; he spoke to her briefly. He was thoughtful for a moment. 'Get hold of Hamilton, Gus Hamilton, the actor.'

Lane nodded. His wife went to the theatre regularly, he knew the name. 'See what he has to offer.'

'Will he have anything?'

'Try it,' said Coffin briefly.

Anyone other than the family who had shown an interest in the child was also bound to be under suspicion. Thus it was inevitable that Gus's name should come up.

As it happened, he did not have to be sought out, he pushed himself into the picture as soon as he heard the news about Tom.

The news did not reach him quickly; he was one of the last to hear. Or so he claimed.

He was told as he walked into the Theatre Workshop the day after Tom had been abducted, which was a Saturday, March 17, to find a group of students for his class talking about it.

One of the girls, a tall, thin red-haired girl who said she admired Nell Casey more than any actress in the world except Stella Pinero and Meryl Streep, was in tears. She was being consoled by a thick-set young man who also admired Nell but meant to keep in well with Gus whom he recognized as a future ikon in the theatre, a role he was planning for himself say a decade after Gus. Olivier was dead, there was a vacancy at the top, someone would fill it, why not Fred Caspar?

'Calm down, Flick, the kid'll turn up, you'll see.'

'But I saw the car. At least, I think I did; I was walking down the road as it sped off.' She pressed her hands together. Even at a moment of genuine emotion she had to play the scene, give a performance.

'What's all this?' Gus had a headache, he'd been drinking the night before, and was in no very good mood, 'Get in line, Felicity, exercises first.' He had found his class a stiff, unsupple group of youngsters and was intent on loosening them up. He amused himself inventing devilish routines for them. 'Walk like a duck, Felicity, walk like a duck.'

Felicity looked agitated and began to wonder if she could mime tail feathers. 'It's the boy, Tom,' she said to put off the moment when she must waddle. 'He's been stolen.'

Gus didn't say anything at first and his expression did not change but his stocky figure seemed to harden as if he had braced all his muscles. He walked the length of the room in silence while they all watched, then he turned and came back.

'You saw this happen?'

'I saw the car. They say he was taken in a car,' said Felicity in a shaky voice . . . God, I'm beginning to quack like a duck, she thought.

'Why didn't you stop it?'

'She couldn't help it,' put in Fred. Although he was violently jealous of Flick who might just conceivably (although how could that be?) have a talent superior to his own, he found her very attractive.

'I didn't know then that Tom had been taken. I only heard about that later and realized I had seen the car.'

'You don't remember the number?' Felicity shook her head dumbly. 'Or the make of the car?'

'It was just a dark old car.' She was miming grief.

'Have you told the police?'

She shook her head. 'No, I've been thinking about it, wondering if I ought.'

Gus got his coat. 'You're coming with me now. I've got my motorbike outside, we can go on that.'

The class, dismissed, was cross. All right for her, was the mutter. Off with Gus, getting all the action. But what about us?

Fred took charge. Ignoring all complaints, he organized his own drill, he wasn't going to call them anything pansy like exercises, they were drill, and you did them or else. No acting ducks, or being a chair, or miming a riverbank complete with rats; he would demand noise, and violence and pain, it would be war. He had always thought he had better ideas than Gus and now was the time to put them into action. He would offer them a slice of life. He had a moment's debate while he considered whether to make them act a massacre or an aircrash. Then he had a better idea. A slice of life.

'Make a circle and scream. High, low, loud, then soft. Then with pain. Now plunge straight in, this is for real: A child, your child, is missing and you want to kill someone. Act Murder.'

To his surprise, the class obeyed.

Gus led Felicity straight up to the desk where a young uniformed police constable was dealing with a woman who had lost her cat. Both parties seemed to feel that something should be done, but while the constable was recommending a masterly inactivity because pussy would come home, the woman wanted a house to house search started at once. It was a valuable cat, a pedigree Burmese, she suspected a neighbour.

Gus cut right across all this, bother cats, what did they count? The woman gave a little scream of rage, but recognizing, not Gus as such, but a primal force, subsided.

'This girl has some information about the kidnapped boy. It's important. Who's in charge?'

'Well, sir . . .'

'Get him.'

Even as she was handed over to the investigating team in the Incident Room, Felicity felt that there was an intensity about Gus that she would rather not have been involved with.

She told her story to a young policewoman, Barclay or something, and was allowed to go. She had half-expected that she would make a statement and have to sign it, but nothing like that happened.

'I've taken it all down,' said the policewoman politely. 'Of course, I may come back to you again with more questions, but at the moment I have everything.'

'I think it was the car I saw,' said Felicity, almost doubting herself.

'Yes, I think it was too. Pity you didn't get a number, but as you say, how could you know?'

'No, I didn't see Tom or anything like that. I know him, he's a nice little boy. But even if I had seen him get in the car I wouldn't have thought anything of it, it would all have seemed perfectly normal. I mean, I would have heard a shout or a fight. I was near enough for that, and he was old enough to shout and fight, but there was nothing.'

She stopped. They were both aware that she had said something important.

That Tom had not struggled, had not called out; he had known his abductor and not feared him.

Or her.

'I saw the back of the driver,' said Felicity, staring straight ahead of her, and not acting now, not a bit. 'I did see the back. Not a very tall person, wearing something dark, blue.'

'A coat?'

'Perhaps a black sweater. Thin arms.'

'A man or a woman?' said Mary Barclay.

Felicity sat thinking, then she shook her head. 'Couldn't tell . . . It just might have been a woman . . . Now I wonder why I think that?' She shook her head again. 'No, I don't know. There might have been something but it's gone.' A hat? No, not a hat, but something womanish.

'Come back if you think of anything.'

'I suppose there's no news?'

'No, 'fraid not.'

No sign of Tom. No one had seen him since Sylvie had seen him playing in the garden.

'People are gone sometimes and never come back.' Felicity was fearful.

'Not often children.'

'Yes, sometimes children.'

Mary Barclay was silent. She remembered the sergeant's son who had gone out one day and not come back. No, they didn't all come back.

'Thank you for coming in, anyway, Felicity. Everything helps.' Felicity smiled nervously and mouthed silent assent. 'Can you get home all right?'

'I've got a lift.' She hoped she had, and that Gus hadn't disappeared. But he was still there when the two of them walked through to the reception area. He was pacing up and down.

'Oh, there you are. So what? Is there any news.' He turned on Mary Barclay. 'It's about time there was. You wouldn't know Felicity here saw the car if I hadn't brought her in.'

'Can I have your name, sir?' asked Mary Barclay.

'Hamilton.'

'Oh, hang on, will you please, Mr Hamilton. I think I've heard your name mentioned. I think the Superintendent would like to talk to you.'

Gus walked impatiently up and down the room while he waited. At some point, Felicity had taken herself off. He seemed to recall a voice saying goodbye and his own answering that he hoped she could get home all right. He didn't recall the answer.

John Coffin was in the room when Gus walked in and he sketched a greeting. Gus knew nothing about police procedure and cared less. If he thought about it all, it would have seemed natural to him that the Head of the Force should be in the room to meet him.

'You kept me waiting,' he said.

'Sorry about that, sir,' said Paul Lane, standing up, and introducing himself. He towered over Gus, which surprised him. Looks smaller than on the stage, he decided.

John Coffin was not introduced and did not explain his presence, although he had taken the lift down from his top floor suite of rooms to be present.

'Good of you to bring that young woman in with the sighting of the car. I don't say we would have missed her, picked her up in the end, I expect, but this is quicker. It's interesting what she had to say. I'll be having a word with her myself.'

Gus nodded.

'You haven't any information for us yourself, have you, sir?' said Lane smoothly.

'No. Wish I had.'

'People often don't realize what they know.'

'If I think of anything, anything, you'll be the first to hear.'

'You take an interest in the little lad.'

'Yes,' said Gus. 'I do. What the hell are you getting at?'

Temper, thought Lane. 'Not getting at anything, sir.'

He was not put out by his Chief's silent presence in one corner of the room, they were old friends and colleagues who had worked together often in the past, but he did regret that other business had not kept the Boss away. Far be it from him to want a riot or a natural disaster in Thameswater but it would have demanded the Chief's attention. The trouble was that John Coffin was a natural detective who had been too successful, the price of his success being removal from what he was good at. So he put his finger in the investigatory pie when he could.

But he's good with men too, Lane loyally reminded himself. Even better with women, if all he had heard was true.

'It's a foul business. Of course I want him found.'

'You won't mind if I ask a few more questions, then, sir?'

'Go ahead. But I don't think I've much to tell.'

'You never know,' said Lane. 'Bits and pieces appear sometimes. All helps.' It was his customary line, he didn't expect to be believed (although it was true), but it was better than silence with an awkward customer. Gus had fallen into that category with his very first words.

An angry man, Paul Lane decided. He glanced at John Coffin, who gave a small nod. You go ahead, he was saying. I'll listen.

Unfortunately, Gus saw and stood up angrily. 'What is this? An inquisition? I came in to help, not to be subjected to this. I'm going. I have nothing to tell you.'

'Where were you yesterday, Mr Hamilton, at the time of the abduction?'

'No bloody where,' said Gus. 'Working on a script in my room. Walking. I don't know. I don't know when it happened.'

'About four-thirty in the afternoon,' said Lane.

'Then I don't know. I took a walk.'

'Do you own a car?'

'No. I do not own a car. But yes, I can drive, and I could hire one.'

There was silence in the room.

'So you could,' said Paul Lane.

Gus got control of himself. An actor after all, Lane mused.

'Why would I be interested in abducting a child I hardly know and only saw for the first time a few days ago?'

'Let's make a case,' said John Coffin, coming forward, 'that you might want to get possession of the boy if you thought he was your own son.'

Gus became very cold. 'If I thought Gus was my son I would want to know him and have him know me, but I would not snatch him.'

'Even if his mother was obstructive?'

'Why don't you talk to her?' Anger was flickering all round Gus now, it was almost visible, like lightning in a storm. 'Yes, ask her. Perhaps she's playing some sort of game.'

'What sort of game?'

'I don't know. Publicity, she's capable of it. She might have some devious scheme. Whatever, she's a casual, careless parent. Talk to her.'

'You don't seem to like Miss Casey?'

'I'm not saying anything about that. Talk to her.' He stood up. 'I'm going. I am afraid you haven't got much from me.'

'Oh, I wouldn't say that,' said John Coffin.

Suddenly, Gus gave his wide, charming smile. 'Is that a threat?' He made a small bow. 'My exit line, I think.'

They let him go. Coffin went to the window and watched the motorbike roar away. He could kill himself on it in that mood, but you knew he never would, a charmed life, Gus had.

'What do you make of that?' asked Paul Lane.

'An angry man,' said Coffin thoughtfully. 'A powerful, imaginative, angry man.'

'Imaginative?' questioned Paul Lane, as they parted.

'Oh yes. Didn't he project a picture of a negligent, selfish, casual mother with her own schemes?'

'A kind of Mother Macbeth?' said Paul Lane. 'But I

think he really believes the child is his. Or thinks that the mother is to blame for what has happened. I don't see him playing those macabre tricks, though. The girl Sylvie had the best opportunity there. Or the mother, although God knows why she should want to do it.

'Likewise the abduction . . . You see the significance of what the girl Felicity had to say?'

'Oh yes, the boy did not call out. Or struggle, and he was big enough and old enough to have a shot at it.'

'Exactly. So he could have known his abductor.'

The Chief Commander left the conference at this point to go off to the House of Commons to see the MP who was making such a nuisance of himself. He didn't want to go, he would have preferred to stay with the teams working on the two big cases on his patch: the hi-jacked coach and the dead Jim Lollard, and the puzzle of the missing child, but his first duty was to defend his Force when under attack, he had to play the politician.

'Keep me in touch,' he said to Paul Lane.

The investigating team had a list. On this list of people under suspicion they had Sylvie, and Nell Casey and Gus Hamilton.

In addition there was always the possibility of an unknown chancer who had grabbed the boy on an impulse. This character might be one of the papershop network.

And there was William Duerden, the alleged child murderer, said to be in the neighbourhood.

The possibilities were wide open. Most of this speculation was kept from the Press, but the media had been told of the missing boy and the coverage was wide.

Tom's picture appeared on the evening news on all television channels. Nell was photographed but had refused, on police advice, to give any interviews. Sylvie had hidden herself in The Albion flat and refused to come out, and the St Luke's Theatre complex, new buildings and old, was besieged by newsmen of all sexes and sizes.

Two days later, when he came back from another visit to the House of Commons (where the MP had been polite but difficult), John Coffin called on Stella Pinero, because you must talk things over with someone and, not having a wife, he had only Stella.

'We are under siege here,' she said. 'And I do not like it. Did you have to fight your way in?' She poured him a drink and went on without waiting for an answer. 'Your sister won't like it if profits are down.'

'They might go up. Thanks for the drink.'

'How was Harry Guffin, MP? I won't vote for him again if he's tiresome to you.'

'He's just doing his job and I'm just trying to do mine.'

'You sound weary.'

'Let's go out and have a meal.'

'At Max's?'

'No, let's go right out of the district.'

Stella studied his face. 'I'll drive, you look tired.' Their relationship was coming to a turning-point, they both knew it but didn't want to dwell on it. It could go either way.

I'd miss him terribly, Stella thought. But it might have to be a parting.

I take too much from Stella, John Coffin thought. I can't let it go on. But what else? Which way? What does she really want?

Stella was never going to say, he knew that, knew her well enough to understand that he would have to read the signs and act. Stella would expect him to do what was required.

'How are you getting on with editing your mother's diaries?'

'Not very well, what with rehearsals for *The Circle*,' admitted Coffin. 'She frightens me a bit. I used to want to get to know her. Now I feel I know her too well but without understanding her.'

'Oh, you're a romantic about family relationships. Not like Letty.'

'I'm not so sure about that: she's got the family habit of jettisoning spouses.' He had done that himself, for that matter. Or been dropped.

Stella gave him a sharp look. 'Letty always comes out of

things with a profit and I bet your mother did. Not sure you do.'

'Thanks.'

'It's a compliment.' The car gathered speed. 'I'm taking you, and it's my treat,' she said, driving briskly along the road which led southwards out of Thameswater. 'You haven't been to this place, but you'll like it. Not smart, but the food's good.'

'Where?' he said suspiciously.

'Close your eyes and wait.'

Five minutes, ten minutes, the roads were clear. 'I know where we are,' he said, without opening his eyes. 'I can smell. That's Deller's.' Deller's was an old soap factory, long since closed, but the smell seemed to hang on forever. 'I know that smell.'

'Of course, you do. Greenwich. You used to live here once. So did I.'

'I hadn't forgotten.' It had been a good while since Stella had worked in a local theatre, closed now too, but he had hung on longer.

'The old Theatre Royal is opening again, did you know that? Was a Bingo Hall, fell on hard times, and has now got an Arts Council subsidy and is going to start up again.'

'No, that's good news.' He was getting out of the car. On one side of the road was the splendid rustic sprawl of Greenwich Park, on the other a row of shops. 'Where are we eating?'

'Can't you smell that too?' She pointed across the road. 'Bert's Diner. The best fish and chips in South London.'

'You know, I think I remember this place,' Coffin said, as they went through the door. 'It used to have a high counter and the top was tin or some metal and the frying went on behind the counter and you got your fish and chips wrapped up in newspaper.'

'It's not like that now.'

'And it's bigger,' said Coffin looking round. The room was divided into two, one part laid out with blue plastic tables and matching chairs, the other devoted to frying and sales. At the blue tables, several parties were eating away happily, and in some cases also washing the meal down with large cups of strong tea. At least, he assumed it was strong, Greenwich had changed drastically indeed if it was weak. The smell of fish and frying pervaded each side about equally. 'Somehow it's grown.'

'Bert bought the shop next door and turned it into a fish restaurant.' She nodded towards a man in a white overall and white cap. 'That's Bert.'

'Not *the* Bert?' Coffin was doing sums in his head.

'Grandson, I think.'

'There used to be a table in the corner, I think,' said Coffin, nodding towards it, 'but nothing like this and I don't remember anyone ever eating at it. It was usually piled high with old newspapers.'

They took a table where they were waited on by Bert himself, who said he didn't remember Mr Coffin, but of course he knew Miss Pinero well, and he didn't recommend the skate tonight but the cod was first-class.

'Do you know, I think I miss the newspapers,' said Coffin, as they waited.

'You get paper plates.' Stella, although elegantly dressed in white slacks and a white jacket, somehow managed to suit her background in a way known only to actresses. Coffin felt he stood out in his dark suit. All the other men were wearing jeans and bright shirts. 'Saves on the washing-up.'

He took a look around. 'Can you get anything to drink beside tea?'

'You'd have loved the tea once.'

'I know, and I bet Bert makes a good cup, but times change.'

'You can have beer. Or wine, he's got a licence.'

'Well, you're driving,' he began.

'And I'm paying.' Stella motioned towards Bert. 'He doesn't keep champagne but he does a nice Bordeaux.'

The fish was as good as Bert had promised and the chipped potatoes, crisp and light, were even better.

Coffin poured the wine. 'I'm glad we came here. It washes the House of Commons out of my mouth.'

'Bad time?'

'I don't relish being told my place in the pecking order. Not very high, it seems.'

'He's a silly fellow, that chap.'

'He's popular,' said Coffin gloomily. The forthcoming election did not seem likely to relieve him of his critic.

'I'm glad to get away tonight myself,' said Stella.

'Yes, I can imagine. How is Nell Casey?'

'I've put her to bed with a sleeping tablet, and Sylvie is staying with me. Had to separate them. Sylvie's watching TV and crying and telephoning her father. In case you wanted to know.'

'All information helps.'

'Well, anything I say tonight is privileged information and not to be passed on to your lot. Agreed?'

'Anything I know is knowledge,' said Coffin oracularly. But Stella seemed satisfied and she laughed. 'What's up?'

'Poor Nell: she thinks you suspect her. You seem to have given her a hard time.'

'Lane can be a bit heavy-handed,' acknowledged Coffin. 'Especially when he's upset and he is distressed over this abduction. We all are. It's a nasty business.'

'But not to blame Nell. Tom's her child.'

'A string of funny incidents,' Coffin said thoughtfully. 'She could have done them.'

Although God knows why. And so could Sylvie have done them. Gus also, for that matter.

Stella whispered, 'I think we've been recognized, they're all watching us.'

Listening too, Coffin thought, unsurprised. The whole district was abuzz with the news of the boy's abduction. He wasn't against that. People on the alert might notice something, hear something. Children did cry. One had to assume that the boy was distressed and would wail.

And if he didn't make a noise, that said something in itself, didn't it?

He decided to talk to Stella. It was what he had sought her out for, to achieve that unloading of worries that a good wife accepted as part of life. Not that Stella was anyone's 'good wife' or ever would be, but a warm, loving presence she was.

And a mother. 'How's your child?' he said.

'Oh fine, she's given up the idea of drama school, indeed of gainful work altogether, as far as I can see, and says she's going to look for someone rich and suitable and then marry and have children. The new generation, you see, different from us.'

'And will she find someone?'

'Has already, I expect, she usually communicates after the fact rather than before.'

'What a cynic you are, Stella.'

He turned his chair so that his back was to the room and his face could not be seen.

'Stella, there's something you don't know.'

And he told her about William Duerden. Stella's eyes grew wide and she made a little noise of protest and horror.

'And this is confidential, Stella.'

'Of course, but if you know about this man, then it must be he who has taken Tom. Oh, I feel quite sick.' Even in her anguish, her diction and delivery were perfect; it was a performance. In miniature, so that the rest of the room could not hear.

But Coffin looked over his shoulder anxiously. No, they were all eating and drinking their tea in peace.

'If I were a doctor, I would say, Yes, that is one possible diagnosis, but there are contra-indications.'

'Talk straight, John,' said Stella, sitting up and looking him in the eye. 'What do you mean?'

'You know already if you think about it.'

Stella ate two chips and a piece of bread and butter (bread and butter was served with your fish and chips whether you asked for it or not) with delicate precision. Then she said: 'I suppose you mean the toy dog, the plaster hand, and the blood on his jersey?'

'Exactly.' He sat back, pleased. His pupil had passed the test. 'Those are pretty personal things. Threats, attacks, levelled at Tom as Tom. How could Duerden know enough about Tom and Nell to do such things? All these episodes look like malevolence directed against Tom by someone who knew him. And that doesn't square with it being Duerden at all.'

'Nell Casey had a fair amount of publicity when she came over. Photographs in the press, something on TV news. I saw them myself. This man could have seen the pictures and marked Tom down.'

'It's possible. Not the way he usually works, though. His habit is just to pick up a child at random.'

'Ugh.'

'As you say. Not a nice man. It'll be a good day's work if we get him.' But he seems to have sunk into the local population without trace. 'But there's something else as well that tells against it being Duerden . . . The boy didn't call out when he was grabbed. He could have known and trusted whoever took him.' He added sombrely: 'For that matter, no one has reported hearing a child cry in a house where no child should be.'

'There might be other children—a family—so that the cry wouldn't be noticed.'

'Not very likely, be too dangerous, you couldn't gag the other kids. They say something in the end. Talk about little Johnny who's come to stay.'

'Unless they are terrified too.'

'Now that is a nasty thought.'

'I don't think I want any more to eat,' said Stella, pushing her plate away. 'A whole houseful of frightened children. Oh no, I can't bear that.'

'It would have to be a school or a hostel or some childminder's group,' said Coffin thoughtfully. 'They're pretty carefully watched and checked, though.' I hope, he said to himself. The papershop group? They had money and connections. Better not say anything to Stella. 'I'll put it to Paul Lane. But he may have thought of it for himself. He's pretty thorough. Casts a wide net with a fine mesh.' And since he was working in a district with a long history of violent crime, he had better. 'But it may just be that the boy is dead.'

Only they had not found his body. Not yet, and four days had passed, soon it would be five, and in such cases every day counted.

CHAPTER 10

Still the evening of March 16

St Luke's Mansions where they both lived was quiet and still when Stella and John Coffin got back. Even the Theatre Workshop was dark, while the building works in the main body of the old church had the desolate air that half-finished work always has when the stonemasons and carpenters have left. But the enterprise was well under way and already, if you stood in the middle of the church, you could see that what was arising around you was an open-plan theatre. The old building was slowly taking on its new character. Badly damaged in the war, left to quietly disintegrate for a decade or so after that, it was being reborn. Hope out of ashes.

Stella yawned. 'I'm really tired, but I must take the old dog out for his late-night walk.'

Bob was a good-natured mongrel into whose body many and diverse breeds must have contributed their genes through generations of ancestors, so that the final effect was a smallish, scruffy, rough-haired basic dog, the type from which all breeds had sprung and to which all would return if left to themselves. He was a gentle soul, but extremely quick to defend himself and those he had taken under his protection. He had once saved Stella's life.

Coffin looked at her fondly: her hair had collapsed into wispy curls about her face, her eyes were shadowy with fatigue, and there was not a trace of make-up (Stella who was so punctilious about grooming) left on eyes or lips.

'Send the old boy down,' he said with sympathy. 'I'll take him. I'd like a stroll.' After all, his code name, as he very well knew, was WALKER. 'Then he can spend the night with me. Give Tiddles some company.'

'He'll like that,' said Stella, yawning. 'He's fond of Tiddles.'

Coffin, with Bob on a leash, set out through the moonlit streets. It was the Chief Commander's habit to make a kind of patrol of his area. Not every night, but frequently.

Soon he was marked by a patrol car, and the message went out: WALKER is loose.

Partly the message was protective, he would be watched over, but it was also a warning, he would be watched for, since it was as well to know what the Chief was doing and where. The odd cigarette, the hasty bite of hamburger, these could be tucked away if he was around. Coffin ran a tight ship and discipline was strict.

He knew what went on, of course, and knew when to turn a discreet blind eye. At the moment, with the MP on the attack, he was not ignoring anything.

Coffin, led by an eager Bob, walked towards Spinnergate Tube station. It was a good spot from which to start a walk. Closed now and quiet, the last train had gone and there would not be another for five hours, when the early morning workmen's train rolled out. Mimsie Marker's newspaper kiosk was locked and shuttered.

No one ever tried to break into Mimsie's little cell, she was reputed to have a good deal of pull among the leading criminal families who might be nastier to meet in the dark than the police. During the day she was attended by a large Alsatian, so it would be a brave soul who tried to mug Mimsie.

Coffin walked on, riverwards. He could smell the river, although not so strongly as in the old days when it had been a working river and full of ships from all over the world. Still, they were coming back, so he was told, and there was always the odd tramp steamer and the pleasure craft.

Not many people about, all seemed quiet, he was glad to note. The two gangs, the Planters and the Dreamers from rival housing estates, had been less noticeable lately. There wasn't so much unemployment as there had been and they were finding recruits harder to come by. As far as he knew, the Dreamers' feeble attempt to set themselves up as drug dealers had foundered owing to business incompetence. They had paid good cash for a dud consignment and been thoroughly beaten up by dealers and users alike for their pains. The local police drug unit having arranged and set up the duff deal had looked on with satisfaction, then arrested all those involved. A real pleasure to do it, the DI in charge had observed.

The Planters might have been expected to take advantage of their rivals' eclipse but their path was hindered by a bitter quarrel between two chieftains, so that they had split into feuding groups. Internecine war might do for them completely.

Other and possibly even nastier groups would spring up to take the place of Planters and Dreamers both in due time, Coffin acknowledged. Life was never going to be easy here, but for the moment the police had the upper hand.

Which made the present situation all the more bitter. He turned his mind to the missing child. Was Tom here, in this large and heavily populated area for the peace of which he was responsible? Or had he already been carried far away?

Or had he gone even further, into that more distant country from which no traveller returns? Was he dead, his body lying somewhere as yet undiscovered?

There was no answer to that. The two of them, dog and man, paused, while Coffin looked at the night sky and Bob conducted a long and apparently satisfying examination of a lamp-post.

A police patrol car passing at the end of the road took note of them and reported back to base: WALKER and dog in Basset Road near to the corner with Hardacre Street. The message was received back at headquarters and duly noted. It was as well to know where WALKER was and what he was up to. The dog was a new one on them, but could be fitted into the Chief Commander's general lifestyle without too much trouble. He was a natural dog-walker. But then a knowledgeable local someone remembered Bob and his part in the Feather Street murders of last summer. 'Miss Pinero took him on,' reported this same knowing character to the rest of the night duty roster. Silence. They all knew of the part played by Stella Pinero in the Chief Commander's life. Sometimes the comments were ribald or even envious, but on the whole they preserved a worldly silence. Coffin was popular, and they were all men, weren't they?

Coffin knew very well what was said and did not care: Stella Pinero did not know but would not have cared if she had known. She might have been deeply pleased.

Coffin and dog passed round the bottom of Feather Street, and Bob looked interested. He had lived there once, a dim memory of something of that sort remained with him, not exactly active but there ready to be revived when needed. Bob's memory of the past was selective, but intelligent and designed to do the best for Bob. Accordingly he also associated Feather Street with scents and smells that had not been totally happy for Bob, so he was willing to plod on.

Coffin tugged at Bob's leash and they climbed the hill back to St Luke's Mansions. Feather Street, a bad business there with all those murders, but it was over and a healing process had taken place. One or two of the Feather Street ladies were in the play-reading circle and he met them still. No ill will there, they thought he made a good butler.

As he turned towards St Luke's Mansions a police car passed, slowed, and then stopped. WDC Mary Barclay got out and walked back towards him.

'We've found the car, sir,' she said. 'Down by the New Canal. Abandoned. No sign of the child.'

'Sure it's the car?'

'We think so, sir. Fits the description.' She paused. 'The boy's shirt was found in it. Bit of blood on it.'

'Ah.' He fell into step beside her. She was a tall girl who walked well. Not pretty perhaps, but with a nice air to her. He liked her.

'The car's been towed away for Forensics to have a go. We've taped off the area where it was found and will be going over it in daylight.'

'Owner of the car?' he queried, not expecting too much.

If the car had been dumped, then the abductor of Tom had felt pretty sure it would not offer much in the way of valuable evidence. On the other hand, criminals didn't know everything, were often too cocky, over-clever for their own good and caught because of it.

'Reported stolen the day before yesterday. An old heap, parked outside a house in Ferry Road and just asking to be nicked.'

'You went down yourself to have a look?'

'The CI was off to a dinner in the City; I was in the office when the news came in. Thought I'd take a look.'

She was keen and he liked that, a nice girl and a good detective. She patted Bob's head; he preserved a cool indifference. Only one woman in his life. At a time, anyway.

'Thought you'd want to know, sir. Sorry if I interrupted your walk.'

'No, you did the right thing.' He smiled at her with more warmth than she had expected, and she relaxed a little. Her spur of the minute decision to jump out and talk to him was not going to rebound on her. She allowed herself a smile back which made her serious, gentle face suddenly pretty.

'Can we give you a lift, sir?'

'No, Bob will want his full walk home or he's going to complain. Or get Miss Pinero up in the night.'

Oh yes, Miss Pinero. She too knew about Stella Pinero.

'One piece of news, sir. I expect it's faxed to you already, but the driver of the coach has come across with a story about the death of Jim Lollard. Looks as if he did it himself.'

'What, the driver?'

'No, Lollard. Not exactly suicide, though,' she appraised. 'More *felo de se*.'

He hadn't heard that phrase used for a long time. Self-murder, an interesting concept. But she was an interesting girl, Mary Barclay, who held her thoughts close to herself until she had something worth saying.

He opened the door for her to get into the car. The driver saluted. ''Evening, sir.' He too was forming a story to tell when he got back. 'Got on like a house on fire, those two.

She's a cool girl, that Barclay. More there than you think.'

'One more thing,' said Mary Barclay before she got into the car. 'I just got the impression that the boy's shirt was left there on purpose. Not by accident. Deliberate.'

'What makes you think that?'

'Draped across the steering-wheel, sir. Not natural, that.'

No, not natural. Smart girl. Just one more little trick, thought Coffin as he walked up the hill. On a par with all the other little tricks.

There were cars parked outside St Luke's Mansions and lights on in Stella's place where he had expected total darkness. Bob could go home for the night, then.

He led Bob across the courtyard to Stella's door and rang the bell. She appeared almost at once, her face free of make-up, hair tied back and wearing a satin robe. But from behind the door came the sound of music and laughter.

He raised an eyebrow. 'Thought you were exhausted?'

'I am, I am,' she said gaily, 'but some friends dropped in and we're talking over the plans for the Festival. Want to come up?'

He shook his head. 'Here's Bob, he's had a good walk and don't let him bully you.'

He smiled as he walked to his own front door and put his key in the lock. Trust Stella. Parties and laughter rose up around her all the time, she didn't seem to plan them or expect them, they just happened.

One thing was sure: Stella would never be a quiet-to-come-home-to woman.

CHAPTER 11

March 19

Other people were troubled on the wet spring night.

The young journalist who had duly passed over his story about Jim Lollard was one of them. Yes, he had told Inspector Young of his talk with Lollard concerning the imminence of another mass crime, and how angry Lollard had been. With the police for never listening to him (especially fierce about the sergeant on the desk who had rebuffed him last). With society for never taking any notice of him.

'It's politics,' he had said, with a little froth of spittle emerging through his overlarge false teeth. 'But just let them wait and see. They need showing. And that neighbour of mine, I'll let her see. Told her to watch who she took in. But does she listen?'

The journalist lived some miles away from Regina Street but he made a journey over that way to stand and stare outside Lollard's house, so newly painted that it put its neighbours to shame. (Not that they were shamed, Regina Street knew no shame.) Queer cove, he thought.

Three streets away from Lollard's house, and over his own shop was the home of the chemist who managed the large pharmacy on the main road near the Spinnergate Tube station. An insomniac, as he took his nightly sedative, he remembered someone to whom he had sold a goodly supply of these excellent tablets, harmless yet helpful when used as indicated on the packet. 'You're going it a bit, Jim, aren't you?' he had said as the man had come back several times. 'Too many of these won't do you any good. They aren't chocolates, you know.' Although they were chocolate-coloured and tasted of vanilla. 'See the doctor, if you're that bad.' The man had indeed looked strung up and tense. Not wild, no, but not relaxed, either, whereas with all the tablets he had he should have looked sozzled.

'You can take them with a cup of coffee, can't you?' Lollard had asked.

'Take them with anything,' he had said, thinking that obviously Jim hadn't touched one yet, which made his shopping even stranger.

Then a woman had come in the shop with a baby who had swallowed her contraceptive pill and in the anxiety to do the right thing by mother and child, Jim had slipped out of the shop and out of his memory.

The baby had been screaming and the mother weeping, not so much for her child, it seemed, but for her lost pill and the danger she was in of 'falling again' if she didn't get the daily dose. As if the pill was magic and another pill wouldn't do.

And the baby had proved not to have taken the pill at all, but to have had it mysteriously, and who knew how, wedged in his nappy.

But Jim Lollard was dead. Dead, so it was reported in the evening paper, from an overdose of sedative tablets which could be used as sleeping tablets.

The chemist guessed he had sold the stuff to Jim, so as he turned restlessly on his pillow he resolved to tell the police tomorrow.

In Regina Street there was one worried landlady who had not received the rent for the let of a room in the house next door, which she was looking after for a neighbour who was in hospital. She hoped she wouldn't be accused of lifting it.

She had tried the tenant's door, third floor back next door, and had got no answer. She hadn't seen him for days and in a quiet way she kept a watch. No sign of Mr Lamartine. Or the other lodger. Where were they?

She found sleep hard to come by and got up to make a cup of tea. Her nerves were jumpy anyway, as she told herself with the self-sympathy of the lonely spirit. She knew about the death of Jim Lollard, and everyone was talking about the missing boy. It had been on the TV news, national, not local, and not to be missed. All of it made for uneasy nights if you were a sensitive soul, as she was.

A sleeping potion would be nice, but people said they were dangerous, habit-forming, and you were better off without them. In any case, she had always avoided anything chemical and artificial even in contraception, relying on luck.

One way and another there were a lot of worried people that night in Spinnergate in John Coffin's territory. The rain disturbed the sleep of the woman in Regina Street, but the journalist was young and slept deeply with no aids, and the chemist was drugged.

The other participant, still more deeply dead to the world and underground, was stirring.

CHAPTER 12

March 20

There was an ancient Romano-British historian, by name Nennius, who said winningly that in writing his history he had 'made a heap of the facts'. The tutor had mentioned Nennius in the course Coffin had embarked on called Tracing your Ancestors, although he could not now remember how Nennius came into it. Perhaps as how you should not do it. Coffin had only attended about two lessons out of six and had not been exactly a star pupil, even before chance had delivered a lot more kin to him than he had expected, but he had always remembered Nennius, for whom he felt a fellow-feeling. Facts did get into heaps. Untidy ones too, usually.

It was at this stage in the working out of the two mysteries of the missing boy and the death of Jim Lollard that John Coffin felt a whole heap of the facts had fallen on his head.

Back in his sitting-room in the tower of the old St Luke's Church, now converted into his 'living area', as the architect liked to say, Coffin went to his desk. On it lay an open copy of *The Circle*, and the box containing his mother's handwritten memoirs which he was editing in a determined but anxious way. Probably he would never submit the memoirs for publication to any publishing house, although they were an interesting social document, to say the least, of the years before and immediately after the war, but he had thought of getting them privately printed. His sister Laetitia had a daughter who might, one day, wish to know about her grandmother's goings-on. He had no child himself and was, on the whole, grateful for it. Life was complicated enough as it was.

He looked down at these two documents: a play written nearly seventy years ago, and a diary whose jaunty, rambling observation on the pleasures of sex had been put down within the last two decades. Mum must have been pretty old by then, he thought, yet she'd been still alive and kicking up her heels and he hadn't known it. Two voices to speak to him if he wanted to listen, Somerset Maugham's and his mother's, but his fax machine and his answering machine were both empty and silent. No messages there about the car or about Jim Lollard.

Tiddles, the cat, came climbing home over the housetops and into the open window, offering a silent mouth of greeting. Coffin picked him up and stroked him absently while he thought things over. *Your coat's a bit wet, boy, so that's why you came in—it's beginning to rain.*

Either his CID were protecting him from overnight worry (unlikely), or they wanted him at arm's length. He would know what was going on, but only when they told him. It was a hint, perhaps, if you liked to look at it that way, that detection was their business and no longer his.

Just as well he had met Mary Barclay. Not that he meant to let them get away with it. He didn't blame Archie Young and Paul Lane for wanting him to keep his finger out of their pie, he would have felt the same himself in their place, but what they overlooked was that his was the ultimate responsibility. The grilling he had had in the House of Commons from the aggressive MP made him only too aware of this. The police were always now under fire, but he was the one who must be judged first and hardest. He accepted that as truth; it was his place; but the other side of the coin was that if he wanted to oversee some investigation, then he would. Bloody well would. He set Tiddles down, giving him an affectionate pat. He sometimes spoke harshly to Tiddles but his hands were gentle. Hands and touch told you so much more than voices and words.

'I was retired once, puss,' he said, 'and then brought back for special duties, and because I had special knowledge I did well out of that, it's why I am where I am now, if that's a good thing, puss. I almost went mad once, Tiddles, only it turned out to be an unusual form of poisoning. I had a wife once as well, but perhaps we should forget about her.' She was dead, anyway, poor girl. Gone to dwell in that other country with so many others.

His hands tightened around the cat. Tiddles gave a muted cry of pain and anger, delivered a sharp scratch and fled.

Coffin apologized to the empty air. 'Sorry, boy.' Tiddles, although officially neutered, was firmly masculine in temperament and behaviour and went courting regularly in the right season (and out of it too, he was not fussy) although nothing came of it.

So Jim Lollard had killed himself, had he? Or so Detective Barclay had said, wording it a bit strangely. The circumstances were strange enough in themselves. That case was going to be one for the books, and another score for Murder Street.

As a well-known local character, Lollard's fame had reached the Chief Commander. Lollard had always been talking about murder and death, he was obsessed with the idea. If Lollard had killed himself then it might have been the death he was looking for.

He took one last look out of his high tower window before going to sleep. The rooftops below were gleaming in the rain, in the distance the street lamps shone in tawny blurred haloes of light, the air smelt sweet.

Looks peaceful enough he thought, but he knew he was deceiving himself. In his wild bailiwick violent and unpleasant events were happening all the time whether he got to know about them or not. Statistics and experience taught it. Steady downpour, though, that usually keeps the gangs off the streets. Both the Planters and the Dreamers hated getting wet, it spoilt their hair and their clothes. Rain does quieten things down.

*

It rained heavily all through the night, seeping into the earth, so that the paper and cardboard around that which was buried in Murder Street began to split apart and the creature inside to burst forth. Still under the earth but soon about to be visible.

Meanwhile, the man who had put the torch to a little business premises in North Spinnergate had already packed his bags and was driving away. Mission accomplished.

In the early morning his fax machine delivered its messages and Coffin read them as he drank coffee.

Better late than never, he thought, and wondered if there was some sort of timing device on his machine so that messages were slow in getting through. Not likely, of course, just his fancy, though an interesting idea. Probably some despatcher tardy about his work.

Amid the usual supply of other messages about a car crash at a traffic lights, two dead; a fire (arson suspected) at a premises on the corner of Magdalen Road and Sweetings Lane, North Spinnergate, shop burned out, the proprietor being questioned; council tenants' protest march over a rent rise (Can't Pay, Won't Pay); and the advice that a gang of Australian pickpockets had arrived as usual at Heathrow for the spring and summer season, were the two pieces of information he was looking for.

The fire in the Magdalen Road and Sweetings Lane area meant something to him, but as yet he was not sure what, and his thoughts were directed strongly to another item.

A fifteen-year-old, dark red Metro, answering the description of the car wanted in the Casey abduction, had been found abandoned on waste ground by the New Canal at 21.03 hours last night by a constable on the beat. The car had attracted his attention and he had examined it. Inside was a child's shirt. Shirt provisionally identified as having been worn by Tom Casey. Blood on it not yet identified.

Get on to that, thought Coffin, it's crucial. It was becoming apparent that this was a case where Forensics were going to be all important.

One last sentence caught his eye and seemed to stand out in large print: a woman's shoe found in the car.

Well, what to make of that? One shoe, and a woman's. A one-legged lady?

Somehow he did not like this discovery of a woman's shoe. It didn't seem natural. What was it Mary Barclay had said about the appearance of the boy's shirt looking 'contrived'? The one shoe looked contrived.

There was nothing more that was new about the missing boy. Or nothing reliable. The usual number of sightings from places as far apart as Cornwall and Berwick-on-Tweed. These would be checked, but would probably lead to nothing. And yet he knew that from one report in a hundred, some vital information might come.

A brief summary of the statement from coach driver Tremble appeared in the next item. Tremble had been questioned yesterday, March 19, in his own home by Inspector Archie Young and had finally admitted to knowing something about the mystery of his coach tour's imprisonment *en masse* and the death of Jim Lollard. The police had suspected all the time that Tremble knew more than he would admit to. After all, he had been driving the coach, hadn't he?

Tremble had confessed to having been paid to run his coach into the old warehouse. Yes, by Jim Lollard himself. Lollard had fed him this story about there having been a mass murder in the place, but he had never believed it. Or even if it was true, he wouldn't have done anything about it. He had his set tour and that was that. But Lollard offered money. Why? Tremble didn't know. No, he had no idea what Lollard had in mind, just thought he was cracked. He had accepted the bribe (if you wanted to call it that, which he didn't) because he needed the cash. No, he didn't know anything else.

Archie Young had added his own comment that he did not believe Tremble on this point, thought he did know more, and would be continuing with his questions. No one told all in a first confession, least of all people like Tremble (no record but one or two near misses and certainly known to the police in his own patch, Loding Avenue district, N.E. London). But it did look as if Jim Lollard had somehow contrived his own death. Couldn't call it suicide, quite.

Progress of a sort, then, on his two main problems. Coffin had another cup of coffee and ate some toast. Tiddles appeared for breakfast and was satisfied with a bowl of dried cat biscuits and some hot milk.

He hesitated whether to tell Stella Pinero the news about the discovery of the car, but he was forestalled by meeting her in the courtyard outside.

'Just on my way to get breakfast at Max's. What about you?' She was wearing jeans and a dark blue sweater but had applied lipstick and a kind of shine on her face which could not be natural but looked good. Very good.

'I've had something. Early for you, isn't it?' Like most theatre people, Stella preferred not to surface till the sun had been up some time.

'Had Nell on the 'phone at what felt like dawn. She'd had a call from your Inspector Young telling her that the car had been found. Empty. Tom wasn't in it. He let her have it straight out, he doesn't wrap things up, that man. Poor Nell. I suppose you've heard all already.'

'Ah,' said Coffin. A rough brown form had rushed past them, giving a small bark as he went. 'Did you know you'd let Bob out?'

'He does what he likes. That means you did know? And probably wouldn't have said.'

'I would have done.'

'Eventually.'

'Now, Stella . . .'

Stella gave a short, unkind laugh which meant I bet, and You never do, and I don't trust you an inch. Not all of which was quite true or even partly true but had some truth in it.

'Nell said that she felt they weren't telling her everything.'

Very likely not. Probably not telling her about the shirt, and almost certainly not about the shoe.

'That was a question,' said Stella, her temper frayed by having to wake up early, by a slight hangover from last night, and the general feeling that life was a bugger.

'I know it was.'

'No wonder they call you pigs.'

Their relationship was taking one of its rapid spirals downward as on a slide in a fairground. They got on a mat, any mat would do, and went swooping down, arguing strongly.

They reached the bottom together.

'See you sometime.' Coffin moved towards his car.

'Right.' Stella never swore outside the theatre (although frequently when inside, they all did) but her lips mouthed the unsayable.

You should always check your car for explosives before getting in, that was the latest security instruction. Coffin did so inspect his car, briefly and without interest. Nothing there. One day there would be, probably, and he hoped he noticed it.

As he drove away, he remembered what was worrying him about the fire in Sweetings Lane, which diverted his mind from the quarrel, near-quarrel, with Stella Pinero. He took the first opportunity that morning to see Superintendent Paul Lane.

Lane was in the temporary Incident Room, into which he had just moved his team, needing more accommodation as the case expanded. It was set up in a caravan in the parking lots across the way from the police headquarters in Spinnergate because once again they had no spare space. The building, a façade of red brick with its interesting air of being a Venetian prison, looked big enough but was proving remarkably inconvenient for modern policing. Temporary huts were often in use, but Lane had his computers and telephones all installed, so that heavy duty cables trailed ominously towards the caravan.

Lane was sitting at his desk contemplating a screen of information on the computer which seemed to be giving him little joy. He stood up as John Coffin came in.

'Not much for me there,' he said. 'I was running over the cases where Duerden was a prime suspect of murder and all those where he might have been involved. No pattern that I can see, just a chancer, that's his style. Neat, quiet little man that no one would look at twice, and that's how he does it. But nothing that helps here. Never goes in for the sort of embroidery we've got here. Could have changed, I suppose. Worked himself up for something a bit more fancy.' He sat down to consider it. Stood up, grunted in disbelief, then sat down again heavily and dragged a packet of cigarettes towards his chief. The air inside the Incident Room was already blue. He did not offer a cigarette to his chief. 'You don't, do you, sir?'

'No, and you shouldn't either. What about the fire in Sweetings Lane? That is the papershop? On the corner of the Lane and Magdalen Road? Used as a letter-box by the paedophile group?'

'Yerss,' said Lane, making a long slow sound of it. 'More than a letter-box, probably had meetings there. Yes, arson all right. A can of petrol popped through the shop window. The owner, he calls himself the manager, but he owns that shop and two others, is in hospital, baddish, but he'll live. Someone had it in for him.'

'Any ideas?'

'He swears he doesn't know who it could be or why. That's lies, of course, he is aware of what his shop is used for. Probably belongs to the club. No, some citizen besides us has a good idea of what goes on there and has had a go.'

'Or it could be the result of a quarrel within the group.'

'Yerss . . . But they're not usually rough with each other. All soft and serious there. No, I reckon it's an outsider.'

'Could be Duerden?'

Lane shrugged. 'Be nice and neat if it was now, wouldn't it?'

'Who's running the investigation?'

'Farmer over the 'Gate, it's his manor. Good man. But

we're keeping in touch. All linked up, anyway, because of the boy.

'Yes, the car.'

Lane stood up again and shifted around uneasily. 'Yes, it's good we've got that. Still, I'd say it was delivered.' He cocked an eyebrow at Coffin.

'So you think he wanted us to find it?' This confirmed what Mary Barclay had said, clever girl. It was on display, meant to be. They were being told something.

'He or she.'

Coffin said: 'You mean the shoe?'

Lane said: 'Yes, a funny thing that. I mean have we got a Cinderella complex here?' He meant it as a joke. 'I'm not sure if I know what to think about the shoe. I'm still thinking. Was it left behind by chance or design? And if the latter, why?' He walked round to Coffin's side of the desk. 'Want to see it? We've still got it here before we let the scientists have a look.'

In a plastic bag was a high-heeled woman's shoe. An elegant shoe of cream leather with a gold trim. Not the sort of shoe to wear every day. Not a cheap shoe, either.

Coffin studied it but without fingering it. The shoe had been worn. A narrow, long, elegant shoe. 'American sizing,' he said. 'Probably an American shoe. Could be bought elsewhere, I suppose.'

'We shall find out that,' said Lane grimly. 'The Caseys have been living in New York. I shall start by asking her.'

Funny thing about shoes, Coffin thought, they told you so much about a person, they told you whether they liked good quality, sober fashion or cheap flashy shoes or expensive stylish stuff. They told you how a person walked, and whether they wore their shoes out or got them repaired.

This shoe did have an air of Nell about it.

Coffin looked at his watch, he was due at a meeting in half an hour and had a twenty-minute drive across the river to the other side of London. 'Is Archie Young around?'

'He was in here a minute ago asking me something. He said he'd be back. He seems to think he's got the Lollard case tied up nicely. He'll tell you about it.'

Coffin walked out and met Archie Young at the door. Young looked warily at his chief. He was feeling successful and buoyant, but experience had taught him that this was the time to be careful, and in many ways John Coffin had been the conscience in his life.

'You couldn't cheat with him,' was how he put it to himself. He knew that he had inside himself a little kernel of cheating, fudging, he preferred to call it, to which he was capable of giving way if he was convinced of the truth of a case, if he had his man but could not get him to court. He did not condemn himself for this, in a pragmatic way he recognized it had to be done occasionally, but he would rather John Coffin never got to know.

He was in such a position now. He knew how Jim Lollard had died but was not quite sure what charge would stick where, while being absolutely sure who deserved punishment. 'I think I know how the coach trick was done and why. Tremble talked in the end.'

'In the end? He's not dead, is he?'

'No, certainly not. Although it was just luck or he might have gone the way of Jim Lollard. No, he's gone home to his loving wife, so he's into happy time. I just meant I had to keep digging.' There was a black note in his voice.

'So?'

'I don't know what we'll get him for. He ought to be done for something.'

'If no crime has been committed—' began Coffin impatiently. He wanted Mary Barclay's words about *felo de se* explained, and quickly. In about five minutes flat, if possible, because that was all the time he had to be illuminated. Archie Young was not wordy but he could be opaque.

'Oh, crime's been committed all right. Tremble is guilty of driving a vehicle with damaged brakes, of driving while under the influence of drugs, of endangering the lives of his passengers, and guilty of having taken a bribe. There ought to be a crime in that lot somewhere.' He handed over a file of papers. 'It's all in there. The statement from the young journalist . . . what he told us about Lollard predicting a mass crime gave us a start. Then a chemist came in with the story that Lollard had been stocking up on the sort of drugs that were used . . . Tremble admits Lollard paid him money to go into the warehouse. Paid him to let Lollard make the coffee and drinks and hand them out. Lollard wanted to stage a crime.'

'Sounds mad.'

'Obsessed, sir. He wanted to be proved right. He'd had a row with the station sergeant at Fowler Street station a few days before. He fancied justification and the publicity. We'd have pinned it on him, of course, but I don't think he cared about that chance.'

'So Lollard paid Tremble to make the detour, drugged the coachload of tourists and then took some of the stuff himself?'

'I don't think he meant to kill himself. Or anyone else. He just wanted to make a show, something mysterious and melodramatic that the newspapers could get hold of. That's why he spoke to the journalist. But he'd had a lot to drink and the drugs and the beer didn't mix. I suppose he was just unlucky. Tremble either didn't get so much of the sedative or wasn't so sensitive to it. That's the medical opinion.'

'Lollard lived in Regina Street, didn't he?'

'Yes, all on his own. Part of the trouble, most of it, in fact. He had too much time to think about living on Murder Street. Ever been there, sir? Regina Street, I mean. Worth a look.' He nearly added, but didn't: on one of your late night walks.

It's a serious business, Coffin thought as he turned away, the death of one man, for whatever frivolous reason.

Sometimes he took himself out of the ranks of driven men, which he had long thought he must be, and became a driving man. A man who pushed events around, usually forward to a conclusion, but sometimes back.

He was pushing his relationship with Stella Pinero backwards now, but other happenings forward.

It was a battle, but he knew himself to be capable of battling.

*

There followed a tumultuous short period for John Coffin. A day of personal crisis. He was into it before he realized what was happening.

His MP critic had proved a more subtle and dangerous enemy than he had grasped.

Devious fellow.

The MP had persuaded two of the other Members whose constituencies came into the area of the Second City to join with him in demanding a commission to 'monitor' the new Force which Coffin commanded.

'I monitor my officers,' he had argued back.

But that wasn't enough apparently. An independent monitoring committee must be set up.

But this was not all: there was a sense of betrayal in the air. One of his senior officers, a man who had come in from another Force but who had started life in the Met and had his own reasons for jealousy, was suspected of handing on information to the MP.

It was bad news and yet no news: he had never liked the man Groden, wished on him as a matter of policy. One of the compromises forced on him that now looked like the disaster most compromises usually are. The news about Groden was passed on to him by an anonymous letter. A letter whose source he could very easily guess but did not mean to run to earth: the woman who ran the computer service. She knew everything and had a mother complex about him. Probably about every man, woman, and animal she came in contact with, but certainly about him.

There was one other arrow aimed at him in this time of crisis: a savagely personal one. His sister Letty whom he had thought to be about to divorce had another message to deliver: a business enterprise in New York on which she had embarked had collapsed. It was likely she would go bankrupt. He knew what that meant: heaven help St Luke's Theatre Workshop and the new theatre now in the building.

And Stella? What would it mean for Stella?

For twenty-four hours the earth shook beneath him. He walked his turret sitting-room overnight, not sleeping, ignoring Tiddles. Letty had enjoined absolute secrecy on him, she might pull through, but not if word got around. Say nothing.

During this time he did not exactly forget either the death of Jim Lollard, or the missing boy. These problems were always there to be thought about but the action was being taken by other people.

Still no trace of Tom. The owner of the burnt-out paper-shop was being questioned. No admission as yet. Nell Casey had been questioned about the shoe but denied that it was hers. He knew these things, but had no solution to offer, and having no solution felt powerless. Chief Commanders ought to see the way forward, know what to do. He did not.

There was a whisky bottle on the table and that was certainly one way out, but not for him. He had tried that sort of oblivion once and it didn't work.

Without knowing it, he fell asleep in his chair with Tiddles on his lap. He woke up with dawn and knew that he was going to fight it out. Even fight for Letty if he had to, although she was no mean fighter herself if it came to that.

Coffin had many social occasions in his life but these days they were often formal, on-show ones, where he had to make a speech, sometimes wear a uniform and silver braid, but anyway be a person of importance.

So the invitation to drinks issued last week by Sir Harry Beauchamp, the distinguished and famous photographer who was also a tenant of St Luke's Mansions, to come round for 'a gathering, my dear boy', had been welcomed as a change. His friend Dick was having the party in the Old Lead Works Art Gallery which he owned and ran.

Sir Harry had moved into St Luke's Mansions at the time of the killings in Feather Street and the murder of a girl in Rope Alley, so he had had his baptism of fire as a resident in the district, but he had taken to it and now proudly called himself a local. He was to be met often in Max's Deli, or drinking in the Theatre Workshop Bar. He had done a whole article for *Vogue* about the Theatre Workshop and its company, illustrated by a dozen or so of his sophisticated, stylish photographs. Stella had been delighted, especially as she got what she called 'best billing' with a plentiful display of her lovely face. Letty Bingham had been very pleased and had promised to come over for the Festival, although she had kept very quiet about this lately and Coffin now knew why.

He could have gone in Stella's company, she was bound to be invited and would certainly go if she was not rehearsing or playing, no one turned down an invitation from Sir Harry, he was too famous and too much-loved by all. But he and Stella were still at odds. Moreover, there was the complication now of Letty's telephone call.

Stella was there, as he had guessed she would be, standing in the middle of the big room, smiling and laughing and looking full of life. She was happy, or as near happy as she expected to be these days.

He stood looking at her. How can you talk to someone when you know something ominous about their future that they do not? How could he talk to her when he knew all her present hopes and ambitions might crumble away, leaving nothing in her hands? So he turned away and talked to someone else, one of the Feather Street ladies who asked him how Tiddles was. The Feather Street ladies marked you by your animals, which they often knew better than they knew you. Oh, you are the owner of the little white dog, they would say, meeting you in a shop. Or: How is the cat today? when you would rather they asked after you.

The room was crowded but he could see Nell Casey there talking to Ellice Eden who was crouching protectively over her. Nell looked pale and thin, but she had put on her clothes carefully and was listening to what Ellice had to say with apparent interest. Her eyes wandered, though, as if she was not so much in this room as she pretended to be.

Coffin wondered what he ought to do about her. Should he speak to her, or tactfully ignore her. She was another one he knew too much about.

He knew now that Nell Casey had a small but interesting record. As a teenager she had done a bit of shoplifting and been caught at it. Scent, make-up and small articles of clothing mostly; she had been what the trade calls 'a grabber': taking a chance and grabbing what she wanted. She had escaped lightly: just a talking-to. Soon after that she had gone to drama school, won prizes and ceased to shoplift. As far as one knew.

He knew this, not from any police record, for none had been kept. She had been a juvenile and treated gently as such. Dismissed, with no prosecution but the order to behave in future. Coffin had been told by a retired copper who had been having a drink with him the day before and indulging in a little reminiscence. 'Gawky, awkward kid, but she had something. When she got on to TV I remembered her. She could be trouble.'

Probably of no importance and no relevance to what had happened now, but it was something to think about.

Sylvie had apparently lived a blameless life, but she had had an unhappy love-affair, to escape which she had taken the job with Nell. Tom, of course, had hardly had time to live a life at all.

Sir Harry approached him from one side and Stella from the other. She got caught up with a trio of young actors and Harry got there first.

He was confidential, in that beautiful, precise, deep voice that he had taught himself, a high cockney whine having come more naturally all those years ago. 'I expect you are wondering why I asked Nell Casey . . . I thought she ought to get out. She brought Ellice with her. He seems to be looking after her these days. Well, she needs someone.' He took Coffin's glass from him and handed him another. 'Have this, it's stronger, I mixed it myself. Dick's so mean with his drinks. Comes of having been born rich. Go on, take a sip, you look as though you need it.' Sir Harry had the photographer's sharp eye and could pick up strain when he saw it.

Coffin took a taste of the drink, which was indeed strong. Strange, too.

Harry lowered his voice. 'I suppose I shouldn't ask if there is any news of the boy?'

'No reason why you shouldn't ask, but no, nothing.' He wasn't being quite truthful. The police always know just that little bit more than they publicize. In this case, they knew that the sighting of a boy like Tom being carried through a crowded South London street by the Elephant and Castle on the afternoon of the day he disappeared was possibly Tom. The person carrying him had been wearing a nurse's green-striped dress (a greeny, as they called them) under a dirty raincoat. Sex hard to distinguish but walked like a woman. The couple had probably taken the Tube. But there was a large car park nearby, could have gone there. So the report had run. Coffin was inclined to accept it. 'I think the child is still alive,' he said in a moderate tone. 'We'll find him.'

'Poor girl.'

Coffin nodded, looking towards Nell still engaged in frantic pretence of animated conversation.

Stella had pushed her way through to him. Harry saw someone across the room and departed. 'Drink up, dear boy.'

'I shouldn't,' said Stella. 'Harry's mixes are lethal.' She ought to know, Coffin thought, her own glass was almost empty. She saw him looking. 'Yes, this is not my first.'

Coffin kept a prudent silence; he knew Stella in this mood.

'I'm not talking to you because I want to . . . No, I want to talk about Nell. I'm seriously worried.'

'I know, Stella.' He was caught by her warm sympathy.

'About the shoe, the one found in the car. Nell said it wasn't hers. I don't think she should have been asked.'

'We have to ask, Stella.'

'Yeah, well, she said it wasn't her shoe . . .'

'I know that.'

Stella looked around the room. 'She really ought to tell you this herself but she's scared. Can't blame her for that. You can be a pretty scarey lot, you know, you boys in blue.'

'I never said we were nice, Stella.' It wasn't a nice job. He waited.

'Now she thinks it is her shoe. Could be.'

Coffin took a deep drink of his strong drink. Vodka, he thought, with more than a touch of something else equally strong, possibly white port.

Stella gave him a long hard look. 'What do you know that we don't know?'

'What a question.'

'*The* question, I should think.'

'Nothing about the shoe.' He looked towards Nell. 'I'll obviously have to talk to her. And she's going to have to tell Lane.' And explain what she's been playing at.

Stella picked up the evasion.

There were tears in Stella's eyes. 'Oh, darling, what is happening to us?'

But he was already looking past her to where Nell stood and thinking that he wished he had Mary Barclay here, she would be the person to do the questioning of Nell Casey.

CHAPTER 13

March 21

It could have been a woman driving the car with the boy in it, that was the knowledge that had seeded some growth in Coffin's brain. Now it was producing an unnatural fruit that he did not like.

Nell's guilt.

He had flirted with the idea of Nell being guilty of something, anything; now there was this business with the shoe so that it looked as if she could be guilty of abducting her own son. Or at least, of hiding him for reasons of her own.

If he was her son.

He knew what he had to do, and it was a nasty, sly trick but he would do it. A doubly sly trick because to do what he wanted he would have to make up with Stella, with whom a slight, residual irritation remained. She might guess it, too, she could be as clever as a waggon load of monkeys when she wanted.

To Stella, he said: I'm going to talk to Nell now, but I'm not going to say much, she'll have to come in to the station tomorrow and do the thing properly then. You going to stay here? I'll come back to you.'

Stella just raised an eyebrow giving him a bare nod. Didn't even hear what I just said, she thought. Pig. Well, that's it. I shall start all over again with someone else. I want a man, a woman like me does. She awarded herself this judgement like a prize. And I should like a man who doesn't smoke, drinks only what I drink, and when, and does his own cooking. Driving too, she added thoughtfully.

She looked round the room to see if she could sight such a man, but all she could see was Nell talking to John Coffin.

That bastard Ellice Eden was still being very protective of her, hadn't moved away, he was staying on the scene, holding her drink for her. Pretending not to listen, of course.

True to his word, Coffin did not stay long with Nell, a few brisk sentences it looked to be, and he came back to Stella, standing there with a withdrawn look, still not really with her.

'What did you say to her?' She didn't want to talk to him, but curiosity was stronger than pride. He didn't answer. Didn't hear me again, she thought, fury bubbling up.

What he had said to Nell was: 'What's this about the shoe?' He too was aware of Ellice Eden hovering.

Nell had turned her head slightly so that Ellice could not see her face. 'I remembered . . . I had a pair like that. Bought them in Macy's. I forgot.' She peered hopefully into Coffin's face. Short-sighted, he diagnosed. Doesn't wear contact lenses or can't. 'I never wore them. Made my feet look too big.' She looked down at her feet, she did have long thin feet. 'So I forgot about them.'

'But you remembered. What made that happen?'

'Suddenly came to me. That's how memory works, isn't it?'

Could do, Coffin had thought, or it could indicate a lie surfacing.

'And then Sylvie said hadn't I had a pair like that,' Nell went on, as if this had been of no importance, 'and reminded me.'

'Do you still have the other shoe?'

Nell shook her head silently.

'Sure?' He studied her face. There had to be another one somewhere, and that somewhere might be of interest.

'Looking,' submitted Nell.

'And you don't know how the one shoe came to be in the car?'

Nell looked him straight in the eye. She shook her head. 'No idea. Can't think. It worries me.'

You certainly have every right to be worried, decided Coffin. It certainly worries me.

'Who's been in your flat recently?'

'Only friends.'

'You'll have to name names.'

'You, Stella, Gus Hamilton came once, Ellice, others from the play.' She looked around helplessly. 'People drift in and out, after rehearsal or before. It's the way things are.'

Easy to pick up a shoe, thought Coffin, if your mind ran that way. Damn it.

'I feel sick,' whispered Nell. 'Right inside me. That's because of Tom.'

He tried to read her face, and couldn't. He could see grief, tension, anxiety, plenty of that, but he didn't know what to make of it: she was an actress.

Across the room, Stella was registering fury and he could read that all right. We must talk, Stella and I, he said silently, I must listen to her more.

But when he had got back to Stella, all he said was: 'Tomorrow Nell Casey will be going in to talk to Paul Lane. I want you to take Sylvie out during that time. Doesn't matter where. Just away. Out of that flat in The Albion. I will come to take you to the flat and then I will stay.'

Stella was silent. 'Are you looking for the boy there?' she asked at last.

'Can you think of a better place?'

He was conscious of carrying around with him a double deceit like a hump on his back. It was a double deceit, because he was using Stella to get Sylvie away, because he was not going to tell anyone, not Paul Lane or Archie Young, and his intention was to request Mary Barclay to meet him there.

His would be the responsibility.

It was a nice day, with the sun shining and a blue sky, but a sudden shower of heavy rain set in as John Coffin and Stella Pinero arrived at The Albion.

'I was going to ask the girl to come for a walk. But I can hardly do so now.' Stella was cross and not worrying about showing it. She had groomed herself with a mathematical precision that made her look hard. She knew it, and didn't care about that, either.

'Take her shopping,' said Coffin. 'Just take her.'

'I believe I would be justified in being angry with you,' said Stella in a quiet civil voice that let him know she was furious. 'But I'll do it. Not for you, though. For Nell and Tom.' She felt as though she ought to cross herself when she said the boy's name, he was so vulnerable, so likely to be dead. And if not dead, then suffering what?

But she was sweet to Sylvie when the girl opened the door, said she thought it would be a good idea for her to get out of the house, so come and have a cup of coffee with her in Max's and then they could decide what to do. Harrods, maybe?

Sylvie's eyes curved with pleasure. 'Oh, Workers for Freedom, please,' she said, her voice reverent and hushed, the voice of the really dedicated shopper. 'And Hyper—Hyper . . . where Princess Diana shops.'

Stella looked surprised, but agreed. The girl knew her fashion onions. It had not been Stella's intention to do any serious shopping, but they were obviously about to do just that. 'Come on, then.' It was to be hoped the girl had the right shiny plastic cards in her purse, but somehow she had that look that said she did.

Sylvie left with Stella without appearing to notice that Coffin remained behind. Clothes had her in their thrall.

Within minutes, Mary Barclay rang the bell. 'I saw them leave.' She stood on the threshold. 'I was told to report to you, sir, and stay as long as wanted.' She waited for him to say something. He didn't, he wasn't even looking at her, but standing there as if he was waiting for the place to speak to him.

She came in and shut the door behind her. Quietly, but there was no one to hear. The boss didn't seem to be getting any answers, either.

After a minute, a clock with a silver chime began to sound the hour in the room down the hall, and Coffin came back to the world where she was. Not a nice world, maybe, but for the moment one they shared.

The flat was very still and quiet once the clock stopped chiming. Someone had had a bath or a shower, you could smell scented essence, piney and bubbly.

'Sir?' she said.

'I want you to look round here. To look for any signs of abnormality, any signs of child abuse.'

Mary Barclay moved her head sharply. Not what she'd expected. 'Alison Jenkins is the expert on that sort of thing.'

'You are the expert on this family.'

'You think I shall find that?' She didn't name it, that horror she was meant to detect. It struck her that her position was ambiguous. What am I being asked to do here?

'I don't know. But I am uneasy.'

'See what I can do, sir.' For some reason that she chose not to determine, she was anxious to keep the formality there. Not that there had been any suggestion she should abandon it. On the contrary, she had never known John Coffin so withdrawn. But you don't know him, she reminded herself, he is the head of a body of which you are a very unimportant member.

'Three rooms. You go round clockwise, I'll go widdershins.' He started to move away. 'Ignore me. Pretend I'm not here.'

Oh yes, sure. Only the boss figure, the top man of her particular tree, he from whom all promotion and favours might flow. Ignore all that? Step carefully, girl, she told herself.

'Right, sir.' She turned her back on him and walked off.

A narrow hallway with the rooms on either side. On the right was the sitting-room, and next to it the kitchen. On the other side were the two bedrooms, Nell's own and the larger one that Sylvie shared with Tom. The bathroom was at the end of the corridor, it had no window.

Coffin took the sitting-room, while Mary Barclay took the bedrooms first. They would both cover all rooms but Coffin had always intended to be the first in the sitting-room. Just in case.

Just in case of what? You don't really expect to find Tom in a cupboard, do you?

It was a big, well-lighted room on a corner with a view down the street as well as sight of the apex of the garden. The furnishings had been done by a professional to make a good letting property, so the face of the room was bland, neutral and uninformative. There were no cupboards.

Nell had kept the room tidy and dusted (or Sylvie had) but otherwise it looked neglected. The real living had been done elsewhere, perhaps in the bedrooms or the kitchen. In Nell's case, probably in the theatre. She might be one of those theatre people who didn't need a home, just a trunk. He could see a few bowls of flowers, but they had a professionally arranged look which meant they had been presents from fans and admirers. Nell must have plenty of those, he speculated, an attractive woman succeeding in her career, her foot firmly on the ladder. There were cards on the flowers still. One said: *From the Friends of the Theatre Workshop. To make you welcome.* The other said: *From Ellice, with love.* Both pots were equally dried out and neglected. Nell was showing no favourites.

Some rooms palely reflect their occupiers, still others send out signals you couldn't miss. This room said nothing about Nell. Negative.

A pale cream and tan sofa with matching chairs which were lined up around a marble-topped table. He touched the table: imitation.

A desk in one corner of the room with another set of neglected plants on it. He opened the top of the desk, but it was empty except for a railway timetable. Perth to Penzance: 1988. Out of date and for another country.

He moved on to the kitchen. The sink was full of almost clean dishes, washed, from the look of them by having the tap run over them, and then left to drain. There was a dishwashing machine in the corner. He pulled it open: full up with the equipment of eating and not emptied. Not washed, either.

Some women liked clean kitchens, others seem not to mind dirt. He had met both kinds.

He opened cupboards and drawers rapidly. 'If I knew what I was looking for it would be easier.'

But he was looking for an idea. An idea that would tell him what Nell Casey was.

'She is not what she seems,' he said under his breath. 'But how do I know that?' The answer was he didn't, that he was guessing, but it wasn't a game.

The bathroom was hung about with pairs of pale drying tights and brief silk undergarments, which looked smaller than they were because they were so crumpled and dry. Several of a more recent crop dripped into the bath.

Clean personally but disorganized was the verdict. But his judgement here was kindly. If I was in the emotional state these two women are, he asked himself, would I wash my socks? The answer was no. Men were probably biologically dirtier animals.

He crossed with Mary Barclay in Nell Casey's bedroom, she was working more slowly than he was. He sat on the window-seat and let her get on with it.

She gave him a brief, grave look and continued her search, which she was conducting with care so that no signs of her progress was left behind her, exactly as he had expected she would do.

Not that much sign would be apparent since Nell was not tidy, depositing her clothes about the room, some on hangers, others dropped on the carpet.

The bed itself looked humped and untidy. But in the middle of the bed, on the turned back duvet, near to the crumpled pillow, she had defiantly deposited one high-heeled shoe.

The shoe. The other shoe, Cinderella's other shoe.

Coffin saw it and Mary Barclay had seen it, but neither of them said anything. What does it say? thought Coffin. It looked like defiance.

Mary moved towards the door. 'Back soon,' she said. 'Meet you back here.'

'Right.' He heaved himself up and went into the room shared by Sylvie and Tom. Sylvie had kept it tidy, carefully separating her territory from Tom's. There was a clear frontier between her possessions and those of Tom. He had plenty: a cupboard full of clothes, all brightly coloured and looking expensive, a cupboard full of toys, a row of picture books. He had a large easel on which he could chalk. He had covered it with scribbles in all colours. Tom had worked hard on that board and no one had touched it since he had.

He turned back into Nell's room where Mary Barclay was waiting.

'Well.'

'She loved the child.'

He nodded.

'Something odd in the bathroom. Did you see?'

He shook his head. 'No.' He had known that if there was anything there of importance, then Mary Barclay would find it.

'You'd better come and look.' She led the way to the bathroom. 'Cupboard on the wall. That lower shelf. It's filled, absolutely filled with—' She threw open the door. Packets and bottles lined the shelves, stacked deep. All new, all unopened. Tights in shiny packets, a silk scarf crammed into a corner, even a man's tie. Armani, nothing cheap. 'What a magpie collection.' She gave Coffin a shrewd, professional look. 'I've seen hoards like this before. Spells shoplifting to me.'

It did to him too. The stuff was new, recently possessed. They would have to take professional psychiatric advice, but what it suggested to him was that Nell, under stress, had gone back to her old vice. 'Go on, tell me what you think.'

'She loves the child. In the drawer by her bed are any number of photographs of him, with her, on his own, playing, asleep. None as a tiny baby. I don't think she had any of those.'

'So no hint of abuse or ill-treatment.'

Mary Barclay shook her head. 'Nothing like that at all. She loved him and I think he loves her. But not quite normal all the same.'

'What do you mean?'

'She had to get him into the country. You can't just bring a child in, can you? You need documents.'

'I suppose he would be on her passport,' said Coffin slowly, saying what he knew she wanted him to say. He watched her face.

'He didn't travel on her passport. Got one of his own. He had a little passport all to himself.'

She produced a big envelope: 'Her passport, his passport. One blue and stamped with the Lion and the Unicorn. The other dark green.'

An American passport. He inspected them gravely.

'He's not her child,' said Coffin, getting up to pace the room. 'I knew there was something wrong. Could smell it. But why would a hardworking actress with a tough career lumber herself with a child?'

Mary Barclay made her kind, serious face look as cynical as she could, she had not enjoyed her tour round Nell's flat, her attempted journey through Nell's mind. Somehow it stank, what she was doing and what they were finding. There was something wrong. 'Maybe she brought him in as a prop.'

And yet she loves him, she told herself.

'Where were these?' Coffin asked, handing the passports back.

'In the drawer of the bedside table. No attempt to hide them.'

'Put them back as they were. What a lot of questions we shall have to be asking that young woman.'

But he thought she had guessed there would be a search of the flat. The way the shoe was arranged was deliberate.

'Let's go down and start asking them.'

Paul Lane and Archie Young, in order of precedence, would not be pleased: he was moving into the case in strength.

CHAPTER 14

Still on March 21

Faced with the shoe on the bed and the passport in the drawer, Nell was defensive, weepy, and in the end, uncommunicative.

'Yes, my shoe. If it matches the one you have got, the one found in the car, then yes, my pair of shoes. Just one more of the creepy things that happened. But I was not driving that car.'

There were none of her fingerprints in the car. Plenty of fingerprints but all probably from the last owner and the owner before that. The steering-wheel and the door had been wiped clean.

'The driver wore gloves,' said Archie Young; he was now assisting fully on the case, the Lollard business having taken a back seat. To him, that was now past history. 'Likely thin rubber. So the science boys say. Surgical gloves. But I'm not looking for a surgeon. You've heard about the sighting of someone in a nurse's dress? Yes, don't know what to make of that.' He gave a bleak smile. 'Casey's fingerprints on the shoe, but she admits it was hers. Is hers.'

He stood in front of John Coffin's desk as if he was a schoolboy awaiting a bad report.

'Yes, I am surprised about the boy not being hers. I've been with Casey a lot lately, and she really loves that child. A lot of emotion there.' He was sensitive enough in his way and he had picked that up. He had a child himself and knew what love was like.

'I've got her waiting for you in the interview room. Barclay is having a cup of tea with her.' He added, with mild surprise, 'They seem to trust each other.'

Nell had repaired her lipstick and with it her morale. 'I hated being questioned that way,' she said to Mary Barclay. 'It made me feel like a criminal, as if it was my fault that Tom has been taken. God knows, I do blame myself but not in that kind of way. What do they think I am?'

You've got to remember she's an actress, Mary Barclay told herself, and can play any part she likes. Loving mother, distraught mother, witch of the woods. 'More tea?'

'Please.'

Mary Barclay put her head round the door and asked the constable outside for two more cups and no sugar. They drank their tea and waited until Coffin, who was taking his time, possibly deliberately, Mary Barclay decided, came down to them.

Nell absorbed the fact that they knew she was not Tom's biological mother without comment.

'I knew you'd get on to it, but I didn't think it was any of your business. I call him my son, he calls me mother. We have that relationship.'

'But not in fact,' said John Coffin. He was studying her unobtrusively. As was natural, she was extremely tense, but he was picking up other undertones as well. Wouldn't mind a look at her medical records, he thought.

'Yes, in fact. Just not genetically.'

'How does it work?' asked Coffin.

'It's just an arrangement between friends. His mother, that mother, I mean, entrusted Tom to me because she couldn't be what she wanted to him.'

'Why not?'

'I'm not going to tell you that. That's her business.'

'We aren't getting very far, are we?'

'It has nothing to do with Tom being abducted.'

'We can't know that.'

Nell was silent. A wetness appeared about her eyes, but she ignored it. 'I always cry when I'm angry. Nothing else.' Eventually she produced from her pocket a crumpled packet of letters.

Coffin took them. Written on cheap, thin paper, in a big scrawling handwriting.

> Dear Nelly—he raised his eyebrows a little at that, but went on reading—I'm glad I've got you to write to. No one else around. This is my address as of now and you can write there but I don't know how long I will be here. But I will also tell you where to write so I can have news of Tommy. I always want news and I know you will write.

'And I do write,' said Nell, as he looked up with a question in his eye.

'Even now? About this business?'

'Later I will,' said Nell. 'Of course, but not in the middle.'

'Supposing she gets to know?'

'She won't.' It was spoken with conviction. Nell knew. 'You'd better read on.'

> You can guess how grateful I am that you are looking after Tommy. If he wants to call you mamma, better let him. Whatever I am going to be to him, it won't be a regular mother and he deserves better than that. The best. I've done what seems best, the attorney who looked after my case says he has done it right. You are to have him, but not adopted, the attorney says it would be too hard to get the papers through, there are so many legal complications since you are, you not a US citizen. But you're to look after him. That's what I want.
>
> Funny how things turn out, isn't it? If I hadn't recog-

nized you and spoken to you in that coffee shop that day and showed you about Tommy, he'd have been in a home by now, poor little bastard.

The next letter had the address of a women's prison in New Jersey and the contents were more of the same.

'What did she do?' asked Coffin.

'Ran away from her husband and then killed her father. Don't ask me to go into that, it's not fancy.'

Coffin read three more letters. They all expressed love and confidence in Nell's care for Tom. Hard to think of him as Tommy. Young as he was, the diminutive did not suit him.

Nell looked at him. 'There you are. Do you think the woman who wrote those letters is likely to be the sort of girl that can be responsible for anything? A poor, beaten-up kid with no friends. No enemies either, as far as I know. Not this side of the Atlantic anyway.'

'How did this woman kill her father?'

'Stabbed him' said Nell, 'and I would have done the same. Only sooner.'

'Are you telling me that Tom is the product of incest?'

'I'm not telling you anything.' She turned her head away. 'We have a life behind us,' said Nell fiercely. 'As well as a life ahead.'

He was conscious of searing anger inside her.

CHAPTER 15

March 22–March 23

'I too have a life ahead of me,' said Stella Pinero when she heard of this interview, or as much as Coffin thought right to tell her. 'I have a Festival to run and a substitute to find for Nell, who is obviously going to drop out of *French Without Tears*.' She sounded more cheerful than might have been expected, although the gossip service having worked with its usual speed, she knew all about Nell's interview and the presence of Mary Barclay. She didn't grudge Mary Barclay her part, she was a professional, thus in the circumstances the right person to accompany John Coffin, but she herself might have been a more valuable source of information on Nell and Tom. Still, it was up to him. If he didn't ask, he wouldn't hear. Was there a faint edge of malice inside her as she thought that? The answer was yes, and she found it satisfying. 'I've interviewed a nice little actress. Just out of RADA with all sorts of medals and prizes, but the best thing is she's a local girl, lives just down the road and she started off in the Drama Department of our local University.' Stella sounded pleased with herself. 'I might get some money out of them for that.'

'I didn't know you were so mercenary,' said Coffin.

'You do know it. Always have been as far as business went, you have to be. Every penny counts in this business. Ask your sister.'

'Ah yes, I will,' said Coffin guiltily: he had had no word from Letty that might mean anything, and from her words Stella was still in a state of innocence about any possible bankruptcy.

The two of them had met on the way to work, Coffin going towards his car, and Stella Pinero towards her office in the Theatre Workshop. It was still just a wooden shack with an electric heater, a fan for hot weather and a desk with two telephones, but she enjoyed exercising her powers.

'Where is Nell?'

'That's the sort of thing you are supposed to know.'

He accepted the rebuke. Stella isn't liking me this morning, he acknowledged. It might be nothing personal; she had these days when she hated the police and disliked him for being part of it. It was an entirely understandable attitude and he accepted it.

'I know she went home. I meant here and now, this morning.'

'As far as I know, she is behind locked doors in The Albion.'

'How did Sylvie do?'

Stella allowed herself a small smile. 'At a conservative estimate she tried on about thirteen outfits, all rejected; wrong shape, wrong colour, and bought one small cotton vest to wear with her jeans. It cost a fortune. Had the right label, though.'

'She's with Nell?'

'With her, of course. She won't go anywhere until she knows about Tom. What ever you think, those two loved the boy.'

'I believe you.'

Love isn't always everything and can sometimes show itself in harsh and terrible ways.

For a few paces their paths lay together. Tiddles, who had come down the staircase with Coffin, paused to look at them, gave a swish of his tail and paced off round the corner. Dog not out today, poor soul, his gait said, I'll do dog for us both.

'I wonder what she's doing up there behind those locked doors?' said Stella.

Coffin shook his head. But, in truth, he knew. She was telephoning the Incident Room every hour to know what was the latest news about Tom. She wanted to know about the car, about the shoe—were there fingerprints on it, and about the bloody shirt. Everything. They told her what they could, repeating themselves patiently.

All that day, while Coffin worked on letters and reports, occasionally thinking of William Duerden, even of Jim Lollard, with all the time that undercurrent of anxiety about Tom, she went on telephoning.

'No, nothing new to report,' the Incident Room would say politely.

Once Mary Barclay took the call, meaning to be kind, and asking if Nell would like her to come into The Albion, but Nell just gave a little scream, might have been of rage, might have been of fear, and put the receiver down.

She telephoned several times more.

Then silence.

*

But by then on that Friday in March, the investigation had taken another direction.

Nell Casey was not forgotten, but they had news about the Papershop Group, which was what they were calling it now.

As always, the patient keeping of records and the matching up of details of persons, names, addresses, car registration numbers and the movements of interesting parties had produced a pattern.

A pattern was something to be treasured in an investigation. The pattern was an intellectual perception, but it formed different shapes in each investigating officer's mind.

Archie Young saw it as an S, a big curling S. He rationalized this by saying to himself: Well, it started on the corner of Sweetings Lane, didn't it?

The owner of the papershop in Magdalen Street by Sweetings Lane had been finally brought to a few reluctant admissions. He did not incriminate himself, nothing as hasty as that, but he did admit to knowing a few people whose tastes might be described, as Young did, as 'bloody perverted'.

Slowly, the police extracted several names and addresses. Some of the names were a surprise, some they knew to be false, but even a lie can be used to lead to the truth.

Take the name Peter Painter, giving an imaginary address in Sydney Street. It did not take a great leap of the imagination to think this character might be the same man who had been convicted of harassing a child and who was then calling himself Sydney Peters who lived in Melbourne Street. He was known to be an Australian. People did give themselves away.

Other names they knew already and could have supplied the addresses themselves. Names well known to them and on a list. On several lists up and down the country probably.

It was hard to say if William Duerden was among these people, under some other name. The papershop owner admitted to at least one new member whom he had not seen lately and who had never had much to say for himself.

With even more than his usual reluctance, the man owned that he knew the name of William Duerden who had paid to have his name on one of their postal lists.

'A corresponding member,' said the man, his eyes behind his spectacles looked pale blue and watery.

Archie Young knew what this meant, those receiving photographs and videos, and he ground his teeth angrily. He was likely to have to see a lot of his dentist if this case went on long.

It was possible that this group had been dispersed by the fire, but the pattern began to hint otherwise. Instead, it led to new territory.

If names and addresses were carefully fudged or false, there was one thing that could not so easily be altered: most of the group that called at the papershop came by car.

True, these cars were parked at a discreet distance from the shop itself. But the police had long been keeping a tally of car numbers, as a matter of routine. There was a list, now in circulation.

The papershop was shuttered, although the owner still lived in what was left of the flat above, but he was not doing any business. He had checked himself out of the hospital against medical advice.

But in an adjoining district, a sharp-eyed and observant police constable had noticed one of the number plates on his list. He noticed it more than once, not always in the same place.

Then he began to observe other interestingly numbered cars also appearing. He too made a list. Certain numbers, not all of them on the first list, but new, kept appearing.

He passed this information on and other officers started to compile other lists.

A group of streets and alleys on the other side of Spinnergate seemed to be the favoured sites. They were marked on a map with red dots which, when joined, snaked across the area in a rough S.

Dates and times of day, when placed on a graph by the

omniscient computer, zigzagged up and down in a regular pattern which signified a habit. These shapes too could be called an S.

There was an attraction sited somewhere in this network of roads which was called the Group. Their habit was creating the pattern.

Hidden in the area was a place, a house or a shop which they had to find.

Inspector Archie Young, who had a tender heart behind his carefully machined exterior, wanted to bash on ahead with all the forces available and take the area apart. He had a disagreement with Superintendent Paul Lane who was for moving more slowly. When Young got home that night, he told his wife how he felt; she was also a policewoman but in a totally different line of work and intellectually a bit above him. She advised him to keep his powder dry and conserve his energies to convince the Chief Commander himself.

'He'll be on your side.'

'Can't go over the Super's head.' He and Paul Lane were on good terms and drank together, but occasionally, as now, the difference in rank showed. 'He's a good judge of a situation.'

'Still, you think he's wrong.'

'I think Duerden is in there somewhere and that he may have the child with him. Or they may have the child, the lot that used the papershop.' That was what he could not bear to think about.

Marg Young went to the kitchen to produce the pudding. She was a good cook but with not much time to perform culinary miracles, and her mother had made the apple pie. There were three more like it in the freezer. Such little secrets were kept from Archie Young.

He cut himself a good slice and poured on the cream. Food soothed him and changed his mood more than alcohol or sex, although he never admitted to this. He kept that secret, his wife kept others, it was the answer to their happy marriage. 'This is tasty. You are a good cook.'

'Of course I am.' He was putting on weight with her

mother's good cooking but now was not the time to tell him. 'You'd better press for what you think is right, as it's so important. And if you are right enough, then you'll get your own way.'

'That's psychic,' he said gloomily.

'You have to be sometimes. If it's so important, and it is, and all you've really got is this hunch, then play that card.' She served herself a modest piece of pie, since she too had a weight problem and skirts were short and tight that season. 'You're seeing The Man himself, aren't you?'

'Yes, tomorrow. We have orders to keep in regular touch with reports.'

'Say your piece then.'

He did, meeting the Chief Commander in Coffin's office by arrangement, but in company with Superintendent Paul Lane, whose silent, cautious presence was damping. Bad mood there, he thought, not without sympathy. He knew that Paul Lane resented the Chief's interest in this case. Not for the first time, either. It was not agreeable to resent someone whom you liked and respected, he was caught in the same position himself. Only I've got two of them, he told himself. The Super and the Chief himself. Both of them. There was also a third, his wife, whose keen, critical mind he found alarming sometimes. Good in bed, but out of it, you had to watch your step. He did so.

Media interest in Tom's disappearance had diminished in the last few days. No news might be good news but it did not fill the papers.

Young was disconcerted to find that John Coffin was not offering total support to him. He was surprised at the pain he felt.

'I don't think we ought to hang about.'

Paul Lane moved irritably in his chair, but he kept quiet.

'That's your view?' Coffin looked from Young to Lane and then back again, reading the difference between them.

'Sure of it, sir,' said Young in an eager voice. 'There's the pattern. It has to mean something.'

'It's not that I dispute that idea,' grunted Lane. 'But the way of going about it. Slow, quiet, that's best.'

'We haven't got the time.' Young was blunt. 'Not in my view.'

For a moment no one spoke, while Coffin shifted the papers on his desk. He had another missive from Harry Guffin to attend to, a letter which might, in its way, be just as important as Tom.

'I agree with both of you,' he said. 'And with neither.'

Young let out a sharp little puff of irritable air through his teeth, not a whistle, more a quiet, involuntary hiss. The fact that he then tried to swallow it only made it worse.

Coffin laughed. 'Yes, Archie, I know how you feel. I don't blame you. I recognize that the papershop regulars have probably established a new pad somewhere north of Spinnergate. But I'm not sure if it brings us any nearer finding the boy. I see that differently.'

Archie Young went red, but he said nothing.

'Leave all the reports with me and I will think about it.' He looked at the clock. Twelve-thirty on a Saturday in spring, but crime was no respecter of day or season and knew no weekends. 'But I'm going to leave the decision of how you go on to you now, Paul. It's your territory.'

Another pause. The Superintendent cleared his throat. 'All right, have it your way, Archie. We go ahead.'

Coffin saw them to the door. Quite unconsciously he held the door in a courtly manner, as instructed last night by the Feather Street lady who was directing *The Circle*. 'You're a butler,' she had said in a firm way. 'Hold the door like a butler. Be courteous.' His body had learnt the lesson.

As Paul Lane and Archie Young left, Lane said: 'I hate it when he has that lordly way with him.'

'He doesn't mean anything.' Young had rather admired it, but well knowing his own manner would not allow of it. You needed to be six foot or over, and thinnish round the waist. He drew his own waist in; he was, alas, putting on the inches.

'And I hate it when he starts plucking ideas out of the

air, which is what he is doing now. I can feel it. There's something ticking away inside him and it's going to be a nuisance to us, you wait and see.'

Coffin went back to his letters, one of which was from his sister Letty and was marginally more optimistic, bankruptcy might not be just round the corner, but she would not be over for some time and it might mean summoning a family conference. Must be for moral support, mused Coffin, she knew he had no money to speak of, and half-brother Will in Scotland would not part with a brass bawbee.

But at the back of his mind was the lost boy.

What he had in mind was what he called the charivari. The carnival, the procession of idiot events: the murdered toy dog, the bloody handprint on the boy's shirt, the telephone call that took Sylvie and Tom away to a non-appointment. The shoe. Do not forget the shoe, which belonged to Nell. What did the shoe mean, if anything?

They were taunts, teases, torments aimed at Nell Casey. They were hung round Nell's head like a crown of thistles.

These ploys were not the style of the dreary pederasts of the Papershop Group. Nor of William Duerden, by all accounts an ignorant chancer.

They had more the mark of the imaginative zeal of Jim Lollard, the self-destructor of Murder Street. But he was dead.

And who had burned the papershop on the corner of Magdalen Street and Sweetings Lane? No news of the arsonist, he noted grimly, that one had got clean away.

That evening, restless and feeling rootless in this city that he loved, he took one of his walks. Almost without conscious planning (only probably deep down inside, he knew exactly where he was going and why) he made his way to Regina Street, otherwise Murder Street.

He could see why it evoked unease: it was an awkward and unpleasing row of houses. Nothing there on which the eye could rest with comfort, each house seemed to quarrel with its neighbour.

But, he had to admit, all seemed quiet tonight. Lights shone behind curtained windows, he could hear the television sending out the noise of instructed laughter. There was a child crying, but it was a quiet noise and soon ceased.

No dead bodies there, he decided. For once, Murder Street was not living up to its name.

Suddenly, he stood quite still. The immensity of the horror of it all struck home. Out there, somewhere, was a child: imprisoned, subjected to God knows what, full of fear and pain.

He felt sick. A knife was in his guts, turning and turning. It was real physical pain.

If he felt like this, how did Nell Casey feel?

He walked back to St Luke's Mansions but instead of walking through the courtyard to his own front door, he went to where his car was parked. Even at that hour, he gave it the quick, automatic check that security demanded, then drove off rapidly. He was almost sure he saw his cat Tiddles sitting in the shadows, watching him.

He drove towards North Spinnergate. He turned towards the area which currently obsessed Inspector Archie Young. The rough oblong was formed by four streets: Clock Street, which ran east to west, Shirley Road, which crossed it at right angles and ran south towards Creek Street, the narrow thoroughfare leading to Bowler Street, which crossed the bottom end of Clock Street. A tiny spur of Shirley Road ran towards the railway line where it ended in an archway, now housing a garage. Coffin knew the garage owner.

None of the roads ran in a straight line and the general shape of the district enclosed was more of a diamond than an oblong, Coffin reflected as he completed the circuit.

Within these four streets was a network of narrow streets lined with houses, shops and small factories. There was a chapel, now secularized, a school and what was once a cinema (and had once been a music hall by the look of it), now a small factory making jeans. A bit of history was embodied in some of the street names: Dalhousie Street, Madras Passage, Jubilee Road, Beckett Street. Tucked away in the north-west corner of the diamond was a little road called, for no reason that anyone remembered, Carnival Alley.

Coffin toured them slowly, mindful that he was probably observed by his own men, if no other. The observer observed.

No doubt frantic radio calls were even then reporting his progress.

He saw nothing that seemed important, the area was quiet, with not much movement. He turned and drove home.

CHAPTER 16

March 24

Archie Young had his way, and his team poured into the area in North Spinnergate to which those they called the Papershop Group seemed attracted. As well as his own men who had been working on the case all along, he was using the radio cars and constables who usually toured the area and knew it well. The first day brought nothing. No interesting cars were sighted parked anywhere, none seen touring the district.

Young had not expected results at once, but it was disappointing. He bit back the thought that some alert might have gone out to the Group. They were an intelligent, sophisticated circle of men and women and would be on their guard.

The next day, the same. Nothing. He reported back to Paul Lane, who said he could have more men if he wanted it, but it didn't look as though anything was going to come of it.

The report duly went to John Coffin, who had other troubles of his own, with the threat of a Parliamentary Commission of Inquiry (which he did not think would come about, but he could not be sure), not to mention the rumours of the formation of a national police force which he thought would happen but not in his time. But it all made for unease.

'Have you any news?' Stella Pinero asked on the telephone that morning. She rang every morning. He thought she was acting as the voice of Nell Casey who no longer telephoned. Relations between him and Stella were still chill.

'No, sorry. You can believe I'd tell you if there was.'

'You know more than you're saying, I expect,' said Stella. 'You always do.'

'Not a lot.' He did not tell her about the police drive on North Spinnergate. But it turned out that he did not have to.

'Mimsie Marker says there's something going on behind the Tube station, that area. Police cars and detectives all over the place, she knew their faces. What is it, John. Have you found a body?'

'No body.'

'But you're looking for one, that's what Mimsie says.'

For once Mimsie had got it wrong. 'She knows more than I do,' he said. 'How's Nell bearing up?'

'Can't get a word out of her. Doesn't answer the telephone nor the doorbell.'

'Well, look after her.'

'I will if I can find her. You don't ask how I am and how my Festival's going.' Stella was crisp and angry, and as usual when in this mood, her delivery was tremendous. 'Well, fine, just fine. I'm well and the bookings are good, thanks for your asking.'

Fill Drury Lane that voice would, Coffin thought as she slammed down the receiver; no, I do her an injustice, every syllable would have registered in the Olivier auditorium itself. He had seen Stella play Lady Macbeth in the National once and saluted her power.

He went back to his own worries, knowing that Archie Young could be relied upon to cover the ground in North Spinnergate. Whether he found anything was another matter.

Back in the North Spinnergate district, the young police constable, Leslie Castle, who had set off the search in the first place, came on duty after making a good breakfast in the canteen. Sausages, bacon, chips and three cups of tea. He was an alert and lively young man with a good degree from Birmingham University, a lot of ambition, and his feet planted firmly on the ground.

The eldest of a large family and still living at home, he had had an argument last night with his younger brother who maintained that aliens were stealing children and taking them away to study. That was where Tom Casey had gone.

'They bring them back, you know, don't keep them. Just want to take a look and make a report, then they dump them on this planet Earth and the kids don't have any idea where they've been. It's all out of this world, you'll see.' And younger brother went back to reading the latest science fiction book which he had just secured from his school library where they were open-minded about what their pupils read as long as they read. 'He'll drop off a spacecraft,' he ended dreamily. He wished it could be him, he'd remember all the details all right.

Not a likely tale, Leslie had thought, as he stepped out, glad it was a fine morning. Nothing extra-terrestrial about this little load of trouble.

He took a personal interest in what was going on, regarding it as down to him. He hoped to transfer to the detective force and he guessed he already had a good mark on his card from his earlier piece of observation, and another one would not do any harm. So he kept his eyes open.

It was a competitive world and you had to look out for yourself. Besides, he liked children. He had a very young brother, a late and unexpected arrival in the family, and he loved the young sprog.

He paced on, through Rocket Street, Forge Street, Needless Passage, thinking as he always did what a silly name for a street, enough to put a street off. Needless Passage did have a sad look to it and seemed to attract more rubbish and old cars than even Carnival Alley, which was a byword for dossers and dirt. In the hierarchy of the streets round here Needless Passage and Carnival Alley did not rank high; if you could live elsewhere, then you did. But there was a nice little café in Carnival Alley much used by lorry-drivers and van men parked illegally near by.

He walked on. Surely there ought to be some sign an intelligent and alert observer could pick up? He turned into Navigation Street and then left into Windward Place, but nothing caught his eye. He continued on thoughtfully. Perhaps that last cup of tea had been a mistake.

He was at the corner of Carnival Alley and the main road that led to the old Chantry Railway station, closed to passengers but used for goods only, when the scream of brakes followed by the sound of metal grinding on to metal told him two cars had hit each other. He hurried down the Alley to the sound of angry voices bitterly accusing each other.

He sighed and hurried forward to deal with the affair before blood flowed.

By the time that the protagonists had been parted, agreed to settle the issue without fisticuffs and had driven off, the matter of the third cup of tea demanded urgent attention.

But Castle knew where to go. He hurried towards the friendly café in Carnival Alley. Harry's Bar would accommodate him.

'A cup of tea?' said the proprietor, as he came back into the café from the washroom.

'Not just now.'

'Was that a crash I heard?'

'Only two old bangers running into each other.' The cars hadn't appeared much worse after their impact than before, not the first collision in their lives. Castle looked round the shop where a nearly full crate of milk waited. 'Lot of milk, you're using, Harry. Trade must be good.'

Harry shrugged. 'I've got a regular customer, comes in and collects the bottles.'

'Wonder he doesn't have them delivered.'

'It's a she. I reckon she's one of those child-minders.

Unregistered, you know, and doesn't want to draw attention to herself.' He looked at Leslie.

'Thanks for the tip, Harry,' said Leslie, after a pause.

'Just telling.'

'Any idea where she comes from?'

'No.' Harry shook his head. 'But it would have to be near, she wouldn't walk far with all those bottles.' He probably did know where she came from, you couldn't hide much round here, but a kind of class loyalty meant that Harry had gone as far as he would for the moment.

Castle acknowledged what he had got. 'You're right. Thanks again. I'll be seeing you.'

Castle turned back into Carnival Alley, and now he looked carefully at every premises he passed. He turned into Russia Lane, looked down Needless Passage and then into Forge Street.

Not a soul about, there rarely was at this time of the day. Forge Street had once had a forge in it and you could still make out the old building now turned into a lock-up for cars. Forge Street was upmarket for the area with a row of three-storey houses perched over narrow basements.

At the end of the road the council's refuse lorry was collecting bags of rubbish. He walked towards it.

One house had a small mountain of black plastic sacks outside, piled up awaiting collection. Leslie remembered the amount of mucky stuff that his small brother had built up as an infant and there had only been one of him.

He went up to look at the house. No. 5, Forge Street. It was newly painted with clean curtains and a brightly polished knocker. It looked very respectable.

But evil things can go on behind respectable front doors. From behind the door, he heard a child cry out.

He hesitated, tempted to bang on the door and rush in, but prudence held him back. He might alert people who would otherwise be caught.

This had to be done properly.

Where children are concerned, Archie Young knew that you had to be both careful and quick. He was both.

He checked that the address in Forge Street was not registered for the care of children. He got the name of the occupant from the electoral roll: Mrs Brownrigg, she had lived there for at least three years.

Then, backed up by a worker from the social welfare department, by a police surgeon, and by Policewoman Alison Jenkins whose speciality this was, he went in.

'You hold up the woman,' he told Alison. 'And I will get into the house. Then you lot follow. But hang on to her. Do you know her?'

Alison shook her head. 'No, she's kept herself well hidden.'

The woman who opened the door to them was tall, nicely built with a neat roll of hair and a blue apron trimly belted at the waist. She looked surprised but not frightened. Behind her, Young could see a tidy hall with a bowl of flowers on the table and the smell of cooking floating towards him. It was midmorning, it smelt like lamb cooking for the next meal. He had to admit that, unregistered or not, this looked a good place.

A faint seed of doubt took root inside him.

'Mrs Brownrigg?' He named himself and produced his identification. 'May we come inside?'

But he was already inside and pushing past her. Behind him he could hear Alison Jenkins's voice talking about illegality and unregistered child-minders, and he could hear the woman protesting. An educated voice.

There was a door at the end of the hall which stood half open. He went through into an anteroom of some sort with hooks for small coats on the walls, and underneath brightly painted lockers decorated with pictures of dogs, cats, cows and even a small friendly-looking lion.

With every step forward this place looked more and more respectable. All right, he said to himself, you may get your head chopped off but this counts, you have to risk it.

He could hear Mrs Brownrigg protesting that she did a good service and Alison Jenkins making a gentle reply. She would not alarm the woman but she would be tough.

He opened the door to the inner room which was the

children's room. It was a big room, bright and cheerful. Two infants, not yet walking, sat inside playpens. Two girls in frilly dresses stood inside a playhouse, and a mixed band of other children, all sizes, ages and colours, disposed themselves around low tables. Some were painting, others dabbing with plasticine, and a couple were studying books.

They were quiet, though, he thought. Of course he had startled them, but he hadn't heard much noise through the door before he came in. All the kids he knew made a big racket.

Well-disciplined, he thought. Was that good or bad?

But at the back of the room, near to the window, a table of four children, two boys and two girls, sat immobile. One girl gave him a quick look and then turned her head away. The other children avoided all eye contact.

That is not good, he said to himself. And his heartbeat quickened and a pain, cold and fierce, went through his guts.

He walked over to them. 'Hello,' he said, and saw, with sadness mixed with venom for those who had caused it, that they looked at him with apprehension and knowledge. 'Don't worry,' he said gently. 'I'm good news.'

But how could you say that to these children and make it mean anything? They had a whole damaged life before them to prove him wrong.

'Alison,' he called. 'Over here.' He pointed towards the tables by the window. 'Look at them.' He turned away. 'Or don't look, even doing that seems to hit like a weapon.'

Alison said gently, 'You go out and deal with the ongoings in the hall. Leave this to me.'

He rode out the storm of protest from Mrs Brownrigg as she was taken away. The cook in the basement kitchen was calmed and interviewed. The woman from the social services department located a roll of children with names and addresses and began the process of getting hold of parents. Other officers started going through the house. It all had to be done and it all had to be done now.

If he was in trouble, he was in it in a big way. But it was worth it. He took a deep breath and remembered one other puzzle.

As things got under control, he drew Alison aside. 'Are you thinking what I'm thinking?'

'Yes.' She nodded.

'He's not here.'

He had a roomful of frightened children, but Tom was not there.

CHAPTER 17

Still that same day in March

John Coffin sat in his office with the late afternoon sunlight on his back and looked at the other two men. He had asked for a tray of sandwiches and coffee to be sent up for the three of them. Himself, the Superintendent and Archie Young, the group which Young was beginning to think of as the War Command. He was taking notes and he observed that John Coffin was taping it all.

He put his pen down and took a bite of ham and bread. No mustard, he thought regretfully, life was getting purer and purer all the time. He would have enjoyed a cigarette but a no-smoking area had been declared about the Chief Commander, so that was out. Probably whisky would go soon. One by one the bodily comforts and supports of the hardworking crime officer were being declared harmful.

Coffin went to his cupboard and brought out a bottle of malt, and offered it around.

'You did a good job,' he said to Archie Young. 'Backed your hunch and got a result.'

'But not the boy.'

'You got a list of the Papershop Group with their names or aliases and their addresses, and evidence good enough to go to court.'

'Underneath the floorboards in the kitchen,' said Archie Young, not without satisfaction. 'Not an original mind, our Mrs Brownrigg.' She had kept a long list with a few pencilled additions, including an address in Regina Street. Murder Street was coming into play again. Archie Young was minded to visit that house. Near old Jim Lollard's place, he thought. 'I reckon she had a poor memory and had to keep things written down.'

'Thank God for that.'

'The woman who did the cooking knew where they were and didn't mind pointing them out. Didn't like Brownrigg. Liked the job, liked the money, but didn't like her employer. Thought there "was something going on."'

'But she didn't report anything until we arrived.'

'That's people,' said Young philosophically. 'But she'll talk now. And so will Brownrigg. Alison's already got her going. She's a marvel, that girl.'

So all that was fine, but had not brought Tom Casey home.

'Back to looking for Duerden?' said Paul Lane.

Regina Street, thought Archie Young instantly. I'm going to have a look for him there. *Say nothing Archie, do it on your own.*

'Possibly. But I don't see it plays that way. Duerden is a chancer, a quick operator, not a fancy planner. And Tom's troubles all seemed custom built for him. They had his name on them. So that means someone close.'

Only two people close to Tom as far as they knew. Nell, Sylvie, and Gus Hamilton in there as an extra to make up the weight.

'I rule out the girl,' said Paul Lane.

'So do I,' agreed Young.

'Yes, she rings true,' said Coffin. 'That leaves Gus Hamilton and Nell Casey.' About equal between those two, he thought. The psychology of Nell he would leave to others. Something odd there underneath the surface, he would swear.

But the Superintendent and the Inspector still quietly stuck to the view that it was Duerden, and whether there was hope in that thought or pure despair they dared not weigh up. Duerden was a bastard.

The repercussions of the records, the names and addresses, discovered in Forge Street spread around the country, up to the Midlands as far as Birmingham and Coventry, to the west to Oxford and in London to districts as far as Hampstead and Woolwich. The house in Regina Street was quiet, the proprietress of the simple lodging-house being in hospital. Archie Young tried a call, but the neighbours said she might have gone to stay with a sister after getting out of hospital, and no, they didn't know her address. He left it there.

A solicitor, and a van driver, a journalist, and a photographer who had won many awards, all these found their lives disorganized in a way they did not care for.

A civil servant and an engineer similarly found their day disturbed. In Woking, a middle-aged man was interrupted while writing a letter.

> My dear boy, he had begun. How I do thank you for introducing me on Friday? A mark of true friendship. I don't know how to thank you for procuring for me what was a truly blissful occasion. I still dream about it. Give me another chance, will you? And send the photographs you promised, they will make it all seem real again.

At this point his wife knocked on the door. 'Sorry to disturb you, dear, but there's someone to see you.' She hesitated. 'He says he's a policeman.'

The letter was never finished.

They were all ordinary men, mostly middle class and well educated. Highly respectable members of society, you would sit next to them on the Underground without alarm.

Shortly before this day, the arsonist of the papershop, who had so triumphantly sped away north, looked to be on the point of resolving his own problems, great as they were, in a terminal way.

His doctors thought so. It was the sort of accident, they said, from which no one recovers.

Looking for evidence of identity, they found his driving licence which named him as Trevor Hinton with an address in Derby. But what they also saw in his wallet gave them pause for thought.

Two photographs: one of a girl child with a smiling face decked in a sunbonnet, and the other, an instant contact print of a man. Or it had been a man.

A consequent search of the wrecked car found an empty petrol can in the boot, together with a length of rope and a spade. There was earth on the spade.

It was not only John Coffin who wanted to see Nell Casey. Stella Pinero was equally anxious to speak to her. As she kept telling everyone, she had a Festival to run, and although she had recast Nell's part in *French Without Tears*, she had hoped to use Nell later in the season in a contemporary piece about women in the police called *Wearing Blue*. She had been keeping quiet about this since she had an idea, (not misplaced) that it would not go down well with John Coffin. The play had won a prize in a drama competition sponsored by their new Thames University, who were financing the production and helping with the cost of mounting a new *King Lear* later in the season. Gus Hamilton was being lined up for Lear, although there was a malicious groundswell that was saying what about him for Goneril? Jealousy and rage, he was good at these emotions.

When several calls at The Albion got no response, Stella became worried and called on John Coffin in his tower retreat. They were neighbours, after all, and old friends and lovers, and if relations were not good just now, if in fact she was madly jealous of that Barclay woman (who was young, young, young), that did not mean she could not call on him in need.

It was the evening of that day on which the conference had been held in his office. As yet the media did not know about the raid on the house in Forge Street, although various lives up and down the country were already being upset, but he knew the silence could not last much longer. He expected there to be a short something on the late evening news and then the media onslaught would begin. He was sitting watching television with the cat on his lap. Tiddles was not pleased to be woken up by the doorbell.

'Hello, sorry to disturb you, but I'm worried about Nell.'

Not the only one, thought Coffin. 'Come in.' As he held the front door open, there was a swish of tail and Tiddles sped through without a backward look, as one escaping from prison, although until that moment he had been wrapped in easy sleep.

'I need to see her,' said Stella. 'God, these stairs, why don't you have a lift put in?'

'Money.'

'Ask your rich sister.'

Ah yes, thought John Coffin guiltily, but how rich is Letty? Still going quietly bankrupt?

'I mean, I've got this casting to settle,' said Stella, reaching the sitting-room and collapsing on the sofa. 'And if I can't get Nell for Judith, then I must look around me.'

Coffin was always surprised how life roared on, heedless, when a major inquiry was taking place. Stella was close to Nell, liked the boy, admired Gus, but still the casting of her plays moved her more passionately. You couldn't call it callousness, it was just business. We do mind more about our own torn fingernail than a death next door. It was a kind of tunnel vision.

'I can't get her to answer the telephone or the bell.'

'Perhaps she isn't there.'

'That's what's worrying me.' She gave him a measured look. 'Or she might be there.' Tied up, unconscious, dead?

So Stella was thinking of something other than her play. As so often, he had underestimated her.

'I want to go into the apartment. I don't want to go on my own, I want you to come with me. If she's there, hurt or whatever, we ought to find her.'

‘I’ll come . . . How were you planning to get in?’

For the first time, Stella looked embarrassed. ‘I have a key . . . As a matter of fact, the apartment is mine. A little investment. I thought my daughter might live in it one day, and meanwhile, I let it out on short lets.’

I do underestimate you, Stella, Coffin thought again. You’re a good business woman. Always have been. Letty knew what she was doing when she let you run the St Luke’s Theatre Complex.

As they went into the apartment in The Albion, he realized he ought to have known that Stella had done the decorations. It had her touch, cool and positive with no dark corners. No wonder it had felt familiar.

It was quiet and still with just a faint memory of the scent Nell used. No sign of Nell herself. They went through all the rooms. Empty and still.

Stella ran a finger across the table. ‘Dust.’ She walked through to the kitchen and opened the refrigerator. A bottle of fruit juice and a withered lettuce. ‘Not much there that’s eatable.’

Coffin had gone across to the telephone. A note addressed to Nell was lying near it. The envelope was sealed. Coffin opened it. ‘Let’s have a look.’

It was from Sylvie. ‘*I’m going to stay with friends, you know the address. I’ll be in touch. I know you’ll understand.*’

‘Nell hasn’t read it,’ said Stella.

‘No.’

‘And Sylvie’s been gone a few days now.’

Three days since the note had been written and Nell had never been home to read it.

Stella had a good look round Nell’s bedroom. She ran her hand through the wardrobe, moving the clothes. ‘Not a lot here, but I don’t know what she had.’ It was all good stuff, very good, not what she herself would leave behind if doing a bunk. At the bottom of the wardrobe was a selection of handbags and a few pieces of luggage. ‘A small case might have gone,’ she said, emerging from the wardrobe, hair ruffled. ‘I remember a shoulder-bag. Don’t see that.’ She had disturbed an album which had been placed with the shoes and bags. It was large, and black. She opened it for a look. 'Left her reviews behind. Goes way back. Begins with a trumpet when she got a medal. Praise from EE. That's Ellice Eden.' She read it with a dash of envy. 'God, he really went over the top there, but he always loves her.' She flipped the pages 'And includes a cutting from *The Times* of last month calling her "a quiet genius". She'll be back. No actress would ever be parted from that little heap.'

Coffin had also been doing a little search. All the stuff that had looked like a shoplifting hoard had disappeared. Quietly disposed of when the police started questioning her, no doubt.

'I'm sure she means to go on performing,' said Coffin, wondering if Nell Casey had ever stopped. 'But where the hell is she now?'

That endless day was still with them. Lane and Young had been dragged from their homes and summoned to St Luke's Mansions by the Chief Commander. No coffee and sandwiches now.

'We should have kept an eye on her,' said Superintendent Paul Lane. 'We should have watched her.'

That they had not was a bad error, but you couldn't do everything. He didn't quite say this but he wanted it to be understood.

'We had no reason to believe she'd go off,' said Archie Young defensively. 'And we had other things on our mind: the Papershop Group, and it looked as though they would lead us to the boy.'

'I thought Mary Barclay was supposed to be keeping in touch with Casey?' said John Coffin.

'I pulled her off that,' admitted Archie Young, 'wanted her to join the unit looking for the boy in North Spinnergate.' It had seemed the right thing to do.

'So what do we assume now? That Casey's gone off with the boy somehow?'

'I think we'd better get hold of Mary Barclay and see what ideas she has to offer,' said John Coffin. 'She's been as close to mother and child as anyone. She might be able to make a guess where the woman could have taken herself.' And if she was likely to have the boy with her. A subject on which, as he remembered, Mary Barclay had remained quietly neutral.

'Miss Pinero must know Casey pretty well,' said Superintendent Lane.

Coffin turned to the fourth member of the party, who had so far not spoken and who was sitting miserably in one corner of the room. Stella looked as though she had been crying.

'What about it, Stella?'

Stella shifted uneasily in her seat. 'Well, you know how it is with actors. Yes, I've worked with her. Once on a series and once on a play that was touring before coming into London. You work together, you're buddies, but then the series or the tour ends and you don't see each other again. I don't know Nell that well.' She shook her head. 'I knew her in the theatre as a theatre person; what she was outside it, and how she grew up, what friends and relations she had, that I don't know.' In a wretched voice, she said: 'I suppose that makes us all sound thoroughly superficial and selfish, but it's the way we have to live . . . You could try Gus Hamilton, but I doubt if he knows much more. Falling in love isn't always an introduction to someone's life. There's Ellice Eden, he's the sort that does research on people, he might know more.'

Gus Hamilton said angrily that no, he didn't know where the bloody woman was and he didn't care. She'd caused enough trouble in his life as it was. Find her and you'd find the kid, that was his opinion. And thank you, he was tired and he'd had a long day, if they cared.

Ellice Eden said he admired Nell Casey enormously as an actress, she had such great potential, but he thought that as a person she was a disaster, and had therefore kept his distance. Neurotics killed you in the end. He feared he could be no help, good night.

*

The Chief Commander took pity on Superintendent Lane and Inspector Young and closed the meeting. 'I'm off to bed. See you in the morning.'

There's a lot happening here, he thought as he turned out the light. *Perhaps I'll give Jumbo Best a ring in the morning. Get him round.* The former Chief Inspector was now the head of a security firm. *He remembered Nell Casey when she was a teenager. He might dredge something up.*

CHAPTER 18

March 26

He did not forget Jumbo but the next day was a busy one. The story of the house in Forge Street and the men who had used it had hit the headlines. At least two TV crews were touring this area of North Spinnergate interviewing those inhabitants who would submit to it (most did so eagerly and incoherently), and a press conference had been called for midday over which he himself must preside, fielding all awkward questions. The name of William Duerden and of the lost boy Tom had already started to appear. Articles on both subjects, strategically placed near to pictures of the house in Forge Street had appeared in the early editions. He had heard that a London evening newspaper was already printing a special supplement on child abuse. (Must have had it in cold store, he thought.) And he knew for a fact, that his MP critic, Harry Guffin, was about to ask a Question in the House.

In the turmoil, although he never forgot the missing boy and his mother, he almost forgot Jumbo.

But Jumbo came to him. Picked up the telephone and spoke to him. 'Saw the papers. You linking this outfit with Duerden?'

'Not sure,' said Coffin carefully.

'I heard you were. Still have my contacts. And Duerden is holed up with the missing kid, so it goes?'

'Not ruling it out,' said Coffin. 'If you've got anything . . .'

'Can't help with that.' Jumbo was regretful. 'But remember talking about the Casey girl?' He didn't wait for an answer. 'Something odd that I remembered . . . There was no prosecution, she just walked out.'

'So you said.'

'But she'd given an address, and later on, out of curiosity I went to have a look. It was the right address, she hadn't given a false one or anything like that, she'd been there. But she hadn't been there long and wasn't there any longer. And it was just one room. She was there all on her own, just a kid.'

'Perhaps her parents were dead.'

'Or kicked her out. Or she kicked herself out. Just a kid in that one room. Abbey Street, it was, back of Costelow's. Remember Costelow's? The old Costelow's,' he said. For there was now a new Costelow's store in a new place, very brassy and bright in a spanking new shopping complex that owing to bad timing and a sales recession had more shops than customers. 'Just thought it might be worth mentioning. It says something about her, doesn't it? Background does help.'

'Certainly does . . . Well, thanks. I'll pass it on to the right quarters and see what comes up . . . You sound very cheerful, you old devil.'

'Not my problem, is it? Yours. Others as well. I hear things.'

I bet you do, thought Coffin as he put the receiver down. The Chief Commander bites the dust. New Force in New City in Trouble, he could hear the voices in the pubs and wine bars.

In the St Luke's Theatre Complex (it's new grand name since the Theatre in the church was now well under construction), the gossip was swirling round and round.

'Probably all set up by Casey for the publicity,' said one

lad who had only just got his Equity card, but he was shouted down for his bad taste.

Nell was popular and although no one wanted to act with children (scene-stealers all), they did not approve of child abduction or child abuse. 'And Nell loved that infant,' that was one thing clearly stated and believed. Some people were suspicious of Sylvie who had been hands off with all who had tried, most people defended any attack on Gus Hamilton on the grounds that he was a marvellous actor and also a powerful and rising figure whose patronage could be valuable and whose animosity (he had the reputation of a long memory) was not to be lightly aroused.

Inspector Archie Young took note of the lodging-house in Abbey Street, back of the old Costelow's, and said he would send someone round for a look, but he doubted they would find Nell Casey there.

She was proving an elusive character, who appeared to have no family and no background. She seemed to have come from nowhere. A brief glimpse of her as a young shop-lifter and then nothing before she turned up in Drama School.

Even that had been no help, for according to the college records, she had received no local authority education grants, her fees had been paid in cash.

That was interesting, Young thought, and raised questions but gave no answers.

Abbey Street, as expected, proved as a source null and void. No one remembered Nell Casey there, it wasn't that sort of street.

'You can't keep Nell down,' said Stella Pinero, when she heard all this. 'She'll be back.'

Just about this time, two lads, home from school on various excuses or none, were out fishing when they saw what looked like a roll of carpet, slowly moving in the water. It was a thin, narrow roll.

The River Thames, as John Coffin had reason to know from earlier cases, is very reluctant to give back its victims. Watermen know that the river hangs on to its bodies, carrying them up and then down the river before depositing them where it fancies.

But this body had got caught in some weeds at the river's edge and did not travel so far from where it had gone in to the water.

The boys were fishing in that part of the Thames which runs between Staines and Wraysbury. After a while, one of them investigated the floating object further, then came back with a white face.

'It's a floater,' he said.

'Better tell someone. The police or something. Telephone. Nine-nine-nine.'

'You go. I'll stay here.'

The one boy went for the police to tell them that they had got a floater, while the other stayed on guard. He kept his distance and sat on the riverbank with his back to the body. All he had seen was blue jeans and a flash of red hair, but he had caught a glimpse of the face. That was enough for him.

The body carried nothing to identify it, nothing in the pockets of the jeans or jacket, and there was no handbag. But it was a woman, and the Thames knew many such.

The police surgeon who was called to certify death was cautious about the cause of that mortality and when it had happened.

'Not a typical death from drowning,' said Dr Salt. 'And I'd say she'd been in the water over a day and less than a week.' He was famous for his circumspection. 'The pathologist will get you much nearer.' He moved his hands delicately over her head, moving the hair aside.

'Not suicide, then?' said the CID man. They were usually suicide. Or accident. 'Wonder if she'd been drinking.'

'She was dead when she went in the river. She had a blow on the head.'

'Might have been drunk and hit her head as she fell.'

'We'll have to see,' said Dr Salt. He arranged for the body to go to the police morgue. 'One good thing, she soon came up. Didn't stay down long.' He hated it when the bodies had been too many weeks in the water. 'No, it didn't keep her down. You can never tell with the old Thames, can you?'

She appeared to have no handbag and no possessions. A search along the river bank produced a blue leather handbag. It was found near the bridge at Staines. It was empty.

'Mugged and then dropped in,' said the CID man. 'I reckon she went in over the bridge at Staines. Or she was driven to Wraysbury and dropped in there. Could have been killed anywhere, of course.'

But she had been found dead on his patch, which made it his business. He went back to his CID headquarters to set the investigation in train. To establish an identity seemed the first requirement.

A day passed, during which the pathologist started his work on his nameless subject.

Body 123, white.

She might have gone unidentified longer if an alert WPC, coming into the morgue on other business, had not seen her face. The WPC was a keen watcher of soaps on TV and had liked the one in which Nell Casey had starred.

She looked and then looked again. 'I'm not sure,' she said, 'but I think . . .'

The investigating officer received the tentative ID with mixed feelings. This was not going to be a case that easily wrapped up. One happy thought soon occurred to him: he must inform the Second City Force, Neil Casey was part of their problem.

And she was a problem: the more he thought about it, the less it looked like a simple mugging.

John Coffin, to whom the news of the finding of Nell's body came after Archie Young and Paul Lane had digested it, was sure it was no mugging.

Inspector Young, not averse to hobnobbing with the top brass, delivered the news himself. 'What the devil was she doing out that way? Of course, she could have been killed anywhere and just dumped, poor cow. But why and how?'

'The post-mortem?'

'Not complete yet.'

'Push them.'

He still had to tell Stella Pinero.

He told her that evening after the performance of *The Circle* where he performed admirably as a butler.

There was a party following it for the cast and friends in the bar of the Theatre Workshop.

'I'm glad that's over,' he said. 'How you do it night after night, I do not know.'

'Nervous, were you?'

'Anxious. Not that I had much to do, but you don't want to make a fool of yourself in public.'

'Ah, there speaks the amateur.' She sipped a glass of the champagne that had been provided by the Friends of St Luke's Theatre. These were the former Friends of the Theatre Workshop who had now adopted a grander title. They always produced champagne for important parties and since several of them (including the one playing Lady Kitty) had performed in *The Circle*, this ranked as an important occasion. 'Still, you did well with what you had. Bit stiff.'

Still cross with me, he thought. Wonder what I've done? Maybe nothing. She might have some private worry of her own, although with Stella, private things usually became public pretty soon.

'That was the producer,' he said in self-defence. 'She said to be formal.'

'Not pompous, though.'

Very cross, he thought.

The party swirled all round him, he could see Gus being charming in one corner, and Ellie Wakeman, current star at the National and his new friend (so they said), keeping close to him. And there was Ellice Eden talking to Lord Bromley, who owned a bank and a newspaper or two and a TV network, and who had been brought along by Ellie Wakeman whose father he was. You had to salute Gus Hamilton, he thought, a very useful contact for him there. Give or take a death or two, Gus never put a foot wrong.

Then he was immediately ashamed of himself for his flippancy. It was true what I thought earlier, we worry more about a pimple on our own face than a great wound on the face of a friend. Even I, who ought to know better, am more anxious about the threat of a Commission of Inquiry into my Force than I am about the death of Nell and the disappearance of the boy.

Not quite true. He put the glass of champagne down. Suddenly it didn't taste so good. Thank God, he thought. I can feel pain now, the proper pain.

'Come outside, Stella.'

'It's raining.'

'Not right outside. Just out into the colonnade.' The architect had created a protected walkway with columns on the outer side which would lead from the main theatre in the old church to the Workshop Theatre.

It had ceased raining but a chill wind was blowing. Stella shivered and drew her wrap closer around her shoulders.

'Oh, come on, if you want to kiss me. I'm too old for this.'

'I don't want to kiss you, Stella.'

'Oh, thanks, it's that pretty policewoman, I suppose. Nice girl and clever, you said so yourself. Young too.'

'Shut up, Stella, and listen.'

There was laughter and music through the open doors to the room where the party roared, and he could hear Lady Kitty still being Lady Kitty to the life, and out here there was a very faint smell of the first spring flowering. Life did go on.

'Nell has been found.'

Stella looked at him and needed no more. 'She's dead, isn't she?'

'Yes.' He put his arms round her. 'I'm so sorry to tell you like this. I should have done it better.'

She didn't move away, but stood still within his embrace. 'No, you did it right. I'd rather have it straight out.'

There was a moment of silence, even the party had gone quiet. Then a door opened and noise and light poured out. The light shone on Stella's face, pointing up her features and leaving her eyes in shadow. She had lost weight, Coffin thought, but weight came and went with Stella, usually on purpose. He hoped she was all right, she worked too hard. He felt a sudden rush of deep affection for her. Darling Stella.

'She killed herself, I suppose?' said Stella. 'What a shame.'

'No, it looks like murder.'

Gus Hamilton had left the party and was walking towards them. Stella saw him, she opened her eyes wide. 'Him?' she breathed.

Coffin shook his head. 'I think not. I don't know.'

Gus came up to them. 'Saw you leave . . . Someone just picked up a newsflash on the local TV programme. Nell, she's been found. She's been murdered.'

'Yes,' said Coffin. 'I'm afraid it looks like that. I am sorry, Hamilton.'

'There was a bit more: seems there's been a suspected child murderer on the loose round here. You kept quiet about that, didn't you?'

'It seemed wiser . . .' began Coffin. Then he saw what was coming.

'You bastard,' said Gus, swinging back his arm and hitting Coffin on the jaw.

CHAPTER 19

Still that same day in March, and then on to the next day.

'Someone will kill Gus one day,' said Stella as she applied hot water to the blood from his nose and cold water to his left eye. She had led Coffin across the courtyard and up the staircase of his own tower. They were in his kitchen. 'You're going to have a tremendous shiner.' Was there a note of satisfaction in her voice?

'If he doesn't kill them first.'

Stella stood back. 'There, I've tidied you up. Say thank you nicely.'

'Thank you, Stella.'

Relations between them had been miraculously restored, they were best friends, tender and true again.

'Where's Gus?'

'Crying on the stairs, I think.'

'Fool.'

'He said he'd stay outside until you said he could come in.' She added in a pleading voice: 'He is very upset . . . Gus always lashes out when he is upset.'

'I've noticed,' said Coffin tartly. 'You can stop throwing water all over me, Stella, I'm all right. Fine, never felt better.' He stood up. 'But thanks for looking after me.'

'You need it sometimes. Here, have a tissue, you're still dripping a bit.'

Gus appeared at the door. 'Can I apologize or would you prefer to shoot me?'

'Come in and sit down.'

'I'll get us all a drink,' said Stella. 'I think we need it, I know I do.'

'Stella, I'm sorry,' said Gus. 'You must be feeling bad, too. Nell's dead. That I know, but how did it happen?'

'She was found in the Thames near Staines, but she was not drowned, she was dead when she went in.'

'So that makes it murder?'

'Probably. We won't know for sure until after the post-mortem. But she had a blow on the head; it may not have killed her.'

'I suppose I'm under suspicion?'

'We're a long way from any definite suspect yet, Hamilton.'

'I'm not sure if I believe that,' said Gus thoughtfully. 'If I was in your shoes, then I'd give me a long hard look . . . I liked Nell, I loved her. Once I loved her, anyway, but our relationship wasn't easy. And it wasn't all my fault. You think Nell was straightforward, she wasn't. Especially about sex. I don't find this easy to say, but for us, it didn't work. I don't know if it was my fault or hers, but it didn't seem to come easy. That was why we quarrelled, really. Well, mostly. There was a rough edge to Nell.'

And to you, Coffin, thought, and wondered how much

truth there was in all this and what weight to put on it. He touched his eye. Sore. A long time since a suspect had hit him.

Gus said: 'And the boy? What about him? There's no sign of him?'

'As yet, no,' said Coffin carefully.

'He's probably dead too, isn't he?'

'The chances are, yes.'

Stella started to cry. 'Oh, please, this is horrible.'

'We have to think about it, Stella. I don't think the police here have handled this well. They've known they had this suspected child murderer on the loose and kept it quiet.'

'We are looking for him,' said Coffin. 'There's been an intensive search for him all this time.'

'And now he's killed Nell and probably the boy before her. Who is he? You don't know. Where is he? You don't know that either. He's there, and you can't find him. You're no bloody good.'

William Duerden had come into the Second City of London and hidden himself in the undergrowth of that crowded metropolis. A hidden tiger looking for his victim.

'That's quite an accusation,' said Coffin quietly. 'I have to hope it's not true.'

Or not all of it. He had his own view of what had happened, and why.

Stella looked at Coffin, wondering if he would defend himself, wanting him to do so, and puzzled that he did not. She knew him so well and he wasn't reacting the way she had expected he would. He always defended himself.

He felt guilty, she said to herself. I feel guilty, Gus feels guilty. But we aren't guilty, Duerden is guilty. This is grief.

She put out a hand and touched Coffin's hand gently. Then she reached out and held Gus's hand.

'Oh, you've hurt your hand, Gus,' she said. 'It's all scratched and torn.'

Gus snatched his hand away. 'It's nothing,' he said.

Next morning, the hunt for William Duerden was in full cry. He had got to be found. Superintendent Paul Lane, assisted by Archie Young, was conducting the investigation in person. He held a press conference in which he explained what was going on. A joint team, Middlesex and Second City, were inquiring into the death of Nell Casey, the media were told. The neighbouring Thameside Forces, covering Surrey, Berkshire and Buckinghamshire, were holding a watching brief.

All secrecy was dropped and photographs of Duerden and also of the boy Tom were seen on television and appeared in all the newspapers. There was not much comment because there was not enough hard news, but there was plenty of publicity.

Here and there a paragraph about the Papershop Group was laid judiciously next to a photograph of Tom or Duerden so that people could draw their own conclusions.

Paul Lane and Archie Young had been on continuous duty for almost twenty-four hours now and did not expect respite. They would be making regular reports to John Coffin.

Duerden had to be found. All channels were open.

'The vanishing man,' said Paul Lane sourly. 'Where the hell is he?'

They went over all that they had on him.

In late February they had received the report from the Merseyside Force that Duerden was believed to be heading their way. He had few friends, except those 'in the trade', and these were naturally secretive, but one of them had passed on this bit of information, passing it in the hope of some small concession for himself.

There had been a reported sighting of him in Spinnergate, walking up and down the parade of shops by the Tube station. Mimsie Marker, no less, who knew of everything secret or otherwise, had told a startled uniformed man in a patrol car that she 'thought she had seen Duerden by the video rental shop on one afternoon, and there he was again now'.

Since at that time Duerden's move towards London was not supposed to be known by the public, the constable asked her what she was talking about. In the space of time it took Mimsie to convince him that she knew, the man, who might or might not have been Duerden, had gone. Mimsie claimed she knew him because his photograph had appeared in the papers when the last little girl had been killed. She saw all the papers and had a very good memory for faces, she said. But she thought he might have been wearing a wig.

Duerden had been more reliably sighted buying a ticket for the Dockland Light Railway.

After that he had disappeared, and except for the reference to him in the records of the Papershop Group, he might never have come south at all. Assuredly he had come south because he knew of them, but they were a cagey, tight-lipped lot who could afford good lawyers. They might be prevailed upon to give information, but had not yet done so.

Not that other reports of where Duerden might be, from the Tower of London to the Bespoke Tailoring Department in Harrods, did not flow in. All pointing nowhere.

'Thirty-two alleged sightings so far,' said Paul Lane sourly. 'And not one of them for real. Except possibly the one with the kid and the woman in a nurse's dress.' He was clinging to that, but it had not led anywhere as yet.

'The Invisible Man,' said Archie Young. 'He's bought another face. Had plastic surgery.'

'That costs.'

'He could do it with make-up.'

'Thirty-two sightings,' said Lane again. 'Thirty-three by now. And not one of them him.'

But the depressing thought was that they could not be sure. He might indeed have been one of those elusive figures.

The thought began to grow that he was indeed among them, wearing a different face.

For Lane and Young the day wore on unprofitably.

Coffin, at home, had received several congratulatory letters and cards on his performance in *The Circle*; he had made an exemplary butler. Marvellous presence, supreme diction. He put on dark spectacles and went out.

WALKER is wearing shades, the message sped as soon as he was sighted. The undertones, the unexpressed jokes going with it, were ribald. Ribald but respectful. And careful. He looked in a mood.

He had requested and received the very first pathology report on Nell Casey's body. It was on his desk. The full forensic reports of the debris on her body and clothes, which might be so helpful, hinting at where Nell had died and at whose hands, would come later. The killer inevitably leaves some trace of himself behind.

Coffin stared at the folder in which the report was placed and had the feeling that it was burning a hole in his desk. He wanted to read it before anything, but he was both more and less than a detective. His telephone was already ringing with the first call of the day and his answering machine had already logged a queue of others.

He picked up the telephone.

When he had dealt with some pressing letters and conducted two short interviews, he picked up the report.

The exact time of Nell Casey's death was hard to establish, the report said, but she had been dead for approximately three days when her body had been found. The remains of food in her stomach suggested that her last meal had been of bread and ham, some form of light lunch was suggested.

She had been hit on the head and then strangled manually. No great pressure would have been needed. She had certainly been dead when dropped into the water.

The detailed examination of Nell's body followed. No rape, no sign of recent sexual intercourse. No disease. A healthy lady.

But was she? What was she really?

This was the point at which Coffin raised his head from the page. 'So that was it? That was what worried me about her and puzzled Jumbo all those years ago? I'd like to know what Gus Hamilton has to say on the subject.'

Attached was a brief report on her clothes and her handbag: so far they had revealed little but might offer more help on a further examination. The handbag was empty. The pockets of her jeans and shirt contained nothing but a handkerchief and a return railway ticket from London to Staines. She had bought the ticket at the London terminus of Waterloo.

He walked to the window to look out. His bit of London stretched below, full of the usual number of crooks, villains, sexual deviants and shysters. Perhaps he had more than average in his new city. But he had a lot of good people and a few saints as well.

People were always unexpected. 'No wonder she was so elusive.' If that was the right word. 'I wonder what they made of her in Abbey Street, back of Costelow's?' The old Costelow's, of course. They must try and flush up someone who had known Nell then. 'I'll tell Lane that.'

He would still have to talk to Stella Pinero, but Lane first.

He reached for the telephone.

Copies of the same report had reached Superintendent Paul Lane and Inspector Archie Young on that very day and been read by them at once. Eyebrows were raised here too.

The report was also read in the Incident Room set up by the banks of the Thames near Staines with which Paul Lane and Archie Young kept in touch by telephone and fax, but here, since they had not known Nell Casey personally, there was less comment. Anything went, was their attitude; near Heathrow as they were, they expected anything and usually got it.

'Well, I'll be blowed,' said Archie Young. 'Who'd have thought it?' He had seen Nell act in her television series and had admired her performance, way above what the series itself seemed to demand. Now he thought he could understand the strange force and power that had come from her. It had come out of what she had gone through, what she had made of herself. Made, was the operative word.

He wasn't a man who usually had a lot of sympathy for

those who did not tread the usual path, it was both a strength and a deficiency in him as a detective, but he had a heart and an imagination and both were touched.

Paul Lane walked into the Incident Room in Spinnergate they had set up to deal with Tom's loss and which had now been expanded to deal with those allied matters of the Papershop Group and the death of Nell Casey. It was one of those cases, the most difficult and yet the most interesting, which sucked other mysteries into it, in itself both the cause and the result of them.

Not that Paul Lane, a pragmatic man, analysed the case thus. A bugger, he called it. But he did sense that with the new information about Nell they might be on the way to solving it.

'So what do you make of it?' he said to Archie Young. 'I see you've got it there in front of you.'

'Dunno. Must help, but I don't guess how.'

'The Old Man wants to see us. Soonest.'

Archie Young looked at his desk. 'One or two things to clear up here first.' They were still preparing a case against Mrs Brownrigg as well as one against the owner of the burnt-out papershop. The various members of the Papershop Group were also being interviewed. Slippery customers, was Archie Young's sour thought, too well-educated and too well-informed about their rights.

'He's coming over here.'

'I hear he's got a black eye.'

'Oh, you've heard that, have you?' Lane too had picked up this item.

'Well, it's interesting.'

A certain bustle at the door, and an undercurrent of suppressed attention among all the other workers in the busy room, announced John Coffin's arrival. One or two of the constables stood up as he came in, others continued with what they were doing, but they all knew he was there. Mary Barclay and Alison Jenkins, who were conferring in one corner of the room, looked at him and then at each other. Neither of them had read the report on Nell Casey's body, but they both knew something important had happened.

Only the man who had just received on his Fax machine what looked like an urgent message ignored Coffin's arrival. He was too busy reading what he had got there. The message said that a man dead as the result of a motorway crash outside Manchester had about him evidence suggesting he was connected with the fire at the papershop, and other more interesting material as well. He had an address on him. The young plainclothes man stood up, intending to hurry the message across to Inspector Young, but was checked by the sight of the Superintendent, the Inspector and the Big White Chief in conference. It was true about the black eye then, he thought; that's what the dark glasses are for.

'You've read it?' said John Coffin. He took off his dark glasses, behind which his eye looked red and puffy rather than black. He offered no explanation, and Archie Young removed his gaze. 'So now we know. She had the Big Operation. She was a manufactured lady. She—he—started life as a lad. Or possibly something halfway between, poor kid.'

'But did it have anything to do with her killing? Can we assume that?' said Paul Lane.

'We can't assume anything. But it fills out the picture. We know what she wanted out of life: she wanted to be a female actress with a child. And she got what she wanted.'

'More than,' said Archie Young. He felt sympathy, unexpectedly so. He was on her side.

'There will be medical records,' said Paul Lane thoughtfully.

Archie Young said: 'We haven't been very lucky in the way of records so far. She covered her tracks.'

'She didn't do that on her own,' said Lane. 'She had help.'

'I believe you.'

'The time to pinpoint is when she lived in Abbey Road behind Costelow's,' said Coffin. 'It must have been then or shortly afterwards that she had the transformation. By the time she got to Drama School in 'seventy-eight, she was female.'

'She was pretty young then, would any reputable doctor undertake the process at such an age?'

'Well, that I don't know, but I would guess there are centres in the Middle East where anything can be done.'

'Expensive and slow,' said Paul Lane. He said again: 'She had help.'

'Yes,' said Coffin, 'she had help. Someone cared. We have to look for the carer.'

'Oh boy,' said Archie Young to himself. 'One step forward and two back.'

'Any idea where to look, sir?' Paul Lane asked Coffin.

'None. Someone there all right, but I can't put a face on him. Or her.'

'What about Duerden? He has money.' William Duerden had been a successful businessman before retiring early to pursue his own particular hobby. He also had a wife and two children. He was living proof that those of perverted tastes are as ordinary as you and I. 'We can't rule him out.'

'So we go on looking for Duerden?' But Lane answered himself, it was a rhetorical question. 'Sure we do.'

Coffin looked at his watch. 'I'm off. Keep me informed.'

'Always busy, eh sir?' said Lane.

'Yes,' and not all of it pleasant business, Coffin thought. He had an appointment to see a lawyer about the threatened inquiry into his Force. He needed to know where he stood.

Before he left, he said: 'Get Hamilton and talk to him again. Find where he was the day Casey died. He's got some interesting-looking scratches on his hands.'

As soon as he had gone, the constable acting as receiver came across with the fax message.

'Thought you should see this sooonest, sir.' He held the fax. 'Manchester have got this man, killed in a motorway pile-up, and he's got arson equipment in his van.' Then he brought out what really mattered. 'And the address of the papershop on a bit of paper in his wallet. They give his ID as Trevor Hinton: his daughter was one of Duerden's alleged victims. They are working on it.'

Paul Lane groaned inside himself: one more CID Force

to link up with and to handle with care. This case was like an octopus, stretching out tentacles everywhere. He supposed he ought to thank God that fifty-two police forces now used HOLMES and were linked into the same computer system.

'He hadn't got Duerden's address on him, had he?' he said. 'Don't answer.' He turned to Archie Young. 'One more fact to feed into the computer.' He paused. 'Still, it's interesting. At least we know what the man had against the Papershop Group.'

'What we've all got,' said Young.

'And perhaps just a little bit more.' Paul Lane's broad shoulders sagged a trifle as if they were bearing too much weight. He had a couple of children himself and this case saddened him above the average, he had learned over the years to keep emotions out of a case as far as possible, but sometimes emotion helped. It fuelled the engine, pushed you on when you were dead beat. This was such a case. Every man in the room would work overtime, not for the money, but because of what the case was.

Lane straightened his shoulders. He passed a hand over his head in a characteristic gesture. Going bald. But going bald nicely, so his wife said.

Archie Young said, 'What's the joke?'

'No joke.'

'I saw you smile.'

'Just remembering something . . . Remembering to see the Chief Commander knows about the Manchester info.'

But Coffin had his own fax and the information was there for him as soon as anybody. Embedded, as it happened, in a lot of other stuff he could have done without.

For him the day passed with that quiet monotony of hard work and no joy that can bring depression. He fought against the depression, turning aside from the whisky that might have been his way out once, and drinking tea and coffee.

It was a bad season. By the end of it he might no longer be head of the New City Force and Stella might no longer have a theatre. No word from Letty, who appeared to have gone to ground: a bad sign. She might be sending a signal he did not want to read.

Something else that Stella would have to be told.

CHAPTER 20

March 27

He went in search of Stella Pinero later that night and found her in her dressing-room removing her make-up. It was her practice to take over a part every so often in one of her productions, thus giving a day off to the actress concerned, and seeing for herself and from the inside how her production was working. Also, it kept the cast on their feet, since they got very little notice, if any, of when the change was going to happen.

Stella was cleaning her face, she threw the wad of tissues into the bin and turned a cheerful smile on him. This smote Coffin to the heart, because he was going to wipe that look off.

'Come in, and sit yourself down. There's some wine over there, rather nasty stuff but it's nicely chilled so you can hardly taste it.' Stella had a cavalier attitude to wine. She stood up and slipped behind a screen. 'Just let me get changed and I'll join you.' Over the screen, she continued to talk. 'I'd forgotten what fun it could be acting in a good team and today it all came back. Lovely people.'

'What play was it?'

'Don't you read the playcards? Or the notices I send you? John van Druten; *There's Always Juliet.* Such a dear little play to do, a fourhander, which is lovely, but of course, you must move with speed and as one. Tonight we did. The audience loved us.'

'Bit out of date, isn't it?' said Coffin morosely, the wine was both strong and horrid.

'Oh no, it plays beautifully, we've had tremendous audience response. Van Druten is having a revival.' She appeared round the screen in jeans and heavy silk shirt. 'What's the matter with you? I mean, more than usual.'

'Thanks.'

'I only meant I know you have a lot on your mind . . . We all have. Gus is going round doing an impersonation of a thundercloud ready to burst. He's trying to be better, though, I will say that for him . . . Your eye looks paler, going yellow, that's a good sign.'

'Come round to Max's. I haven't eaten.' And neither had cat Tiddles, shopping was imperative. 'I must get some food for the cat.'

'I can give you a tin of dogfood.' Stella loved her old mongrel, adopted as an orphan.

'Oh, I don't think Tiddles would like that,' said Coffin doubtfully.

'Can't read, can he?'

Privately, Coffin thought Tiddles could read, or as much as suited that intelligent animal. It was, anyway, very hard to deceive him, and not worth trying because he had his own means of fighting back. Like chewing up your letters, or opening a book and clawing the pages. The typewriter could also have a very strange effect on him that was better not dwelt upon. 'I'll get something fishy from Max.'

Stella walked along beside him, talking cheerfully. Which belied the dialogue going on inside her. So the moment was approaching that she had dreaded. It was going to be goodbye and we will always be best friends. She had heard that dialogue in the past, rather too often in fact, sometimes playing one part and sometimes the other.

So when, over a slice of rich pâté which was by no means what a lady who watched her weight ought to eat, but food does furnish the spirits, Coffin said: 'I want to talk to you about Nell Casey, something to tell you.' Stella felt her fears lift. She put down her fork. 'Go on. I'm listening.'

'Ah,' she said with sympathy when he had finished. 'What a fight she must have had. She was she, no doubt about it, she was right to decide the way she did, but I bet it cost . . . Money as well as emotion,' said Stella thoughtfully. 'Poor Nell, poor girl. Oh, she would have hated us finding out in this kind of way. I mean, she might have gone public herself but she would have wanted to choose the time and place.'

'You're taking it well.'

'What did you think I'd do? Throw up my hands in horror? You're talking to a grown-up lady who knows what the real world is about. I think it would be nice if nature provided us with a kind of zip so we could change sex when we wanted. I know I've wanted to, more than once. Men get all the best parts as you get older.'

'You'll never get old, Stella,' said Coffin, laughing.

'Think so? But of course you don't. That's the kind of thing people say when they know that growing old is exactly what you've done already. We've known each other a long while, you and I, so we ought to be honest with each other.'

'You're always that, Stella.'

'And you?'

'Most of the time.' So then he told her about Letty's threatened bankruptcy.

'Oh, I knew about that, well, more or less, I have my channels, you know. I didn't want to worry you. As long as we can keep our apartments . . . I don't own mine completely, do you?'

'No, borrowed the money from Letty.'

'Me too.'

'Never mind. I still own that place of mine in Greenwich. We can always share a roof.' Of course, he might not have a job either, but he wouldn't worry her with that now.

Max served them the omelette they had ordered, his head raised carefully high to indicate he had not been listening and had not heard a word they had said, but he had already reported it to his wife, and caused his youngest daughter, whose innocence must be protected, to be sent to bed.

'It does explain a lot about Nell,' said Stella, 'a kind of brittleness, and the glitter she had. It seemed artificial, and it was in a way, as I see now.' She ate a mouthful of omelette. 'Lovely, Max, thank you, just how I like it.'

'*Baveuse*,' he said.

'Exactly.' That meant runny inside? Well, Max must know. She protected her silk shirt carefully with the napkin, she didn't want any *baveuse* on her shirt. 'And it explains the way she looked, her bones, so strong and clean. A lot of great beauties are a bit androgynous, you know, and Nell was a beauty.'

Max put down a pot of coffee and cups on the table before her, regretfully aware that he had missed something while he fetched the coffee. Stella stirred her cup, black, no sugar.

'Gus knew, of course. Not with his mind perhaps, but underneath, emotionally, like an animal would. That explains why their sex life never worked. And his anger.' She hesitated. 'You don't think that Gus . . . the scratches on his hands. You saw them?'

'I saw them. I don't know, Stella, but we will find out.'

They sat over the coffee.

'No news of Tom?'

'We'll find him,' said Coffin, with a confidence he could not trust.

They walked out into the night. 'I feel better now I've told you,' he said. Everything, or nearly everything.

'I was jealous of that policewoman, Mary Barclay.'

'Nothing there.' He took her hand.

Stella smiled, pressed his hand, and looked inside herself to see what she felt. But oh, I think there was, said a voice in her head, and might be again. That was how things went.

The two walked back together to the St Luke's complex of theatre and old church (so soon to be the new theatre) and apartments.

Big playbills shouted the names of Gus Hamilton and Stella Pinero and Nell Casey and little Nancy Fotheringham. A great review by Ellice Eden was splashed across the front.

In the evening while the performance was on these names were in lights. But now the lights were out.

CHAPTER 21

March 28

Afterwards, Archie Young said this was a day that should never have happened. They should have got there first.

Gus Hamilton was asked to go down to the New City Police Headquarters and duly went. He did not complain, for Gus he was docile. He said he had just been conducting his normal life during the days of Nell's absence. He had been preparing for a performance, performing (two matinees, he pointed out, didn't leave much time for anything else), teaching his drama class, and getting his hair cut. 'Just living,' he said. He could produce various witnesses. There was the girl he was living with at the moment, although she had been working away from London for at least one of those days. Doing a commercial, people had to live.

He had damaged his hands pruning his roses, yes, he had a garden, and although he hated looking after it, he could not afford a gardener and the neighbours had complained that his rambler rose was invading their garden.

He submitted to having samples of his skin and tissues taken.

There was no further report as yet from the police forensic team on Nell, but if she had blood and skin under her nails and they matched with Hamilton, bad luck for him, thought Archie Young. But he still admired Gus as an actor. Good face on the chap too, but sulky-looking. A lot of anger there. Violence never seemed far away.

They let Gus go home: they could check his roses later,

but he wasn't a fool; one way and another, they would appear pruned.

The ID check on the Manchester car crash victim had confirmed the name of Trevor Hinton. One of the child victims whom Duerden was suspected of killing was Clarissa Hinton. Hinton, who had been a soldier in Ulster, had been known to be following up his own leads on Duerden.

'Looks as though he found something, and got as far as the Papershop Group,' said Archie Young to the Superintendent. 'Wish he'd left an address or something. We do need to find the boy. He can't be alive now, can he?'

Paul Lane said nothing. He had sent his own family away to visit his parents in Galloway. Just for a holiday, of course.

But it was their first break.

And as such, duly transmitted to John Coffin, who was engaged in drawing up his defences against the threatened Commission of Inquiry. His whole area was quiet at the moment, but you could never tell now when racial or social differences would burst out. Who wanted a riot? There was very often some group working on the idea.

A quick result on the Casey affair, mother and child, would do good. He feared for Tom now. Everyone did.

Late on the afternoon of that day, a pleasant-faced middle-aged woman got out of a taxi in Regina Street and limped to her own front door. Mrs Bradstock had been a passenger on the ill-fated Tremble Tour, having been specially invited with a free ticket by her neighbour, Jim Lollard. Out of malice, she now believed, seeing all that had happened.

I shouldn't have laughed at him and his mass murders, she thought as she fumbled for her doorkey. That was him paying me out, the old devil.

She had not been one of those made very ill by the sedative drugs, she was a lady of strong constitution, but she had slipped on a rug in hospital and broken a bone in her hip. So there she had had to stay for longer than she fancied. After which she had gone to recuperate with her sister, but Emmy was getting more and more difficult, and she had suddenly decided to come home.

Home was best, and she had hated being away, but she had a couple of lodgers, quiet men, and she had dropped a note to Mr Hinton asking him to water the plants. She had also asked her neighbour to keep an eye on the house, collect the rent and pay for the milk, that sort of thing.

She let herself in, the house felt and smelt empty, so both lodgers were out, which she didn't mind, not fancying to engage in conversation before a cup of tea. She noticed at once that the house was stuffy and unaired. Well, men, she thought, never open a window.

And don't do much washing-up, either, she decided after a quick limp into her kitchen revealed a sinkful of dirty dishes. Not much of a hand with the pot plants either, she thought, observing her row of wilted primulas and geraniums.

'Thought better of you,' she said aloud, as she put the kettle on for a cup of tea. Tea first, then unpack, then look at the garden. It would be dark, but there would be a moon. She had been a countrywoman and knew the waxing and the waning of the moon.

She had two cups of strong, hot tea, and a slice of shortbread. Emmy might be getting madder and madder but she still baked a good round of shortbread.

Then she got up to look at her garden. She was quite right, there was a lovely moon.

The moon shone down on John Coffin also and on The Albion where so much of the mystery had started.

He was in the garden there because the cat Tiddles had been missing for almost twelve hours now and that was a long time for Tiddles to be absent from his feeding bowl.

But it was moonlight and spring was on the way, and although Tiddles was officially neutered, his hormones did not always seem to know it. Coffin was not really worried, but he did his duty as a loyal cat-owner and conducted a hunt in the nearby gardens and shrubberies.

He saw a flash of green eyes from behind a rose-bush.

'Devil,' he said fondly. 'There you are.' A whisker twitched, the bushes moved and Tiddles sped off, uttering a mawkish cry like a child in pain.

Coffin straightened his back and stared at the moon. He believed in lateral thinking, and he was remembering something. A cry.

He turned his steps towards Regina Street. It was a longish walk but he stepped out. He had remembered the night walk when he had heard a child crying in Regina Street.

Extremely unlikely, he told himself as he walked, that it was Tom. But he was going towards Murder Street.

WALKER is out and going south, reported the patrol car when it passed him.

Regina Street looked calm and quiet. He passed Lollard's house, now closed and shuttered. A few yards down the street a shabby white van was parked with the words HOUSE CLEANING decorating the side. The van itself could have done with a wash.

Sign of the times, he thought. No more servants, just cleaning teams. Stella had told him how difficult it was to get the theatre cleaned.

He walked on, still feeling restless. Then, a few houses along, the front door opened and a woman came out. She stood on the steps and stared about her.

Coffin came up to her. 'Anything I can do?'

'Are you a policeman?'

'I am, as a matter of fact.'

'You've been quick. I've only just telephoned. They said they'd sent a car.'

'What is it?'

She held the door open. 'Come and have a look.' She was talking as she bustled through the hall and towards the back door. 'I've been in hospital and then staying with my sister. Had enough and come back . . . It's the garden.' She threw open the back door. 'Look.' She pointed. In the middle of a small rosebed was a long, low mound. 'That wasn't there before, and I don't like it. Something's been buried there.'

'Could be,' said Coffin.

'Well, I want it dug up. Could be a bomb or lot of explosives or drugs. Anyway, it's not natural and not right in my garden and I want it looked at.'

There was a shout from the front door. 'Anyone there?' A uniformed constable found his way through the hall and out to the garden. 'Trouble here, is there?' He had a slightly aggressive, urgent way with him as if he was prepared to be trouble himself if he didn't find any. A young man, still in his early twenties and impatient. 'Come on, mother, what is it?'

She pointed: 'Look! That happened while I was away. In hospital.'

He was puzzled but trying to find his feet. Also, there was something about the man present who was saying nothing that worried him. 'You've been burgled? Someone's broken in?'

'No, no, I've been dug up and that's not right.'

The constable took a look at the rosebed. 'See what you mean, but it doesn't look dangerous. Leave it for tonight and we'll have a go tomorrow.'

'No, tonight,' said John Coffin. He came forward from the shadows.

'You lodging here, sir?' The constable was aware that Mrs Bradstock took in lodgers.

'No.' Coffin took a step forward and the moon shone on his face.

Mrs Bradstock gave a shriek of eldritch amusement. 'He's one of you, he's a copper.'

The constable's companion in the patrol car had grown impatient waiting and came through the garden door. 'What's up here, Jim, want any help?' Then, sharper than his companion, he recognized John Coffin, took a step back and saluted. ''Evening, sir. What's the trouble?'

While they had been talking, Mrs Bradstock had picked up the small spade that had been left by the mound and was moving the earth. Suddenly she stopped, dropped the spade and turned her head towards them. From her country childhood came memories of farmyard smells, she knew what she was smelling.

'That's death there,' she said. 'It's a grave.'

A group was gathered in Mrs Bradstock's garden. John Coffin, who had been there all the time, the police surgeon and the Scene of the Crime officer, who had arrived next. Archie Young, who had been at a concert with his wife, had hurried and got there just after Paul Lane, who had been morosely watching TV on his own, his wife and family being away. This case is marking us out, he thought, those of us who have children and those who don't. We all mind, but if we've got kids we take it more personally. The telephone call summoning him to Murder Street had been almost welcome.

He had joined the group as they stood around the improvised grave.

A smallish figure, buried just beneath the earth, fully clothed, with a notice wrapped in a transparent plastic envelope and tied to his chest.

WILLIAM DUERDEN

executed

March 6th

I only buried you, you bugger, because I didn't want to spoil this nice lady's house.

'Yes, that's my lodger. One of them. Mr Lamartine, that's what I called him.' Mrs Bradstock looked bemused. 'No, you needn't lead me away, I can bear to look. Hasn't changed all that much, has he? But I didn't know that was a wig.' The tumble of blonde hair had come adrift from the head and lay on the earth.

Later, inside the house and taking another cup of tea with a touch of something a little bit stronger in it, because after all, in spite of what she had said, she was unnerved—Mr Lamartine had been strangled, and that does not improve the features—the questions started and she did her best. Paul Lane asked the questions, while John Coffin listened.

'How long was he with you?'

'About a month, Jim Lollard said he was a weird one. Takes one to know one.'

'Did he say why he had come to you?'

'Everyone knows I let rooms. Never permanent, can't do with permanent and I advertise in shops. Put a card in the window. He said he'd seen it. No, he didn't say which but I use lots of places. Newsagents, post offices, video shops, that kind of place.'

'Did he say what had brought him to this district?'

'He said he had friends.'

A simple truth. William Duerden did speak the truth when he could.

They left Mrs Bradstock still sipping tea but wondering whether she should go to bed here or return to her sister's house. The police had offered her a lift, but Em was not likely to be welcoming. Words had passed that would be remembered. Better to stay here. Otherwise the neighbours would think she was dead and that would never do. She didn't feel haunted, although that might come later. Still, there were a lot of memories walking around Regina Street already. Could ghosts haunt ghosts?

That must be the whisky talking, she thought. Stop it, girl. You've got the police here. All over the place. You are not alone.

She took a quick look out of the landing window on the way to bed. Yes there they were.

'Well, we know one thing now, don't we?' said Coffin, back in the garden. By now a few neighbours had come to their windows to look and speculate. 'If the inscription is to be believed, and I see no reason for a lie; Duerden died before Tom Casey went missing, before Nell was killed. Of all the crimes he was guilty of this is not one of them.'

He had come here because he had remembered a child crying and he had arrived for the unburying of the dead William Duerden.

'We ought to have got him before this,' said Archie Lane. He turned away and looked at the garden wall. Whether you've got kids or not, you mind this sort of case. In fact, I think you feel it worse. I don't blame the chap who killed Duerden and fired the papershop. I'd have done it myself.'

He turned back to look at the others. 'And where's the boy? We've got Duerden but we haven't got him.'

And no idea where to look. All the leads they had followed had led nowhere. He had gone off in a car which might or might not have been driven by a woman and had never been seen again.

No one went to bed that night, and the long day went on.

CHAPTER 22

March 28 and onward

The long day wore on, becoming a day of thirty-six hours, of forty-eight hours, it was going on for ever. They were making newspaper headlines, grabbing the media attention worldwide. Several contingents of the press wer camping out in Murder Street, but they too were getting no sleep.

Stella Pinero reported that bookings for all the Festival plays were up and some plays, those with Gus Hamilton in, were sold out.

Gus, who was followed everywhere by photographers and newsmen, was saying nothing. He had been interviewed again and again by different police questioners, they had asked the same questions over and over in different ways, but Gus always repeated the same story. He knew nothing, had been at home. No witnesses except when he was working. There were traces of skin and blood caught underneath Nell's fingernails but the work on the traces was not yet conclusive.

'It's not magic,' the forensic scientist had said to Archie Young. 'And we're not able to pull things out of hat to order. I can't, as yet, say there's a match. Give me time. I can't go ahead of the evidence. You shouldn't want me to.'

Mary Barclay was in close touch with Sylvie, visiting her for a talk nearly every day in the hope that something might pop out that would help them to find the boy.

Copies of such reports as she was able to make were passed on to John Coffin where they added to the bulk of similar reports on his desk. But he read them all carefully.

She's a good girl, he thought. She'll do well in the Force, very well. I must see she makes the right moves. That's the best way for our relationship to go. I can't do better, and if I try to get closer, then I may very well do worse. He had the slight, sickish feeling in the pit of the stomach that in younger days he had called a depression. Now he knew it was just his body warning him that events were moving. The trouble was that it never put a label on the warning.

His legal advisers had told him that it would be wise to let them send a team of three to survey the New City Force and draw up a report. It would provide the basis for his defence if it was needed. They did not say that he too would be investigated and reported upon, but he knew it would be so. The investigator investigated.

He read Mary Barclay's latest again.

> I asked Sylvie once more if Miss Casey had mentioned anyone she had quarrelled with. Or any person who could have a grudge against her. Sylvie said No, everyone loved her.
>
> Then she said: Perhaps not everyone. Miss Casey had said that once she had upset a friend very badly. (Or lover, Sylvie could not be specific on this.) But Nell had defended herself, it hadn't been her fault. Things had been bad for a bit, but this friend understood her better now. Nell had said that she knew she alienated some people, it was the way she was built, she'd been born that way and it couldn't be helped, but life rolled on like a river and you went with it.
>
> No names, Mary Barclay had reported, none mentioned and Sylvie could make no guesses. But since it was at the time when the strange things had started to happen (the affair of the toy dog, the blood on the boy's shirt and so on) perhaps we should try to follow this up.

Life rolled on like a river, she said that? Strange she should have used that metaphor and Sylvie have remembered it and passed it on.

Nell had died in a river.

He put down the report and went to the window. There, just beyond his view was the River Thames, rolling on its way to the sea. For a while it had carried Nell Casey's body with it. Did it now carry the body of Tom?

In the pocket of Nell's jeans had been a return railway ticket to Staines. Nell had known where she was going.

A phone call from Inspector Young came through at that moment. 'I'm dead keen to nail Hamilton for this. I want to take him into custody.'

'Have you got anything new?'

'Yes. He's gone off. I think we can get him though, because he's taken his car. The girl he is living with said he went off late last night. They had heard about the finding of Duerden's body and it upset Hamilton.'

'Who told them?'

There was a moment of silence, then Young said with reluctance, 'Seems she has a cousin who works on the telephone at HQ.'

'There's always someone,' said Coffin. 'I suppose she's been feeding them with information all the time?'

'Probably, sir.'

Look good on my Inquiry Report, thought Coffin: Security Poor, that would be an easy judgement.

'The Superintendent supports me in this, sir.'

'Then go for Hamilton, you didn't need to clear with me.'

'Thought we'd better,' said Young. On account of Miss Pinero. But he didn't say this aloud, nor did he have to.

Into the pause, Coffin put a query: 'Have you noted Barclay's reports on her talks with Sylvie?'

'Yes, as soon as they come in. The girl's out of it, though.'

'Agreed. But did the last report say anything to you?'

Young took a deep breath. Should he say yes or No? 'Not really, sir.'

Coffin said: 'You've got an Interforces Unit going on the

Casey death, haven't you? Then get a search undertaken for a riverside house, a weekend retreat, that sort of thing. Between Staines and Windsor, I would say. Find all likely houses and check them over . . . The most likely site would be near the castle.'

'What will we be looking for, sir?'

'Anything that has worried the neighbours,' said Coffin crisply.

Archie Young put down the telephone at his end. 'I shall have to think of another way of putting it to those other poor sods,' he decided. 'I'll say: We have information that . . .'

He moved across to the Incident Room which was dealing with this multiple crime with arms like an octopus. Here he set in motion the search demanded by the Chief Commander. He could do no other.

I do hate it when he goes extra-terrestrial, he told himself. When he repeated this comment to the Superintendent, all Lane said was: 'He's a difficult man to decode.'

The long day went on.

The reaches of the River Thames between Staines and Windsor are fringed with houses running down to the water, some with boathouse. Houseboats, barges, and all types of small river craft are moored along its banks.

The river itself is lined with meadows, sheltered by trees and dotted here and there with small islands. On one such island, at Runnymede, was the Great Charter sealed. King John had come out from his castle at Windsor to meet his angry baronage. They had more soldiers than he had and a better grasp of political and military realities. Surrounded on an island, a small one at that, there wasn't much the King could do if he wanted to get off without one of those unfortunate accidents that could happen to a mediaeval king who lost control of his great magnates.

Many of these river homes are weekend or summer places, deserted in the winter, left locked up and empty.

One way and another, the police teams sent out had plenty to look at. No shortage of choice, especially, as one constable said to his mate: You didn't know exactly what you were looking for.

Trouble, was the answer. Something out of the ordinary.

Coffin dealt with a series of routine matters, heard with some satisfaction that his MP critic was about to be involved in litigation himself—his wife was divorcing him—and took a message from his sister in New York that she was on her way over. Not to meet her at Heathrow.

Wouldn't think of it, he told himself.

The news came in much more quickly than he had expected. Somehow he had thought that Gus Hamilton might get there first and that the place he was interested in would be found through him, but Gus had proved elusive.

The call came through in the early dusk of that day. Which day was it? He too had not slept and was suffering a time wastage.

'We have a choice of two places on offer. Want to hear the details sir?' Archie Young had got his second or third wind and sounded cheerful. 'One is a houseboat on the river near to Eton. The locals say they have heard voices and seen lights at night, which was not what they expected as the owner is abroad. They were about to tell the police themselves: they think a young couple are squatting there.'

'And the other place?'

'It's a small kind of villa, actually on one those little islands . . . Signs of life seen there at night and by day sometimes. Not usual, owner hardly ever comes.'

'Access?' asked Coffin.

'You walk across a wooden bridge.'

'And where is it?'

'Not far from Runnymede and the John Kennedy Memorial. There's a good road and car park not far away.'

'That's the place to go for. Are you watching it?'

'Watching both.'

'Hold on, I'm coming.'

It would only take forty minutes with a fast car and clear road. A helicopter would be quicker. There was a helicopter. He justifed the use of the helicopter to himself.

*

A small group of police were there waiting for Coffin in the car park on the banks of the River Thames at Runnymede.

A wind had got up and it was raining.

'What's he expecting to find?' asked a sergeant of the local outfit.

'A body,' said Young, turning up his coat collar. 'He's lucky that way. A joke. Don't bother to laugh.'

'I wasn't.'

Young had a sergeant with him. Paul Lane was coming out with the Chief Commander.

'They're here,' said the local man.

The helicopter dropped neatly into the open field beyond the car park. Young saw that Mary Barclay made a third member of the party. He hurried forward. 'We have to move on by car, it's just down the road.'

Quietly three cars left the car park and took the road which wound parallel with the river. Out of the corner of his eye, Young saw that Mary Barclay gave John Coffin a small nod, then got into another car and drove off in the opposite direction.

'What the devil's she up to?' he asked himself as the car procession sped on. There was a right turn and they were in a cul-de-sac of houses on the river bank. A narrow lane led to the river.

At the end of the lane was the bridge to the island.

Coffin looked at in the moonlight. 'Does it have a name, this island?'

'Duck Island, I think,' said the local man.

But there was no ducks, or if there were then they were safely asleep.

'Let's go, then.'

The party swept down the lane towards the river. A figure moved out of the shadows. The local CID Inspector acknowledged his salute, and a murmur of conversation passed between them. Then he turned to John Coffin.

'The car you were interested in has been found. Parked on the road not far from here. No one in it.'

'Hamilton can't be far away. Let's get to the house.' Before Gus, if possible.

Archie Young muttered: 'What's Hamilton playing at?' The comment was to himself but Coffin heard him.

'What would you be up to in the circumstances?'

'Looking to protect myself,' said Young.

'I think he has something else on his mind.' Something more violent. 'Go on looking for him. He's got to be close.'

Across the wooden bridge, over the dark river and into the greater darkness around the low building in front of them. It was surrounded by a shrubbery and small trees. A path went from the river to a door set in a porch.

There was a small boathouse with a name on it: Camelot.

'Wouldn't you know,' said Coffin to himself. '"By the margins willow-veiled, Slide the heavy barges trailed."'

'What's that, sir?'

'Nothing. Just a quotation.' Tennyson, not the *Morte D'Arthur* but the romantic idyll of the Lady of Shalott.

Another figure moved out of the bushes. 'Someone has gone in. A man. Couldn't see much detail, he went in through a window.'

'How long ago?' Coffin looked at the house which still showed no sign of life, but the curtains were drawn tightly at one window.

'Barely a minute. I think he must have heard the cars and that gave him the push.'

'Right. In we go, then.'

No need any longer for silence or quiet. The door was forced open and they were crowding into the hall. The house smelt damp and sour. Unused, empty. But to the right a line of light shone under a door.

John Coffin threw open the door.

It was a room used as a bedroom. In one corner was a child's cot and in it, tethered by a kind of harness, stood Tom. He was surrounded by various games and toys, there was a mug of milk and another of water within his reach. He looked bewildered, lost and frightened, and there was a strong smell suggesting that his toilet arrangements had been shifty, but he was alive.

A door led to a bathroom. Coffin could see in and see a

reflection of man's figure in a looking-glass over the basin. The man was trying to hide behind the door.

'You can come out, Gus,' he said.

Gus Hamilton slowly appeared.

'You're too late and in the wrong place. Ellice Eden was taken into custody a few hours ago, on my instructions as soon as I heard of this place.'

As the newspapers reported later, he was helping with their inquiries. But he would not be walking free. The forensic evidence matching his blood to that on the shirt and on the model of a child's hand was there, as was the fact that Ellice Eden's handlotion, so carefully and lavishly applied, had left traces on almost everything he had touched.

'I wouldn't have killed him,' said Gus Hamilton, sitting in the police car with John Coffin. 'But, by God, I'd have beaten him up. As soon as I was told what had happened to Nell, I knew Ellice Eden had to be behind it all, although I didn't know why.'

'I think you do,' said Coffin.

Gus said slowly, 'I suppose it was all to do with that boy who died in Australia. I knew that Ellice thought he was the great white hope of the future for the stage. I suppose he loved him, and he blamed me and Nell for his death. The boy was mad for Nell those weeks on the tour. He was a neurotic, had had a bad time as he grew up. Brutal father, that sort of thing. We didn't know his history, his rages, his despairs, we saw those, but not through to the great depressions he had inside him.' He looked at Coffin. 'Not Nell's fault, not really. I mean, I didn't think people killed themselves over sex these days.'

'All the time,' said Coffin. 'So?'

'I remembered this place. I was never here, but I knew of it. And I thought of the boy . . . I wasn't sure exactly which house but I was going to find it. In the end you lot pointed it out to me . . . I thought the boy would be here, but I thought he would be dead.'

'No, I don't believe Eden wanted to kill the child, he was

looked after. Just to torment Nell. But when she came here looking for the child, then he was willing enough to kill her.' Or perhaps he had meant to do so all along.

'He's off his rocker, you know,' said Gus confidently.

'Not for me to say. Leave that to the psychologist.' Through the car window he saw Mary Barclay accompanied by a woman in a nurse's uniform carrying Tom away to an ambulance. No physical wounds were apparent, but there must be some emotional ones. A tough little begger, though, he was smiling at the nurse.

Archie Young came over to the car. 'All tidied up, sir. Good job Barclay came along.'

He sounded exhausted but relieved. 'Pity we couldn't have got here before.'

But the long day was over.

CHAPTER 23

On several April days

I have loved two things in my life [wrote Elliee Eden]. The theatre and that boy who died in Australia . . . I might have loved Nell Casey. Yes, I did love Nell, and I have been her helper. I saw her/him first in a bar off Piccadilly. A gawky adolescent trying to be a sophisticated female, all of sixteen acting thirty. So lost and touching. She said she was an orphan, but I have always had my doubts about that. But I pretended to believe her. I gave her a meal and got the story out of her. She went to Amsterdam for the operation, but I expect you know that by now, and then I paid for drama school for her. Cash, I didn't want to be too closely linked.

By that time, I had met HIM. Ah, that was different.

'He never used his name,' said Coffin to Stella Pinero, 'never once, it was as if he couldn't. And he has never spoken . . . Oh, asked for his lawyer and things he wants and thinks he ought to have in prison, but not a word of what went on.'

'But he writes?'

'Oh yes, all the time. Sometimes the same story all over again, word for word.'

> He was a genius, you see. Far and away the best hope of his generation. Nell was good but he was different. Nell met HIM through me. Came together to my house on the river, my little hideaway. Folly, folly, all is folly.

'Gus Hamilton says everyone knew about his so-called hideaway but he'd never been invited there himself.'

'Oh yes, we all know,' agreed Stella. 'I was never asked. You had to be a bit special for that. Poor Nell, poor Ellice. What a business, what a rotten business.'

They were sitting in the bar of the Theatre Workshop. No one else was there.

'I wouldn't trust Ellice too far,' she said. 'He mayn't be as mad as he's acting. He is quite an actor. He liked a bit of drama. You can tell that from the drama he created for Nell and Tom.'

> As soon as I heard about HIS death, I vowed to get back at Nell Casey. I held her responsible for the death of a great and lovely talent. I had loved Nell too and helped her (although I liked her better as a boy). She was beautiful as a boy, immensely appealing, so talented. I was willing to help pay for what she wanted, an operation and tuition at a drama school. She seemed so vulnerable and lost. Or so I thought. I didn't know her then. Or did the operation change her?
>
> I arranged and paid for her operation, while deploring it, and she repaid me by seducing HIM, lightly and without caring. Then she dropped him. She was a destroyer. It wasn't Hamilton, it was her. I have letters from HIM to prove it. Pure anguish. Hard as nails, our Nell, but the boy was her weak spot. That and her career, and I

thought I could get both. Torment her through the boy, and then break her career. Good tricks with the boy, I thought, I remembered what I'd been like as a boy and what my mother had feared for me. Hieronyms Bosch country.

It all comes out of self, you know, truth and lies both. I like playacting and dressing up, cross dressing it's called, isn't it? I dressed up when I took the boy. Nurse Eden. When Nell was in the States she was out of my reach, but she came back. I got her the job over here with Stella Pinero. I didn't want to kill her, though, I would have delivered the boy back, I rather liked him, but she remembered me going into her bedroom and guessed I had taken her shoe. The one shoe. I overreached myself there, I freely admit. She knew this place and came here to look for Tom. Unluckily I was here too. I came regularly, of course. The boy was well looked after. A visitor, not a hostage. Nell should have behaved and he would have come back. She shouldn't have attacked me. It was self-defence on my part, but I lost my head. I admit that freely too.

'Did he?' asked Coffin. 'Did he get the job for Nell?'

'No one influences me,' said Stella. 'But he might have given a push. He was a power. You have to admit that.' She got up to get some coffee. No one was serving at the bar, they were looking after themselves. 'He's not claiming it wasn't him, then?'

'Hardly could. His forearms and hands are scratched, and there is a match with the tissues under Nell's nails. It was his blood on the china hand and on the shirt. He cut himself on purpose. And in his bedroom we found a wig and a nurse's uniform which he wore when he abducted Tom. I suppose the child, who one way and another had been looked after by various people, thought a nurse sent was safe enough. Eden's defence will be that it was a revenge scheme that got out of hand.'

'What about Gus's scratches?'

'I think that may have been the girlfriend,' Coffin

allowed himself a smile. 'I believe she may have heard about Ellie Wakeman.'

'I'd heard she'd got a temper.'

'They're a match, in that case.'

'I'm told that Mary Barclay was the real star of the show. Arriving with a nurse and all equipment for the child . . . Where is Tom?'

'In care.'

'What's going to happen to him?'

'The best possible thing: he will probably go back to his mother. She is out of prison and reputed to be anxious for a reunion.'

'Good. You've acquired a cat after one murder and I've acquired a dog. I don't think either of us could take on a child.'

'You've got a daughter,' said Coffin.

'Do you miss not having a child?'

'Yes.'

'Put in a bid for Tom.' He shook his head silently. 'Marry someone still young enough to give you one.'

'You mean Mary Barclay? No, Stella. I thought you and I were going to share a roof?' It was said as a joke, wouldn't really do in his job even these days. Respectably married or nothing. Nothing too noticeable, anyway. Of course, he might be looking for a new job. There was still that Inquiry hanging over his head.

Stella started to laugh. It was wonderful to laugh again, she was so glad she could do it.

Ellice Eden wrote:

> It was quite easy to put into effect my little teases with the child. I went round to view where Nell was staying that first night after seeing her in the bar. I was overstimulated, I suppose. Imagination working overtime. I knew about the boy, although I pretended I did not. I always know the gossip. Didn't know where the child came from, of course . . . I saw the dog in the garden that night and thought about the burial. I had the shoebox that was used in my car, the bit of wood on which I

wrote TOM was a plant marker from one of the rose-trees . . . I was still there when Nell came down. I saw her, watched . . . Didn't see Stella, I was home by then. But I could not sleep. Still in overdrive, so I went back and moved the dog, and put the little hand (a small treasure from my collection, said to be the hand of one of Charles Dickens's daughters), in position. The blood was my own.

Even Ellice Eden himself wondered if he had been a little mad at that point. It was a good defence point, anyway. He would suggest it. He frowned. He had prowled up and down the stairs that evening even before seeing Nell in the bar, wondering if he should call. He did not like that memory. It was not worthy of him. Yes, that was the moment that the fire had started to burn. I should have strangled Nell then, not the dog.

No, no, the killing was an accident. Cling to that thought.

I had heard the story that the child-killer was in the neighbourhood which gave substance to what I was doing and put fear into Nell Casey. But I want to make it quite clear that I never knew William Duerden and never met him or the so-called Papershop Group. My tastes are quite other, thank you.

I don't imagine I shall be incarcerated for very long. Self-defence, you see, Nell Casey came at me like a tiger. You can kill without noticing you have done it and for a little while I did not. Come round, Nell, I said, stop playing the fool.

For a while I thought of killing myself, but even though HE whom I loved has gone, I want to go on living.

I shall be back to the theatre.

The Theatre needs such as me.

'I see now,' said John Coffin, 'that the business of strangling the toy dog was a substitute, a rehearsal if you like, for strangling Nell. And the blood on the plaster hand was a unconscious confession of guilt. "My hand is bloody," he was saying. I wonder if he realizes that now?'

'I might make use of Ellice,' said Stella. 'Do a real drama based on the case. Very much in at the moment, that sort of thing. Might ask Letty what she thinks. Saw her this morning. New emerald earrings and a suit from Bill Blass. I think we can say the money troubles are over. She didn't say, but I believe there might be a new husband on the way . . . And she wants to talk to you about your late mother.'

'I shan't listen,' said Coffin. 'I've got my own worries.'

'Oh, you must go on acting, stay with the Play Reading Group. You have a real gift for butlers and they are thinking of doing *The Admirable Crichton.*'

'You know, Stella,' said Coffin, remembering something. 'When I saw the dead face of William Duerden, I thought I had seen it before . . . There was a chap who came to the Reading Group once or twice and never came again. Couldn't have been him, could it?'

'Even murderers must have hobbies, I suppose,' said Stella.

But it was Ellice Eden who had the last laugh. He discovered after all that he could die: he hanged himself in the cell in the remand prison when he was left alone for half an hour. Usually there were three other prisoners with him.

Before dying he had made a valid will and with the will was a letter to be sent to John Coffin.

> As the days have passed [he wrote], I have come to realize that what moved me was a profound and overwhelming jealousy. I was jealous of what Casey was, what she had done and what she had it in her to do. It was a very destructive emotion and it has destroyed us both.

In his will he left half of his comfortable fortune to the child Tom.

I owe him something, and unlike some, I pay my debts, and you know, he was a great character. He laughed at me when I picked him up as Nurse Eden. He knew I was a joke. I'm afraid he was bored while he was with me. Not afraid, but bored. The money is to make up.

The other half of his fortune went to found two drama scholarships to be called The Nell Casey Scholarship for men and The Peter Astell, for that was HIS name, for women. A condition of the bequest was that Gus Hamilton be chairman of the judging panel for the rest of his life.

Thus ensuring that every year Gus would have to think of the name of those two people.

But before all this there was one last scene involving Jim Lollard to be played out.

John Coffin was informed of it in person by the head of the Second City Security Unit.

'We didn't write old Lollard off,' said Superintendent Ascot (soon to be promoted to Chief Superintendent as a result of his current work). 'That would have been foolish, we can't afford to ignore any source, so we went through his house with a fine-tooth comb.' The Superintendent used the cliché with relish. 'And the stuff that man had! Papers piled everywhere, or pinned on to the backs of doors, with a diary here and notebook there, and a kind of a tally board of dates and events on the wall. A life work, it was.' He gave a bleak smile. 'And we got interested in a man he called Michael Henry. Henry had taken a flat in Regina Street, just down the road from where Lollard lived. He appeared to be running a mobile housecleaning operation from a small van.'

'Go on,' said Coffin. He had seen that van himself.

'Good cover, anyway, and he had probably had some genuine jobs in South London. He worked with a small team of two men and two women. We've got the lot. We'll never know what excited Lollard's suspicions, anything or nothing, but he was right. We took a chance and searched the flat.'

'And found what?'

'A good quantity of explosive and bomb-making material. Together with guns, and a list of addresses.'

Two addresses in particular had attracted their attention.

One was that of the Police Headquarters.

'And the other was your own address, sir, in St Luke's Mansions.'

'To be expected, I suppose.' He was probably on several lists, but in spite of himself, Coffin felt a chill. This was real.

'And there was a date, attached to a note of the theatre there. Henry had a ground plan of the place. The bar and restaurant were starred in red. Apparently he had got himself a cleaning job there, we have checked with Miss Pinero. But I'm not sure how much cleaning was planned.' Ascot passed a document across. 'Take a look, sir.'

Coffin read slowly and sombrely. There was indeed a date, about three weeks ahead. The day on which the Festival was due to hold a big reception, to be attended by a number of great theatrical figures. He was going to be there himself.

A time was noted down: twenty-two–thirty hours.

There did not seem much doubt that at ten-thirty on the evening of that day in April a bomb had been due to explode, nicely timed to do the maximum damage. He did not need to speculate on the number of the casualties: they would have been massive.

He raised his head from his reading and took a deep breath. 'Lollard was not so far wrong. Mass murder, was it? That would have been a day all right.'

A day on which he would have lived, and possibly died, on his very own Murder Street.